Justice and Mercy

Books by Rod Miller

Rawhide Robinson *series*
Rawhide Robinson Rides the Range
Rawhide Robinson Rides the Tabby Trail
Rawhide Robinson Rides a Dromedary
Rawhide Robinson Rides a Wormhole

Novels
Cold as the Clay
Father unto Many Sons
Pinebox Collins
Silver Screen Cowboy
A Thousand Dead Horses
All My Sins Remembered
OUTLAWMAN
Justice and Mercy

Coming Soon!
With a Kiss I Die
And the River Ran Red
This Thy Brother
The Mail Must Get Through
Where the Long Trail Ends

For more information
visit: www.SpeakingVolumes.us

Justice and Mercy

Rod Miller

SPEAKING VOLUMES, LLC
NAPLES, FLORIDA
2024

Justice and Mercy

Copyright © 2024 by Rod Miller

All rights reserved. No part of this book may be reproduced or transmitted in any form or by any means without written permission.

ISBN 979-8-89022-155-1

*Dedicated to my grandchildren:
Sydney, Ian, Delilah, and Irie*

Chapter One

In the bottom of the valley is a river. It is deep enough in crossing that a rider must float out of the saddle and hang to the horn for a time as the horse paddles through the depths. Or, in times past, pay the toll to ride the ferry. The river meanders, the current strong and steady but not swift. Except in spring, when snowmelt from the mountains comes down with a force that scours the bed and banks. Long ago—long, long ago—the surge ate its way through the neck of an oxbow and the river made an island. Someday, sediment will cut off the old channel and that part of the river will become an oxbow lake. Someday. But for now, what once was the bar of the meander is an island.

Because the island is there, a rider nowadays need not take the ferry or float out of the saddle as his mount paddles through the depths. That is because bridges link the island to the mainland on either side, connecting to the only road that both enters and leaves the valley. So, a horse and rider, or a team and wagon, or a stagecoach, or any other conveyance, or a drove of livestock can cross from one side of the river to the other and no one gets wet. At the downstream end of the island the ferry lies abandoned, put out of business when the builder of the bridges graded bypass roads linking the thoroughfare to the bridges, relieving travelers of the need to float and the ferryman of a job.

The island is not a big island, but it is big enough to host a small town. A small town, but not so small that it cannot provide for the wants and needs of the residents of the big valley. Some of those people reside on cow outfits and sheep raising operations scattered across the valley. Others in mining camps and logging camps on the slopes of the mountains. And some live in the town.

West of the river, the valley is labeled on maps as part of Jefferson County, most of which is on the other side of the mountains. East of the river is Adams County. Again, most of the settled part of that county is on the other side of the other mountains. Neither county cares much about the isolated valley over the mountains and pays little attention to its governance.

As for the island, being in the middle of the river that defines the county lines, it is neither here nor there. It is not in Adams County. Nor is it in Jefferson County.

And that is why Justice Payne, the man who built the bridges, built his town on the island.

Justice Payne ruled his town through a variety of offices, including mayor, toll and tax collector, real estate magnate, business owner, and judge. For the latter office, he had neither license nor diploma. What he did have was a stock answer for any and all who questioned his qualifications to pass judgment on his fellow man. "Why, my middle name is Justice!" he always said. "Or it would be if it wasn't my given name."

The performance of his passing judgment was a casual affair. Court was held in the main room of his Cactus Thorn Saloon. A table, temporarily perched on a raised platform where dancing girls normally plied their trade, served as the bench. The trappings of his office consisted of a wool blanket woven by Navajos, a gavel, and a thick, oversized book with a scuffed and worn leather cover. Also present, save on rare occasions, was the judge's three-legged dog, Twah, perched on a pillow atop a bar stool beside the bench.

This morning, however, was different.

This morning, Justice Payne was at work in his butcher shop—a trade he had plied elsewhere in his travels, as he was adept with knife and cleaver. The bell on the door announced the arrival of his associate in law enforcement, Luther, wearing the badge of town marshal, pinned to his chest by appointment of Justice Payne.

"Luther, what is it? Can't you see I'm busy? I've got this sheep to dress."

The marshal reached out through the open door and pulled in, by the scruff of his collar, Giacomo Moretti.

"Giacomo," Justice said with a sigh. "What has he done this time?"

Giacomo Moretti filled several important positions on the island, among them town drunk, layabout, loafer, gossip, and—when conditions required—casual laborer.

Luther gave his prisoner a shake. "He was found in the back room of the bakery this morning. He'd jimmied the door, it looked like."

"My bakery?"

"Yessir."

Whack!

The cleaver in Justice Payne's hand struck the butcher block. Never one to waste motion, the same strike parted a mutton chop from the rack.

"Court is now in session!" Justice said. "Giacomo, what the hell were you doing in my bakery?"

"Only getting out of the weather, Justi—"

"When court is in session, you will address me as 'Your Honor,' or be found in contempt!"

"Aw, hell, Justice—Your Honor—we're in the butcher shop."

"That matters not a whit. I see no need to drag you over to the Cactus Thorn and go through all the rigmarole and legal niceties on your account. When I say court is in session, court is in session whenever—and wherever—I say it is!"

Whack!

Another mutton chop fell from the rack.

"Now, as you were saying . . . ."

Giacomo Moretti hemmed and hawed, hoping something reasonable might work its way through his stupor. It did not, so he told the truth. "It's the ovens. Them ovens in the back are always warm. I like to curl up next to them to keep the chill off."

"You mean to say you've done it before?"

Moretti blanched. "I . . . I . . ."

Whack!

"Guilty!"

"But your honor!"

"Quiet! Giacomo, I am inclined to sentence you to three days chained to the whipping post on the town square with a diet of bread and water. But I see from the crumbs down your front that you have already been helping yourself to my bread while lodging in the bakery!"

Moretti cleared his throat. "Only a yeast roll, Your Honor. I never had a loaf or anything. Just one little roll—a right tasty one, I might add."

"Empty your pockets!"

Giacomo Moretti sidled up to the butcher block. From a coat pocket came an empty wine bottle. An inside pocket produced a ball of assorted kinds and colors of string knotted together. From one pants pocket came a tarnished watch on a chain, correct in its timekeeping twice a day at seventeen minutes past eight. From the other pocket, Moretti spilled a handful of coins onto the block, totaling a dollar and twenty-seven cents.

"Giacomo Moretti, having been found guilty as charged of breaking and entering, loitering, unlawful domicile, and partaking of bread unpaid for, I fine you one dollar—plus court costs in the amount of twenty-seven cents."

Whack!

And another chop fell.

"But Justice—Your Honor—a buck twenty-seven is all I've got to my name!"

"Silence! I warn you, Giacomo, you are treading dangerously close to a charge of vagrancy! Court is adjourned."

Whack!

The *when* of Justice Payne's arrival in the town on the island was well known—he arrived there before the town did, and his coming to the island is the very reason for the town being there. There is, however, a mystery concerning the *whence* and *why* of his arrival.

The most popular conjecture placed his previous habitation in Canada, most often at or near Fort McLeod. A Canadian origin carried weight with some, for despite the Englishness of Fort McLeod and the surname Payne, there was an indescribable hint of Frenchness about the man.

Others insisted he had migrated from the opposite direction, coming north from Chihuahua, or perhaps Sonora. Others chose another compass point and claimed Justice Payne hailed from California. Still others had him crossing the plains from the East, somewhere near Cincinnati—or was it Cleveland?

The fact is no one knew whence he came. Except, of course, for Justice Payne himself and he wasn't telling.

Why he was here stirred up even more hypotheses.

He had fled at the point of a gun wielded by the jealous cuckolded husband of a paramour. He was absconding from the law—accused, according to the conjecture of various citizens, of murder, robbery, claim jumping, perpetrating a confidence scheme, bribing public officials, or a number of other departures from legal and acceptable behavior.

Others insisted he had been convicted of one or more of those—or other—offenses and was on the lam, having escaped from prison.

He was a deserter from military service.

Hiding out from an abandoned wife and family.

Avoiding punishment for wrongs committed against a crime syndicate.

Broken and mourning the loss of loved ones.

Again, only Justice Payne could speak with any authority about his history. And again, he chose to remain silent.

With court out of session and the sheep carcass reduced to saleable cuts of meat, Justice Payne washed up, hung the sign in the door advising prospective customers to seek him out three doors down at the Cactus Thorn Saloon should the butcher normally on duty—abed with the croup—not make it to work.

He locked the door and with the toe of his boot nudged the dog sleeping on the porch awake, then dropped a trimming from the meat, which Twah snatched out of the air with a snap of his jaws. After clapping his teeth together enough to serve as chewing, Twah gulped down the treat, hoisted himself to his feet—all three of them—and followed his master along the planks. As Justice stepped through one side of the saloon's swinging doors, the dog slithered under the other one.

"Justice! How the hell are you?"

The judge smiled at the young woman propped at the end of the bar. "Just fine, Al. Just fine."

Al—short for Alice—called the dog over, squatted to its level, and ruffled its ears. The dog endured the scratching and smooching with a smile on its face, then flopped down and rolled onto its back for a session of belly rubbing, which the woman was pleased to provide.

The woman, slight of frame and short of hair, fooled the uninitiated with her appearance. Dressed in clothes cut for and more suited to a man, right down to the cartridge belt and holstered revolver, many took her for such. Once they learned better, some considered her being female an invitation to misbehave. Al's job was that of bouncer for the Cactus Thorn Saloon, employed to maintain order and decorum, and expel those from the premises whose behavior crossed whatever line she saw fit to draw between acceptable and unacceptable activity.

It was a job she was good at, despite her small size, atypical sex, and unconventional appearance. Many a former patron had found themselves with the barrel of her pistol violating the sanctity of a nostril, felt the strength of its steel barrel against the back of the head, or skidded face first through whatever befouled the street after being pitched and heaved through the magic of leverage out of the saloon, across the plank porch, and onto the street.

The judge shook his head at the display of affection between mutt and muscle. "You'll spoil that damn dog, Al."

"Ah, you've been saying that ever since he hobbled into town and it ain't happened yet."

Justice snorted. "I'll be in my office."

"Office" is a word used advisedly for where the judge was going. Tucked into the back of the saloon, a sidewall away from the hallway that led to the barroom's back door and to the jakes beyond, and a back wall away from the alley behind the building, was Justice Payne's home.

Upon entry—by invitation only—through a nondescript door, one finds oneself in what could be variously described as a sitting room or parlor. The room does double duty as an office of sorts, with a rolltop desk shoved against the wall, and next to it a mostly empty filing cabinet. A combination safe was concealed, if not hidden, in the lower part of a nearby highboy. The chest's upper-half drawers stored a miscellany of papers—not well organized—related to the judge's legal and business interests.

Separated from the sitting room by a curtain, a sparsely furnished bedroom. A man of his means certainly could have built a palatial mansion on the island, but Justice Payne preferred to keep his money in more active investments with a more predictable rate of return. Rental properties, both leased lots and owned buildings, provided monthly income. The judge's businesses included the butcher shop, the bakery, the bank, the Cactus Thorn Saloon, and a café. While he employed workers to run the businesses day to day, the owner took an active interest in all his enterprises and might darken the door at any time, tie on an apron, and go to work.

All of it proved profitable. Life on the island was good. In addition to a steady and comfortable income, Justice Payne enjoyed generally cordial relations with employees and tenants alike.

Except for one.

And that one was Mercy O'Malley, proprietor, madam, and sometime participant in the work that went on at Mercy O'Malley's House of Passion.

Chapter Two

Mercy O'Malley sat at the window in her upper-floor suite, her hands busy with needlework interrupted with watching the people coming and going on the road, and the river flowing under the Adams County bridge. She wondered if she, like the Lady of Shallot, should abandon this cursed island, lay herself in the bottom of a boat, and float away to take her chances somewhere downstream.

Nothing would make Justice Payne happier.

And that was reason enough to abandon the idea. She determined to stay at Mercy O'Malley's House of Passion—if only to annoy the judge.

Setting aside embroidery hoop, needle, and thread, she left the room and walked down the hallway, knocking on each door along the way. The day was well into afternoon, and it was time for the girls to get out of bed and get ready to go back to bed—but not to sleep.

She reached the balcony above the parlor and saw Luther, the town marshal, taking his ease in an overstuffed chair in the corner. He sat, hat in hands, slowly rotating it around and around by its brim. He looked up at Mercy as she came down the stairs.

"Luther! What are you doing here? How did you get in?"

Luther did not stand. He smiled at the madam. "Oh, I got a key from the judge."

"Oh? And what is Justice Payne doing with a key to my house?"

"The judge, well, you know, he's got keys to all his properties. In case of an emergency, you know."

Mercy laughed, but not because she found it amusing. "Is that right? What kind of emergency do you suppose might be found here, within these walls?"

"Can't say," Luther said with a shrug. "That's just what he says."

"Hmmph. Now, for my other question. What are you doing here?"

Now, Luther stood. With a smile, he held his hat over his heart. "I've come to call on Miss Rose."

"Good Lord, Luther! It ain't but two o'clock in the afternoon! Rose is still abed."

Luther's face fell.

"What's so special about Rose, anyhow?"

Luther smiled. "I couldn't rightly say, Miss Mercy. But Miss Rose, well . . . she just, well, she's just as cute as a button. And she treats me right nice."

"You're sweet on her, ain't you Luther."

With a blush coloring his face, Luther admitted that was the case. And he assured Mercy that his intentions toward Miss Rose were altogether honorable.

"Be that as it may, it's too early to see the girls, honorable intentions or otherwise. Come back when we're open and the girls are ready for business."

Again, Luther had the look of a man whose favorite horse had pulled up lame.

"Go on now," Mercy said.

"Ain't no need for him to rush off," came a voice from the balcony. Leaning on the rail, dressed in her nightgown and a sultry, come-hither smile, was Rose's co-worker, Miss Violet. "C'mon up, Luther. I'll take real good care of you." She yawned, then turned and started down the hallway to her room.

"Yes, Miss Violet. Thank you, Miss Violet," Luther said, a big grin slicing his face.

Mercy stopped him at the bottom of the stairs. "Hold on there, Luther. You just said you was sweet on Miss Rose."

"Oh, I am, Miss Mercy. I surely am."

"And yet here you are, on the way to call on Violet."

Luther's brow furrowed like a plowed field as he stared at Mercy. The very notion that his affection for Rose should somehow affect the opportunity for a romp with Violet escaped him. He shrugged, and plopped an oversized boot on the bottom step of the stairway to heaven.

Mercy tugged on his shirtsleeve, stopping him mid stride. "Before you go, Marshal, I'll have that key."

Wagging his head like a dog shaking off water, Luther said, "Oh no, ma'am! I couldn't do that!"

"And why not, boyo?"

"Why, the judge would have my hide!"

Mercy smiled. "He don't know you've got that key."

Luther swallowed hard.

"Well? Does he?"

Luther stammered and stuttered and hemmed and hawed before he found the ability to answer in the negative.

"Hand it over!"

Luther handed her the key and begged her not to tell the judge where she got it.

"What's the matter, Luther? You afraid of Justice? A big, strong boy like you?"

"Well, it ain't that. Not exactly. It's just that . . . it's just . . . well . . . ."

"I swear, Luther! You ain't no better where the judge is concerned than what that three-legged dog of his is! The both of you don't want nothing more from life than for him to say, 'good boy!' and pat you on the head."

Luther stood, head bowed, one foot still propped on the bottom step and the other on the floor.

"Oh, be gone with you!" Mercy said, and swatted Luther on the backside.

The town marshal climbed the steps two at a time on his way to his assignation with Miss Violet, smiling at the prospect despite his stated affection for Miss Rose.

For convenience, all the girls at Mercy O'Malley's House of Passion carried the names of flowers. As the girls came and went from the island, the names were left behind by those leaving, waiting to be reassigned to new arrivals as need required. Miss Rose. Miss Violet. Posy. Lily. Hyacinth. Daisy. Camellia. Amaryllis. Petunia. Marigold. Iris. Mercy O'Malley had a bouquet of floral monikers that never wilted.

Allowing a few minutes for Luther to get settled, Mercy climbed the steps and again made the rounds of the rooms lining the upper hallway, knocking on each door and urging the girls to be up and about. All, of course, except Violet.

Even at her tender age—an age, at least, much younger than that typical of others achieving her level of accomplishment in her chosen profession—Mercy O'Malley had lived the equivalent of a long and eventful life. Forced out of Ireland in the bloom of young womanhood when her entire family perished from a fever, and lacking any hope of a living in a land ravished by famine, she stowed away aboard a steamship bound for the more promising shores of America. The ship berthed in Boston Harbor and the crew bundled the girl off onto the wharf with less ceremony than that given a bolt of Irish linen or bale of spun cotton goods.

Tromping the streets of Boston in search of employment, the girl found *Help Wanted* signs in many a shop window, but penciled beneath those words on one and all was the exception: *No Irish Need Apply*. A toff in a top hat and long-tailed coat found her huddled in a doorway begging handouts one day and offered her a job as a domestic servant in his palatial household. Giddy with good fortune, she strapped on the proffered apron and went to work. But the job was short-lived. Mercy O'Malley left the house as eagerly as she had arrived upon learning, within days, that her employer expected more from her than household duties.

While far from ideal, she found other work as a waitress, barmaid, and all-around dogsbody in a grog shop near the seaport, serving drinks to seamen, sailors, and longshoremen, and performing other chores as assigned by the keeper of the house. Unlike those demanded by her previous employer, Mercy found the chores required of her acceptable. At the same time, she learned from the women she worked with that there were more profitable ways to make a living, whether instead of or in addition to slinging drinks. Acceptance of the fact that her body was a valuable commodity came some time after realization of the same. But, eventually, she succumbed to the lure of filthy lucre and learned to hoist her skirts for coin.

Plying the world's oldest profession—which, as it happened, Mercy O'Malley was well suited for and particularly accomplished at—provided the working girl the opportunity to live beyond comfort in the posh cities of the East, and her purse swelled. Boston, Baltimore, Philadelphia, New York, and New Orleans each held her interest for a time. But, as with many in America, the pull of the West tugged at her as it had Europeans from the first moment they set foot on the continent. Chicago. St. Louis. Kansas City. Denver. Salt Lake City. San Francisco. All served their purpose in the education of Mercy O'Malley.

Then, having "seen the elephant" and most everything else the budding nation had to offer, Mercy decided to try a more settled life in a smaller town with a slower pace. A place where she might find the opportunity to run her own house of ill repute, with the profits lining her own purse rather than the pockets of another.

A wish which eventually found Mercy O'Malley in the town on the island in the river, proprietor of Mercy O'Malley's House of Passion.

While Mercy O'Malley was, beyond question, proprietor of Mercy O'Malley's House of Passion, she did not own the building in which the enterprise was housed. The structure, like every other on the island, carried the name of Justice Payne on its title. But through employing against her landlord an irresistible combination of feminine wiles, superior intellect, and ingenuity, Mercy had negotiated the most favorable lease of any in the town, as well as a likewise advantageous tax rate.

It had not come easy. When first arriving in the town, Mercy had taken a room at the hotel and assessed the economic opportunities on the island by plying her trade in a quiet way, prospecting in the saloon and on the streets.

Before long, Justice Payne became aware of unauthorized financial activity taking place in his town—an exchange of wealth that did not provide the percentage due him, owing to his position as lord and master of all he surveyed.

This, he could not allow.

Whack!

The gavel fell hard on the little wooden block on the table on the platform in the saloon. "Come to order! Court is now in session!" Justice Payne hollered over the din in the barroom, and punctuated the call with another whack of the wooden hammer.

As was always the case when court was in session, the bar remained open and drinks continued to be served. But the patrons were expected to pay attention to the proceedings, and the barmaids went about their business quietly. Outbursts were treated as contempt of court or disorderly conduct, depending on the whim of the judge, with fines assessed and collected for the tiniest infraction.

"Mercy O'Malley, you are the defendant in this case. Rise and approach the bench!"

Whack!

The woman sashayed up to the bench and faced the judge, arms akimbo and feet in a wide stance. "On what charge?"

Justice Payne leaned forward and looked down his nose at the woman before him. "That remains to be seen. It has come to the attention of the court—"

"Court!" Mercy said. "You call this a court? Why, you ain't nothin' but a pompous ass wrapped in a Navajo blanket and holding a hammer, sitting behind a table in a two-bit saloon! What passes for 'law' around here is as watered down as the drinks!"

Whack!

"And what's that three-legged dog doing there on that stool? He the clerk of your court or some such?"

The challenge caused raucous laughter throughout the barroom.

Whack!

"Order! Silence!" the judge hollered. He did not threaten to clear the courtroom, however, as such extreme action would cut into profits from the sale of drinks. Again, he leaned forward to address the defendant. "Miss O'Malley, while the formalities and legal niceties may be somewhat lacking in our humble town, the rulings of this court nevertheless carry the weight of law. Now, then, confine your talk to answering my questions or it will not go well for you."

The judge reached out and scratched the dog's ears. "And, for your information, Twah is here merely as an observer, as he always is in my court."

In truth, Justice Payne's three-legged dog served a much more important role in the judge's courtroom, and in his other endeavors. Justice was convinced that Twah had a finely refined sense of character and an unassailable knack for discerning truth from lies. His growling at a scofflaw signaled suspicion; barking at the defendant indicated guilt beyond question. Oh, the judge continued the proceedings despite the dog's judgments, if only for show, but it cannot be denied that Twah determined to a great extent the guilt or innocence of the defendant and the severity of the sentence Justice imposed.

"Miss O'Malley, as I was saying prior to your interruption, it has come to the attention of this court that you have been seen receiving gentleman callers at your lodgings at the hotel."

"Is there some law against it, judge?"

Justice sat upright, unaccustomed as he was to being questioned in his own courtroom.

"Well? Is there?"

The befuddled judge pulled close the big leather-bound book sitting on the table. He opened it, flipped back and forth through the oversized pages as if seeking something specific among them. He ran his finger down the text on a particular page, turned to a new page and repeated the action, and again on yet another page. At length, he slammed the book shut, the report of it nearly as loud as a whack of his gavel.

The judge cleared his throat. "It is an important question you raise, Miss O'Malley. One that carries considerable legal import. The answer, it seems, lies in the purpose of those visits, and the activity that takes place within the confines of the abode."

"That's a lot of twaddle. What I do in my own room is my own business."

"That may well be true in most instances. But, in your case, where payment is made in exchange for services rendered, there are exceptions in the law."

Mercy O'Malley snorted. "Oh? And what the hell is that supposed to mean?"

"It comes down to this, Miss O'Malley—what services are you providing, and are your patrons, in fact, paying you for those services?"

The defendant stretched to her full height. Insignificant though that height might be in terms of feet and inches, it was sufficient to cause Justice Payne to lean back in his chair. "Damn right they pay me," she said. "You don't think I work for nothin' do you?"

"That is quite enough of that—I will ask the questions and you will answer them. Now, having admitted you accept payment for your services, tell the court exactly what those services are."

"Like hell I will!"

Whack!

"Miss O'Malley! Answer the question!"

Mercy O'Malley shifted her weight from one foot to the other. She swallowed hard. She took a deep breath. She smiled. "Would you like a list, you lecherous old turd?"

Whack!

"Mercy O'Malley! You will respect the solemnity of these proceedings! You will address me as 'Your Honor' or, at the very least, as 'Judge.' Do you understand? Now, answer the question!"

Mercy told the judge it was a difficult question to answer, as her patrons were many, and the services they require were varied.

"Come on, Miss O'Malley. Stop prevaricating. We all know what you are up to in there."

"Oh? Why don't you tell me, then?" Mercy waved an arm to include the customers in the barroom. "Tell us all!"

The attentions of all present, by the way, were riveted on the proceedings. Drinks sat on tables untouched by drinkers, serving girls stood with empty trays hanging from their hands, bartenders leaned with elbows on the bar and towels slung over their shoulders.

It was a situation that did not go unnoticed by Justice Payne. He squirmed in his seat, wanting nothing more at this point than for the trial to end. "Please, Miss O'Malley. A few examples will serve. What is it you do with the men who come to your room?"

Mercy looked about, seeing she had command of the room. Even the dog sat upright, propped on his one front leg, his eyes fixed on her. A faint smile passed her lips so quickly that only the most attentive noticed. "As I said, it ain't a simple question. Men want different things."

"Go on. Please, go on."

"Well—*Your Honor*," again, the fleeting smile, "some of them men come to me for singing lessons."

Silence was loud in the room.

"Some of them want to learn or practice reading—I use the Bible, mostly. Others come to see me to get their fortunes told—I got a tarot deck, but I can also use tea leaves or palm reading."

A few snickers and repressed giggles sounded here and there in the room.

"There's some that wants fashion advice. One man, he don't want nothing more than to have me help him tie his necktie—see, he can't get a nice, even knot to save him."

The laughter in the saloon-turned-courtroom grew more pronounced.

"I do light tailoring for some, maybe replace a button or mend a tear. Some, believe it or not, want to learn to sew themselves, or take up needlepoint. I've been known to give piano lessons, but I ain't got a piano at present. I do teach mouth harp, though!"

The laughter, while still restrained, was more general.

Whack!

Mercy did not let up. "There's some that come to see me wanting nothing more than talk—they're maybe having marital troubles, or wanting advice on child rearing."

More laughter.

Whack!

Whack!

Whack!

"Silence! The court will come to order!"

Whack!

"Quiet, I say!"

Whack!

Whack!

It took a while, but the judge's remonstrations and the pounding of the gavel eventually brought the laughter to a halt—or, perhaps it had run its course—and the judge returned to his questioning of the defendant.

"Miss O'Malley! Singing lessons? Mouth harp? Tea leaves? Needlepoint? Do you expect this court to believe that sort of thing is what goes on when men come to your room?"

Mercy smiled. "Sure, judge. Can you prove different?"

Justice Payne sat upright. "Miss O'Malley! We all know better!"

"You do, do you? How is that? You been peeping, Judge? Is that it? You been sneaking around peeking through my window curtains, have you?"

Whack!

"Of course not!"

Mercy smiled again. "Then you don't know for sure just what I do in there, do you, *Your Honor*?"

"Well . . . I . . . it . . ." The judge cleared his throat. "Case dismissed!"

Whack!

Cheers erupted throughout the courtroom.

Chapter Three

Justice Payne sat in his desk chair, feet propped on a low table, thumbing through a handful of papers plucked from a disorderly pile. "We've got to figure out a way to bring in more cash, Luther."

"Gosh, I don't know, Judge. You got money coming in from the Cactus Thorn. The take from the café. There's money from the bakery. Heck, that ain't even the half of it. There's the bank, y'know, and all them lease and rent payments you get from all the buildings there is in town. Golly, I collect enough in taxes ever' month to where the vault in the bank can't hold it all. And that don't even count what you got in that safe over there in that cupboard."

Justice tossed away the papers he held and they floated and fluttered down onto the jumble of pages on the table. "It ain't enough, Luther. There's things I want to do." He took in a long, slow breath and let it out the same way. "I don't suppose you've got any ideas?"

The question was rhetorical, as the judge knew full well that the man he had appointed town marshal would have no ideas. In fact, he was of the opinion that Luther had never had an idea in his life—which was why he had appointed the boy to the office.

Luther was last in a long line of sons of a rancher who ran a rawhide and greasy sack outfit at the far edge of the valley. Even after spending the entirety of his boyhood and a goodly portion of his youth among horses and cattle, Luther lacked what his father called "cow sense," the ability required of a good cowboy to think like and outthink his charges. He was likewise bereft of "horse sense" as well. He had a knack for being in the wrong place when working cattle, coming too late to where he was needed, spooking the bovines unnecessarily, could not get the hang of a catch rope, bucked off horses a kid could ride, left too many gates open, and otherwise proved his unsuitability for the life of a cowboy.

And so, following the last of a countless number of tantrums and tirades in his attempts to educate the boy, the rancher sent his youngest son down the road kicking horse turds, as they say. In other words, for the benefit of the uninitiated, the father fired his youngest son. Gave him the sack. Let him go. Gave him the axe. Terminated him. Gave him the boot. Drummed him out. Showed him the door. Sent him packing.

Harsh treatment, perhaps. But, from the father's standpoint, it was an act of love. He knew Luther did not have what it takes for life on a ranch, and understood the necessity of the boy finding his way elsewhere, in another line of work. And, given the cowman's low opinion of town life, he figured Luther's size and strength and handsome face would serve him well among the wan and weak who plied their various trades in the town.

Luther wandered the streets for a time, doing odd jobs and setting his hand to any task he could find. For a young man of his appetites, casual labor barely provided enough remuneration to keep his belly from shrinking up to where his belt buckle bounced off his backbone.

But his performance did not go unnoticed. Justice Payne, who kept an eye on all things in his town, took note of Luther's eagerness to work, his apparent willingness to do whatever was asked of him, and his ability to carry out simple instructions and follow orders—if the task at hand was not too complicated. The judge balanced those qualities against the boy's seeming lack of initiative and inability to forge an original thought. His bigness and bulk offered benefits as well, hinting at sinister skills lurking beneath his affable manner.

All in all, Luther looked like the ideal candidate to wear the badge of town marshal, serving as the judge's assistant in maintaining law and order in the town on the island. Justice offered the job like a bolt from the blue one cloudless afternoon.

"Gee willikers, Judge! Me? Town marshal? You sure?"

"Sure I'm sure, Luther. I seldom do anything unless I am sure about it. You will learn that about me, given time."

"But, gosh! I don't know nothin' about the law—all the rules and such."

"Don't you worry about that, son. Just follow my lead and you will be fine. I'll tell you what to do and when to do it. And, if need be, how to do it."

"Golly gee! I can't hardly believe it!"

"You'll be paid a salary, son—not a big one, mind you, but it's steady. On top of that, you'll be given free room and board at the widow Ellis's boardinghouse—a significant improvement over sleeping in the haystack at the livery stable."

The boy's enthusiasm could hardly be curbed, and his attachment to the law on the island—that being the judge—started strong and grew stronger with the passage of time.

Justice Payne's faith in the boy proved well founded. All these months later, Luther had served him well. For example, there was no ordinance in the town forbidding the carrying of firearms. Enforcing a gun ban seemed to the judge a losing proposition—cowboys, miners, and loggers came to town to rid themselves of the jingle in their jeans every payday. Arresting and trying them for packing pistols would not prove nearly as profitable as their parting with their pay in more profitable places, such as the Cactus Thorn Saloon.

There was, however, a standing law against firing weapons on the island. Should someone in their cups take to shooting out the stars, Luther would effect an arrest, disarm the miscreant, and chain him to the whipping post until the judge saw fit to hold court. But violations were rare, most celebrants finding ways to blow off steam that did not involve burning gunpowder. The idea for that particular law took root in Justice Payne's garden of illegalities soon after Luther pinned on the badge.

The ordinance got its first test when a logger from one of the camps in the mountains was in an overly festive mood one Saturday night. Alice (call me Al) had already found it necessary to pitch him out of the Cactus Thorn on his nose for repeatedly ignoring her instruction to stop dancing on the bar. Not that there was anything wrong with dancing on the bar *per se*—it was just that the logger's hobnail boots made a mess of its polished surface and marred the finish, which would not do.

Said woodchopper dusted himself off and, rather than face further embarrassment at being manhandled by the diminutive Al, set off in search of other entertainments. Standing in the street in the moonlight, the lumberman developed a fascination with the letter "O" on the various and sundry signboards lining the thoroughfare. Dry Goods. Tooth Extraction. Rooms and Hotel on the same sign! Cactus Thorn Saloon. For reasons only he understood, the logger decided the letter "O" formed a perfect target—a natural bullseye to test his marksmanship.

He unholstered his revolver, checked his loads, and proceeded to penetrate the signboards. Being three sheets to the wind, and an average pistoleer at best, his aim was less than true and he punched holes in the signs outside the target letters much more often than his slugs struck within the ring of them. But his success at raising a ruckus was greater, and the racket rousted Luther from his bed at widow Ellis's boardinghouse.

The marshal, the top end of his long johns framed by hat and trousers tucked into boots, marched half-dressed toward the sound of gunfire, having forgotten in his haste to arm himself. He shrugged off the lack of a revolver in his resolve to enforce the law regardless.

"Hey! You! Leave off all that shooting!"

The offender, struggling to stay upright and on his feet, turned to face the oncoming threat to his spree. "Aw, to hell with you," he said, weaving the smoking pistol in the general direction of the law officer.

"Gimme that," Luther said, and reached out and grabbed the barrel of the gun and pulled it away from the logger. "Ouch! Darn!" he said, tossing the pistol to his other hand. Again, he caught it by the barrel, heated by burning powder and escaping lead. He repeated the motion a few more times before it dawned on him to grasp the handle of the gun as God and Mister Colt intended. "You can't shoot here in town," he said through clenched jaws, shaking his free hand, then shifting the pistol to the other hand to free up the other for wafting and waving. "It's ag'in the law."

By this time, the lumberman realized he was empty handed and unhappy about it. He said—more slurred, really—some naughty words and took a swing at the lawman. Luther saw it coming through his pain and dodged the blow. He told the scofflaw not to do that, but dodged another punch. Shoving the pistol into the waistband of his pants, he placed his fist against the other man's chin with considerable speed, and the logger sagged to the ground, the blow having unhinged his knees and released his eyeballs from their anchors.

Luther rolled the woodchopper over and slapped his cheeks a time or two in a futile attempt to rouse him from his slumber. He yawned, grasped the man's belt in the vicinity of the buckle, hoisted him off the ground with one hand and carried him off as if he were a feed sack with a handle.

Come the sunrise, the logger awakened chained to the whipping post in the town square with no recollection of how he came to be there. Or why. But whatever it was, he suspected it was a bad thing and that did nothing to improve his mood. Holding his head as still as possible, he pulled himself upright hand over hand up the post. He found particularly annoying the shackle around his ankle, to which was attached a chain attached to a ring in the post. The ogling and giggling of the town's citizens as they passed by on their way to start the day did nothing to improve his mood. By the time Luther arrived, he was on full boil.

"Who the hell are you?"

Luther smiled. "You mean you don't remember me?"

The man shook his head, gritting his teeth and wincing at the unexpected pain.

The lawman drew aside the lapel of his vest to reveal the badge pinned to his shirt.

"You're the sonofabitch that locked me up here, I guess."

Luther nodded.

The lumberman lashed out with a roundhouse punch that caused considerable pain—but only to his own aching head. Luther, however, dodged the blow and felt not a thing. He grabbed a fistful of the prisoner's shirtfront and lifted him off the ground, shaking him like a coyote with a cottontail rabbit in its jaws. He lowered the man to the ground and told him to sit still, then knelt down and unlocked the shackle. As he stood, he grabbed the scruff of the man's collar and lifted him to his feet as well.

Luther half dragged and half carried the prisoner down the street as the man attempted to keep up with long strides and hops and skips. The lawman stopped at the scene of the crime, gave the miscreant a good shake to get his attention, then guided a visual tour of his attempted marksmanship in violation of the law, pointing out bullet hole after bullet hole in signboards, penetrating and splintering the wood sometimes near but more often far from the targeted letter "O."

"What happens now?" the culprit said, somewhat chagrined at his unlawful behavior, and embarrassed in no small way at his poor aim.

"Well, I talked to the judge. He's seized your pistol—says it ain't much good anyhow—and if you confess your guilt to me, a fine will be assessed and you'll be let go. If that ain't to your liking, I can chain you back up to that post and you can set there till the judge takes a notion to hold court. If that was to happen, I can promise you the consequences of your misdeeds will be much more severe." Luther recited the speech as if it had been drilled into his head nearly word for word, which, in fact, it had.

"How much is the fine?"

"How much you got?"

The malefactor gleaned every pocket in his apparel, harvesting coins and folding money, even finding a few bills folded up and stuffed into the top of his boots. The leftovers from his week's work and night of partying amounted to something less than five dollars.

"It looks like I got about four dollars and eighty-two cents here. Don't know what the hell happened to the rest of it. I had a lot more when I came to town."

Luther shook his head slowly and clicked his tongue. "I'm awful sorry. The judge, he said the fine for what you done is five dollars." He grabbed his prisoner by the arm and started back to the town square and the whipping post and the shackle and chain.

The prisoner held back. "Hold on! I ain't but eighteen cents short—hell, that ain't even two bits. You wouldn't hold a man for less than a quarter would you?" He swallowed hard. "If I ain't back up at the camp in time for work in the morning I'll lose my job."

Luther stopped, took off his hat, and scratched his head. He bowed his head and rotated his hat by the brim. "Gosh, I can't think of what to do. It does seem a shame for a man to lose his job over eighteen cents."

He shrugged. "Still, I got to go by what the judge says. He's the law around here, not me."

The scofflaw said, "Wait! I got an idea." He unbuckled his gun belt and started thumbing cartridges out of the loops. "Look! These bullets is worth at least two cents apiece—I paid more'n that for them. There's fourteen of them here."

"What does that come to?"

"Twenty-eight cents, at least. Way more than what'll make up the rest of the fine."

Luther thought for a long minute. He shook his head. "I don't know." His eyes widened and he smiled at the rare occurrence of what may well be an idea, but was most assuredly a thought. "Tell you what—throw in that gun belt and holster, and I think I can talk the judge into it. But just in case, you had best light out of here in a hurry. If you're gone, I can't very well lock you up if he don't go for it.'

Mingled as it was with the throbbing in his head, the ache in his bones, and the inferno in his stomach, the logger did not know if he was pleased with the dispensation of the law or not. But he opted to call it a day and hoof it out of town and make his way back to his place of employment while he still had a job.

But all that was in the past. So many fines for various misdeeds had been collected since then, that particular one and many others had receded so deep into the dimness that only serious thought could recall them, if at all. Right now, Justice Payne was concerned with more immediate problems—such as how to increase the amount of money in his possession. Luther was no help—which was no surprise.

The judge let his feet drop off the low table and hoisted himself to stand upright. He moseyed over to the rolltop desk and extracted a bottle of whiskey from one of the cubbyholes. A glass came to hand from a drawer. He poured himself a drink as he pondered his problem. He did not pour a libation for Luther—the boy did not like the taste of liquor, and the judge did not want to encourage any change in that regard. There was something intriguing about the boy's innocence—relative, that is, to his own lack of it. He took a sip, rolled the liquid around his tongue, swallowed, then emptied the rest of the glass in a single gulp.

"That damn woman," he said, turning toward his town marshal.

"You mean that one that you had in court the other day? Mercy O'Malley?"

"Yes, dammit!" He slammed the empty glass down on the top of the desk. "Her! She's the answer. I know damn well there's money to be made there. I've just got to figure out how to get at it."

Chapter Four

The seduction of Mercy O'Malley had been a lengthy, drawn-out, complicated, exasperating, and frustrating affair for Justice Payne. Seduction, that is, in the sense of setting her up in business in such a way that the judge would reap the profits of her management and labor.

Not that Mercy was in any way opposed to setting up shop in a more formal manner—that, after all, was her very reason for being in the town on the island.

But the young woman proved a more formidable opponent than Justice was accustomed to dealing with. In fact, he had never before encountered a negotiator with her acumen and tenacity. Hidden inside her diminutive frame stood an outsized business sense and mental toughness that would stand shoulder to shoulder with that of the captains of industry at work in big cities building their empires of profitability. She could calculate figures in her head faster than a Chinese accountant at his abacus. She computed percentages and fractions, denominators and numerators, sums and tallies in a trice. Her ability to foresee and forecast, to appraise and assess, to gauge and guesstimate far outpaced the judge's ability to keep up.

Still and all, Justice Payne was no neophyte. What he lacked in alacrity he made up for in persistence and pigheadedness. He did not become sole owner of a town on an island and master of all he surveyed—at least as far as the waters' edge—through stupidity. Justice and Mercy argued and contended, disputed and debated, squabbled and quibbled, agitated and expostulated for hours on end, through days and nights innumerable, over weeks seemingly infinite.

"Damn it all, Mercy O'Malley! I swear you are the most intractable soul I have ever had the misfortune to contend with!"

"I could say the same of you, Judge. Only except that back in Ireland our neighbor had a hog. That pig had an endless appetite and never was content with what was put in front of him. Many's the time he would break out of his pen and through the hedge and into our potato field and help himself to a repast of my Pap's spuds. Much like you, that hog could never get enough, and like you again, he did not care whose pocket—or potato field—he picked!"

"Good Lord, woman! What on earth do pigs and potatoes have to do with it? Stick to the matter at hand!"

Mercy grinned, in marked contrast to the judge's florid frown. "Bear with me, Justice. It shall all come clear.

"My Pap, he warned that neighbor—the one what owned the hog—time and again to keep his pig penned. But the man, stubborn as that oversized shoat, contended it was not up to him to keep the pig out of our potatoes, but that it was Pap's duty to keep his potatoes out of the pig."

Justice slapped the tabletop. "Mercy sakes alive, woman! You are talking in circles! Get back to business!"

"Here's the thing, Judge. My Pap, he saw he was never goin' to get anywhere with that neighbor. There wasn't much he could do to the man without runnin' afoul of the law. But the pig, now that was another matter altogether. One dark night he caught the hog rootin' in the potato patch. The next morning, there was no sign of the porker—unless you was to sneak into Pap's smokehouse."

The judge sighed, long and labored. "I still don't get it, girl. If you've something to say, just say it—enough with this bogtrotter version of a parable."

Mercy sniffed and snorted. "Why it's as plain to see as the fat on a flitch of bacon. That pig, by never bein' satisfied with what he had, and, beyond that, the taking of what rightfully belonged to another, ended up with nothing. Nary a thing."

"And?"

"And that's the road down which you are heading, Justice. If you cannot come to terms that's fair to me and fair to you, you'll end up with naught."

The judge stewed for several minutes, then frustration bubbled up into a boil. "Damn it all, woman! You talk as though your demands are equitable. Bear in mind that this island is mine. The land on which the lot lies is mine. The materials from which the house will be built are mine! The expense to furnish it will be mine!" With that, he pounded the table with the palm of his hand as if striking the gavel to finalize a finding in court.

Mercy O'Malley allowed him to steam for a time, then reached across the table and laid her tiny hand atop the judge's larger appendage. She smiled. "You go on ahead then, Justice my friend. You build 'your' house on 'your' lot. Build it just as we've discussed—sizable and swank. Furnish it all opulent and plush-like, like we said. You go ahead, Judge. You do it. You build your house."

Of a sudden, Mercy stood, propped herself on her hands and leaned over the table until her nose nearly touched that of the judge, and shouted. "And what the bloody hell will you have, Justice? A big, expensive, empty building!"

She huffed and sat down. "Keep in mind that with all you've got, you ain't got the knowhow nor wherewithal to bring in girls to work the place. You ain't got the foggiest idea how to run the business. It ain't as simple as slingin' drinks, nor slicin' meat, nor kneadin' dough, nor stuffin' money into a safe, nor any other kind of job or business you've ever laid a hand to. These is girls, we're talkin' about here. Women! They're human bein's with minds and bodies of their own, and keeping them happy and hard at work is a thing you know nothing about and ain't likely to figure out anytime soon, if ever!"

The rant had taken all the air out of the room. Mercy and Justice sat silent for a time, waiting for tempers to temper. With emotions on a more even keel, they carried on discussions late into the night. They did not reach agreement that night, nor during a long string of similar nights. But, in the end, Justice was tempered by Mercy, and he succumbed to her wishes, mostly. The contract they signed had, as all good contracts do, something for each party in its provisions.

Convinced—or, more likely, worn down—that the negotiations were fair and equitable when he put pen to paper and formalized the agreement with his signature, it did not take long for the judge to come to believe that he had been taken advantage of. Mercy had hornswoggled him. He felt duped and deceived. Believed he had been bamboozled.

As he watched the comings and goings at Mercy O'Malley's House of Passion, then entered his share of the takings in his ledgers—inadequate as those books were—he grew increasingly annoyed and irate with his business partner. It was an itch he couldn't scratch.

But it was more than that. The belief that he had been outdone by a slip of a girl messed with his mind more than the numbers in the ledgers—sizable figures though they might be—frustrated his finances. He could not get over the notion that his pelf from the House of Passion was overshadowed by the profits Mercy O'Malley reaped.

His resentment of the woman increased with every passing day. His fruitless attempts to renegotiate their contract were unceasing. His annoyance at her success—even as it enriched him—intensified.

But, so far as Mercy was concerned, a deal was a deal. Justice Payne could suck eggs.

Opening the House of Passion for business was no small job. It is unlikely that anyone lacking Mercy O'Malley's knowledge and experience could have done it. She mailed missives to denizens of the demimonde in cities and towns far and wide, announcing the pending curtain raising on her palace. She stockpiled replies from applicants and selected candidates for further scrutiny, checked references, arranged interviews, and lined up a stellar stable of paramount paramours for the inaugural. Filed away for future reference, other candidates ensured profitable recruitment in days and years to come.

The house itself received similar scrutiny. From flocked wallpaper to fringed curtains, soft rugs to softer chairs, smooth whiskey to shiny silver, she inspected and supervised and rejected and approved with a critical eye and demanding expectations.

Through it all, and despite demands and standards that far surpassed those of Justice Payne, Mercy O'Malley maintained friendly relations and cordial connections with one and all. For all save the judge, doing business with the madam proved a pleasure.

Her popularity not only continued after throwing open the doors of Mercy O'Malley's House of Passion, it increased. Patrons were accommodated with kindness. She encouraged and rewarded good behavior and maintained order in her house with a firm but fair hand. The working girls, being the source of her bread and butter, were cosseted and coddled. Working hours were arranged to fulfill demand without overtaxing the workers. Meals were munificent, fringe benefits generous, pay surpassed ample and approached plentiful. And the ladies were allowed to pocket any tips that came their way.

All in all, Mercy's flower girls and the town maintained neighborly relations. The house was calm and quiet, serene and restful, creating no disturbances in the neighborhood. Even in her dealings with the judge, Mercy was meticulous, providing an accurate accounting of income in order to pay Justice his proper portion of the profits, and lease payments and assessed taxes handed over to Luther in a timely manner and always with a smile.

The only fly in the ointment, as it were, was the preacher. His house of worship, on the opposite side of the town from Mercy O'Malley's House of Passion, often resounded with sermons decrying the "Sin and depravity, the corruption and immorality across town." Few worshipers—at least among the males in the pews—paid it any attention. None of the wives suspected their contented husbands of any dalliances outside the marriage bed, including the sermonizer's spouse.

And far be it from Mercy O'Malley or any of her charges to allay those beliefs.

For his part, Justice Payne squirreled away his share of the wealth the house created. One might expect him to do so with a smile on his face, but such was not the case. Instead, he resented every cent. Every decimal point, every dime, every dollar entered in his ledgers riled him, knowing, as he did from her bank deposits, that Mercy's share far surpassed his own. And he suspected his bank saw only a fraction of her funds. He knew for a fact that a fireproof combination safe had been delivered to the house. He was aware of wire transfers from the telegraph office to far-off banks in big cities.

He believed, most of all, that Mercy had taken advantage of him in their business arrangement. Never mind that he fancied himself a tough negotiator and hard dealer. For a fact, his confidence in his skills only made it worse, as it implied her abilities surpassed his own.

As a result, at the same time Mercy O'Malley fostered friendly relations in the town, Justice Payne's sour mood and bruised ego led to testiness and bitterness that diminished his esteem on the island.

"I don't see why you're so aggravated, Judge," Luther said one day on the heels of Justice's tirade after entering his income from the floral establishment in his ledgers. "That's a right smart of money she handed over."

"Yeah, right. And I suppose she allowed you to climb the stairs to see that girl Rosy for free. I can't imagine any other reason for that smile on your face."

Luther's smile widened. "Oh, no, Judge—you're wrong. Miss Rose was busy. Miss Mercy fixed me up with a new girl. Her name's Daisy." He smiled again, stretched, and sighed.

Justice snorted. "So I suppose it's all over with Rose, then."

"Oh, no! She's still my one heart's desire, Miss Rose is."

The judge shook his head. "I don't understand you one little bit, Luther. You keep mooning after that girl, even knowing what she does for a living."

With a furrowed brow, Luther asked what he meant.

"Good Lord, boy! She's with other men all the time! And you know damn well what I mean by 'with' them."

"I don't see as that makes any difference," Luther said with a shrug. "Heck, I take my pleasure with some of them other girls from time to time, and that don't bother Miss Rose none."

The judge could only shake his head. "Well, never mind all that. The fact remains that that woman is taking advantage of me! She's taking more money out of that house than I am. It just isn't right. That's not how it's supposed to be."

Luther furrowed his brow and pursed his lips, pondering what the judge said. "I don't know, Judge. Seems like she—her girls, anyways—does all the work. Mercy runs the place. Heck, far as I know, you don't ever even go over there to check up on things."

Justice fumed. "Good hell, boy! That's why I've got you!" The judge slapped the desk. Twah, sleeping on a pillow on a chair, moaned and twitched. "And don't forget that I own that damn building! And every stick of furniture and every pane of window glass in it! I own the very ground it stands on! The street out front! The whole damn town! The entire island, for God's sake!"

Whack!

He pounded the desk again. The dog twitched at the report, halfway opened its eyes, then closed them again, uninterested in the cause of the disturbance.

Chapter Five

Twah lay stretched out across the end of the bar in the Cactus Thorn Saloon, his tail dangling off one side and his head the other. The time being barely past the dinner hour, few patrons and little activity kept him company. When the swinging doors flapped, he would scramble to roll onto his belly, then hoist himself up on the prop of his front leg to examine the entrant. If his finely tuned sense of character detected no threat, Twah would plop back down to his favored position and Alice (call me Al), the grog shop's bouncer, would give him a gentle pat and ruffle his fur. But should a growl rumble from deep down in his throat, and the hairs along his spine stand erect, tickling the palm of Al's hand tangled in the fur, the bouncer would slide off the stool upon which she sat, forewarned and on high alert.

The dog's assessment of the latest entrant into the Cactus Thorn left no reason for alarm. Al tousled his pelt, gave him a "good dog," then greeted the new customer with a warm welcome. He was a regular, known to while away many an afternoon nursing a glass or three of beer.

"How's it going, Al?"

"Far as I know, it ain't goin' nowhere. Everything seems to be stayin' put."

The man sat down two stools away from Al and took a sip from the beer mug that appeared in front of him as if by prior arrangement. "I guess that's a good thing."

"I reckon so."

"Too much excitement ain't good for a man. Upsets my digestion."

Al smiled. Given the size of the man's middle, that could prove a major malady.

"You know, Al, I've lived a good many years and seen a good deal of country. And I've got to say, I ain't never seen, in all my travels, no other lady bouncer than yourself."

Al shrugged. "Guess I can't comment on that, seein' as how I ain't never seen nowhere outside this here valley."

The man shook his head and chuckled softly. "I must say, however, that you seem eminently suited to the task. I recollect one time, not so long ago, seeing you escort a man nearly twice your size out the door—and he was not the least bit cooperative. And yet you pitched him into the street like nobody's business."

Again, the shrug. "I've done the same thing too many times to know which particular incident you're talking about."

"That's just the thing, Al. You're no more than a slip of a girl, yet you have an uncanny ability to manhandle relative behemoths. How do you do it?"

After a moment's consideration, Al said, "I don't rightly know what you mean by 'behemoth,' that being a word I ain't never heard before. But it has the sound of a big word, so I reckon it means big."

"You are correct." The man wet his tongue with beer from the mug. "But that is not the point—how is it you are able to better bigger, stronger men with seeming ease?"

"I ain't never give it much thought, now I think of it. I just go about doing what needs to be done whenever it needs doing. I reckon it has to do with my raising. I growed up on a ranch out yonder way in the valley," she said with a vague wave of her arm. "Had me six big brothers, I did. They never had no notion of what to do with a girl, so they rassled and grappled with me all my time growin' up, just like I was one of them.

"Besides that, me being raised on a ranch and all, I did my share of work come roundup and branding time. Flanking and legging down two-or-three-hundred-pound calves is a whole lot more of a job than throwing down a man that weighs maybe only half or two-thirds that much."

She smiled. "I guess it don't hurt none that I am well-schooled in what needs to be done to turn them big bull calves that's been hid out in the brush all summer into steers." Al blushed at the thought of what she had just said. "Not that I ever did nothing like that to no man, see—it's just that . . . well, I guess . . . hell, I don't know. Somehow it just makes a man seem all the more easier to handle, knowing that."

The sipper nodded slowly and squirmed a bit on his seat. "I see."

"And the men that's causing trouble in here is usually so drunk they couldn't hit the ground with their hat if given three tries, so it ain't like they're in any condition to fight back to where it amounts to much."

The man nodded again, and studied the bouncer for a long minute. "Another thing that gives me pause—and meaning no disrespect—why is it you dress in male habiliments?"

"Habiliments?"

"Clothing. You wear that hat, a man's shirt, trousers, and high-topped boots. Your hair is cut short, as well. You look like a cowboy."

"I guess I don't know no better. Like I said, I growed up with six big brothers. My Ma died right shortly after birthing me, so all I ever knowed was the ways of menfolk. And all I ever had to wear was hand-me-downs. Oh, I had Aunt Alice, but I only seen her on occasion. Not enough, I guess, for her to have much to do with my raisin'."

"Do you not ever yearn to be more, for want of a better word, lady-like?"

Al blushed. "Aw, shucks, Mister—that don't mean nothing to me. Oh, I have got all gussied up in a frilly dress, with painted lips and smudges on my eyelids, and face powder and reddened cheeks and all that. Did it when first I come to town to make my way." She sighed and shook her head. "It just never took with me, for some reason." Then Al's eyes widened and her eyebrows arched and she sat up straight on her stool. "But don't you go getting the wrong idea, Mister—I looked right fine, all fixed up like that. Why, I could've strolled into Mercy O'Malley's House of Passion and put every girl there to shame. So, I guess it's enough to know for my own self that underneath all these men's clothes—habiliments, like you say—I'm a right purty girl."

The man nodded his agreement. "I would not doubt it for even a moment."

The door flapped open again and Twah sprung to attention. But it was only Luther, the town marshal, so the three-legged dog flopped back down, again assuming his preferred position.

From where he sat, the beer sipper watched Al's expression soften and heard her sharp intake of breath. He fancied he could hear her heart pounding as well, but knew it was only his imagination. On second thought, he believed the notion might be real.

"Hey, Al," the marshal said.

"Good afternoon to you, Luther."

The marshal stopped and looked around the barroom, his thumbs hitched in his gun belt. "Any trouble?"

"Nope. Quiet as a coyote sneaking up on a jackrabbit."

Luther sighed. "Oh, well. All right, then. I guess that's a good thing." He stood for a time, looking around the saloon, hoping he had missed something that needed his attention. He found nothing.

"Say, Al, is he back there?" Luther said, pointing with his chin toward the rear of the saloon.

"The judge, you mean?"

"Sure. Who else?"

"Yeah, he's back there. Come in maybe an hour ago. Ain't been back out since, lessen he snuck out the back door. But I reckon Twah here would've took note of that."

Luther nodded one time and set out toward the hallway at the back of the saloon. Even from a distance, Al and the beer sipper heard his knock on the door of Justice Payne's office.

"Come on in," Luther heard the judge say. "There is no need to break down the door."

"Sorry 'bout that, Judge," the marshal said as he stepped into the room.

"What is it you need?"

"Oh, nothin'. It's pretty quiet out there. Just thought I'd drop by and see if there's anything you need. Al said you was back here."

"Is Twah with her?"

"Yessir. He's sittin'—layin'—out there on the bar like he does."

With a shake of his head and a sigh, Justice Payne shared his opinion—one Luther had heard voiced many times before—that Al was going to spoil the dog. Then the judge leaned back in his chair and studied his town marshal for a time. "Come to think of it, Luther, I'm glad you're here. There is something I'd like to discuss with you—an idea I've had."

Luther stood to his full height and smiled. "Golly! Why sure, Judge. Happy to help out!"

"You remember our talk about my wanting to get more money coming in?"

"Sure."

"Well, that's what my idea is all about." Justice stood and tugged at the lapels of his vest, took his suit coat from its hook and put it on, then took his hat from its hook. "Come with me."

Twah propped himself up on his front leg when he heard the men coming through the saloon. He whimpered and wagged his tail, but the judge paid him no mind. Al patted him on the head and nuzzled his neck and whispered sweet nothings in his ear. When the doors flapped shut, the dog again assumed his position, laying across the bar with his head flopped over one edge and his tail off the other.

Outside, the judge stood in the shade of the porch roof over the sidewalk in front of the saloon and surveyed the main street of his town. A few pedestrians were evident up and down the street, walking along the board sidewalks and crossing the street, coming and going in and out of the various places of business. Horsemen rode by from time to time, and now and then a wagon or buggy drove past. Saddle mounts were tethered to hitch rails here and there, and a few wagons were parked in front of a few stores.

"Take a look around, Luther. What do you see?"

With furrowed brow, Luther studied the scene to see if he had missed something, anything. "Gosh, I don't know, Judge. Just the usual stuff. Nothin' special far as I can see."

The judge said nothing for a long minute.

Luther broke into a sweat. He swallowed hard. "What is it, Judge? Is there something I missed?"

"No. No, Luther. Not at all. But I want you to notice how easy it is for folks to get around this afternoon."

"Sure."

"Now, then. Tell me what it will be like on this very street come Saturday."

"Aw, shucks, Judge. It'll be right crowded, what with all the folks comin' to town from out on the ranches to take care of whatever business needs tendin' to. And the cowboys and ranch hands will all show up come afternoon to blow off steam. Same with the boys from the loggin' camps and the mines. Heck, a man can't hardly get across the street there's so much traffic—but most of it ain't goin' nowhere. There's horses tied up everywhere. Wagons all over the place—so many they can't hardly get around. And down by Miss Mercy's place, it's worst of all. There ain't room to take a breath there's so many horses tied up down there."

The judge nodded. "Right you are, boy. Now, what's the problem with all that?"

Luther smiled. "Aw, heck, Judge! There ain't no problem a-tall."

"Oh? And why is that?"

"Well, heck, all them folks is spendin' money. Lots of it in places what you own. Why, even what they spend in other places means more tax money comin' in for you."

Justice laid a hand on the marshal's shoulder. "Now, just imagine, Luther, if the street was not all tangled up with parked wagons and tied-up horses. Think how much better it would be."

Luther worried over the idea for a time, then gave up and confessed to the judge that he did not understand.

"It's simple, boy. The easier it is for people to come and go on the street, the easier it is for them to get into and out of the shops. That means it will be easier for them to spend money—more money in more places! Do you see?"

Justice Payne could see that Luther was struggling with the notion. But he gave him time, enjoying watching the boy try to sort it out. When he figured the marshal had suffered enough, he said, "Think about it. If, say, some woman has in mind to buy herself a new hat, but there are so many wagons and buggies and such parked in the street, and all those others trying to get through all that mess—not to mention all those on horseback—that she dare not try to cross the street to get to the millinery shop.

"Or say some rancher wants to lay in a supply of pinto beans to see his outfit through the winter. But he can't see a way to get through the congestion to get down to the mercantile, and he sees that if he did manage to get down there, there are so many wagons parked out front he could not navigate his way into and out of the store anyway. Well, then, he'll do just what the lady wanting a hat would do—keep his money in his pocket and await a better day. And what if he or she decides in the interim that she really don't need that new hat after all, or that his cook can scrape by on what beans they've already got? Do you see it boy? The money we might have made from those transactions is gone! Poof! Business lost. Not a penny for our pockets.

"We must do something about it, Luther!" The judge emphasized the statement with a slap of the balled fist of one hand into the palm of the other.

Whack!

Luther, overwhelmed with the onslaught of ifs and ands, all but trembled in his boots. All color had drained from his face, beads of perspiration sparkled on his face. His breathing was shallow. "Wha . . . what—what can we do, judge?"

Justice Payne smiled. "I know just what to do, Luther. That is the idea I mentioned earlier. Not only will it make us more money from increased commerce through controlling traffic congestion on our main street, it will, in and of itself, provide a source of additional revenue—with little to no expense against it! I tell you, Luther, it is nothing short of brilliant!"

Sensing little would be required of him in the way of thinking, the marshal calmed down. What he did not know was that the judge's big idea would mean a lot more work for him, especially on Saturdays, when demand for his services was already at its peak. But extra work, as Justice Payne well knew, would not distress Luther in the least. At least, not like thinking would.

The judge smiled, more pleased with himself than usual. The only hair in the biscuit was the fact that Mercy O'Malley's House of Passion would likewise do even more business once his scheme took hold. But he was willing to overlook that, so excited was he at the prospect.

Justice Payne clapped his hands together, then scrubbed the palms against one another, eager to get started. "The first thing you need to do, Luther, is get on down to the newspaper office and have the printer there make up some handbills."

Chapter Six

The announcement of Justice Payne's latest scheme soon papered every porch post, bulletin board, telegraph pole, and previously blank wall all up and down the main street of his town on the island. People stopped to read the notice, a matter of only a few seconds, then shook their heads in wonder and walked—or rode, or drove—away.

<u>NO PARKING!</u>
ON THIS STREET
<u>ON SATURDAYS</u>
horses or wheeled vehicles!
violators will be
FINED!
conveyances of
repeat offenders will be
IMPOUNDED!
city ord. no. 374
<u>strictly enforced!</u>

Mercy O'Malley stormed through the swinging doors of the Cactus Thorn Saloon, wrapped in a bathrobe and waving a wrinkled paper torn from the gate post in the picket fence fronting her House of Passion. Although white, the handbill did not represent a flag of surrender. Not in any sense of the word.

Sensing something amiss, Twah roused himself from his sleep and struggled upright to prop himself on his front leg. A growl rumbled deep in his throat, but stopped short when he realized it was only Mercy

O'Malley and that there was most likely more bark than bite in her ire, strident though it may be.

"Where is he?" she said through gritted teeth.

"Who?"

"Damn it, Al! You know who! Is he back there?"

"If you mean the judge, he ain't."

"Where the hell is he?"

Al shrugged. "Can't say. He ain't been in here at all today." She shrugged again. "Could be most anywhere. It's his town."

The doors were already swinging shut before the enunciation of Al's last syllable. Despite being clad only in carpet slippers, Mercy's feet resounded on the board sidewalk as she made her way to the butcher shop. Justice was not there. She stopped in at the bank. He was not there. Nor was he at the café, in the hotel lobby, or among the loafers around the cracker barrel in the mercantile.

"Aha!" she said upon entering the bakery. "Hiding out in here, are you, Justice!"

Justice Payne stood at a table behind the counter, an apron wrapped around his waist. One hand held a spreader, the other a bowl of icing which he was slathering onto a tray of cinnamon rolls. "Hiding? I am not hiding. I am at work in one of my many enterprises—which is more than what you are doing, it would seem."

Mercy waved the paper. "What is the meaning of this?"

"You can read, Mercy. Its meaning seems clear enough, even to one of limited education."

"Of course I can read it! There ain't no doubt who cooked up such a cockamamie lot of nonsense. What I would like to know is *why*. What on earth could you be thinking? If you was thinking at all, which I doubt."

Justice and Mercy

Justice set the bowl aside, licked the icing from the blade of the spreader and dropped it onto the table. "I shall explain, Mercy, if you can rein in your tongue. The thing gallops on and on like a racehorse."

Mercy snorted and nodded her head with a snap. "Thoroughbred, too, it is. Go on then—explain yourself."

The judge shared his opinion, now oft repeated to concerned citizens, that traffic congestion on the street hindered commerce. While he admitted to Mercy that prohibiting parking might seem counterintuitive ("cockeyed," to use his actual terminology), ridding the street of its clutter of tethered and parked horses and wagons would improve traffic flow, allowing more shoppers unhindered access to more shops and stores, and that easier access meant more customers, and more customers meant more sales, which meant more money for more merchants. He neglected, of course, to mention that all those "mores" meant more for him, most of all.

"Why, you're daft, Justice!"

"Stop and think about it for a minute. Look at your own place. On any Saturday there are horses tied to horses out front of your house. Three deep at the hitch rail, tied to practically every picket on the fence, tethered to tree limbs, even ground-tied cowhorses cluttering up the street. And when buggies or buckboards or carriages are parked there—which they usually are—it makes it even worse."

Mercy sniffed. "Just goes to show how popular my place is."

"So you think. But look at it through the eyes of a longing logger. All it says to him is that wading through all those animals—not to mention the dung heaps piling up—may well make getting through the gate more trouble than its worth. Not to mention he'll think the place is overrun with customers and he'll be wasting half the day waiting.

"Face it, Mercy O'Malley. Even as popular as your House of Passion is, who knows how many prospective patrons you're missing out on on account of the street being crowded with parked animals and wagons and the like?"

The madam thought it over as she tore bits off a hard roll she had lifted from a basket on the shelf, chewing each bite slowly as she mentally masticated the judge's contentions and conclusions. "Mayhap you've got a point. But answer me this: where are the boys to tie their horses when they come to visit, if not on the street?"

"Oh, for heaven's sake, Mercy O'Malley! You know full well there are side streets and back alleys aplenty in this town. More than enough room for parking, without cluttering up the main street. And heaven forbid one of your 'boys' should part with fifty cents to stable his horse at the livery barn."

"*Your* livery barn, Justice. But you've a point, at that. Leastways as far as the alleys is concerned. But them boys would agree with me, to a man, when I say they'd find more satisfaction spreading that half dollar among my flowerbeds than spending it at your barn."

The judge smiled. "Well, you have me there, Mercy. What say we all calm down and give this ordinance a chance?"

Mercy shrugged and allowed that she would keep her powder dry for a few Saturdays and see how it went. But, if not satisfied with the results of the experiment, she warned, she would shoot off her mouth loud and long.

Come Saturday, Luther wore himself out carrying out his duties as town marshal, mostly enforcing the new ordinance against parking on the main street. It got to where he was so run down he felt like a centipede with sore feet. He wore out his stub of a pencil writing citations faster than he could whittle a fresh point with his pocketknife.

But he did not notice much difference in the flow of traffic. People read the signs. Now and then Luther heard laughter, from time to time he heard cussing. He watched a particularly aggravated citizen tear down a handbill, wad it up, and toss it into the street to be trampled and tromped. Another especially agitated man ripped one off a porch post and lit a match to it, then used the flaming notice to light a cigar, staring at the marshal with a mean smile the entire time. Another angry someone tugged on his gloves and threw road apples at one of the signs.

When handing out tickets, Luther was called names he had never heard before. Cuss words that had never rattled his eardrums assailed him in waves. And excuses! By two o'clock he had heard them all.

"Sign? What sign? I didn't see no sign."

"I thought it was a joke, so I never paid it any attention."

"I just had my hair fixed, and if I'm out in this wind any longer, it'll be ruined!"

"Hell, Marshal! You know I can't read a word. How d'you 'spect me to know what that sign says?"

"Something's covered up most of the sign, so couldn't read it." (Perhaps he referred to the one previously pelted with poop.)

"I only parked here to haul my liquored-up and passed-out buddy from out of the saloon. He's so damn big and fat there ain't no way I can carry him any farther than this!"

"I've got a duck in the oven, and it's almost done. I just need to run into the store there for a can of peaches for dessert. If I don't hurry, that duck will be overcooked and dry. I'll only be a minute."

"This horse has throwed a shoe—if I go to move him, he could pull up lame."

"Hell, Marshal! I don't dare move this here wagon—it's got a bad wheel that's about to bust! I gotta wait here for the wheelwright to bring a spare."

"Can't you see how I'm limping? You can't expect me to walk no farther than this!"

"It looks like rain, and I didn't want to get caught out in it."

"That sign says you can't park here on Saturday. Thing is, Luther, I was drunk last night, and I fell asleep right here in the wagon—so it was Friday when I parked here, not Saturday."

There were some, most, who pulled the assessed penalty from their pockets and paid Luther, even if they weren't happy about it. The judge had declared what he called "a mere two dollars" fine as punishment for a first offense, since the law was new and would take some getting used to.

Those who refused to fork it over—the most vociferous and raucous offenders—were escorted down to the town square. Rather than impede commerce at the Cactus Thorn Saloon on a busy Saturday, Justice had set up traffic court there on the square, next to the whipping post. His table and chair, hauled out from the saloon, held his big leather-bound book, his gavel, and the block upon which he struck the wooden hammer. He even took the trouble to wrap himself in the Navajo blanket that served as his ceremonial robes when court was in session. Twah, of course, lay on his cushion atop a stool next to the judge's bench.

Justice heard the same excuses the marshal had heard, and, like Luther, refused to let them stand in the way of justice.

Whack!

Whack!

Whack!

He hit the block smartly with each finding of guilt. Some of the most clamorous complainers were called out for contempt of court and assessed additional fines and penalties.

Whack!

Justice and Mercy

Some offenders cast down parking tickets to be stepped on, stomped on, and ground into the dirt. Others tore them to shreds and tossed them into the air like so much anti-celebratory confetti.

Whack!

One miner, dissatisfied with the situation, drew his pistol in a threatening manner, but holstered it when Twah leapt from his perch on the stool beside the bench and bit him on the ankle. The mucker's impertinence earned him an additional fine for contempt of court and yet another for disorderly conduct.

Whack!

Much murmuring and significant squawking accompanied the payment of penalties. The judge, however, did show mercy in one sense by accepting IOUs from those short of cash. All in all, the day's take was sufficient for the judge to call the program profitable, if too soon to call the experiment a success. Once the citizenry and visiting out-of-towners grew familiar with the parking proscription, he would be able to assess its effect on commerce and the attendant taxes collected.

Still and all, as he counted currency and stacked coins at the end of the day, he determined it all worthwhile, even in the face of public outcry. In other words, Justice was convinced that his gain was well worth their pain. Should conditions demand he abandon the ordinance and remove it from the canon of municipal codes at some future date, the funds generated by its enforcement on this inaugural day proved well worth the effort.

Luther did not agree.

The exhausted, overworked, drooping long arm of the law sat atop the edge of a water trough out front of the Cactus Thorn Saloon. His boots stood beside him on the main street, socks sticking out the tops. The cuffs of his pants were rolled above his knees, his feet immersed in the water. One hand—the one that had wielded the pencil all day—

was likewise submerged in the hope of relieving muscle strain and reducing swelling.

Alice (call me Al) stood on the saloon's porch in the fading light, her concern for Luther drawing her away from her post at the end of the bar. But Twah was on duty, perched there and propped on his front leg. Should any disturbance occur, or foul play threaten, the dog would summon her with a bark.

"You all right there, Luther?"

"Al, I don't believe I have ever been this wore out. Gosh darn it, even my ears is tired from hearing all them complaints from people about this here new parking ordinance the judge has put in place."

"Can I get you something to drink? A cold beer, maybe? A glass of wine? Whiskey?"

"Nah. My mouth is too tired to swallow. I spent all day talkin' to them that was talkin' at me. I think I used up a whole year's supply of words just today. So if you don't mind, don't ask me no more questions that I can't answer with only a 'yes' or a 'no.'"

"Sure." She sidled over to the edge of the porch and sat, dangling her legs over the side and swinging them back and forth. "Y'know, Luther, my place is lots closer than what yours is. Would you like me to walk you over there? I'll tuck you into bed so's you can get some rest. It's right quiet there, and there won't be nobody to disturb you. Even if the judge wants you for something, he wouldn't never think to look for you there."

Luther shook his head so lickety-split it made his hat shake and rattle. His eyes grew so wide the irises would have looked like yolks in eggs fried sunny side up had they been yellow rather than blue. The paleness of his face as the blood beneath the skin depleted added to the cackleberry effect. Or it would have were it not for the dark maw of his mouth as it hung open as far as the jawbones allowed.

Barely seated, Al was back on her feet in a trice. "Good Lord, Luther—what is it? You'd think I'd offered somethin' indecent! It weren't nothin' but a kindness. I never meant I'd stay there with you, for goodness' sake! I'd of just curled up somewheres here in a corner of the Cactus Thorn to sleep after closing up."

Al snorted and stomped her foot, the report echoing in the space beneath the boards like rolling thunder. "I can't believe you'd think such a thing of me!" She stomped again. "I guess it must be all that time you spend over at Mercy O'Malley's place that puts such thoughts into your mind. Well! I never. . . ." She turned and tromped her way back into the Cactus Thorn, the swinging doors banging back and forth and back and forth and back and forth and back and forth in her wake.

It took ten minutes beyond a quarter of an hour for Luther to recover and regain normal breathing. His initial shock at his misunderstanding of Al's offer, compounded by the vehemence of her reaction to his mistake, on top of the stress and strain of a long day of law enforcement had him so worn out and weary, and now depressed and disconsolate, that he was half tempted to slide on into the water trough, sink to the bottom, and stay there.

Chapter Seven

The effect of the parking—or no parking—ordinance spread far beyond the boundaries of the town and the island and the banks of the river. Citizens of the valley—those not residing in the town—took umbrage at the assessed fines they were forced to pay. Some crossed the mountains to visit the county seats of Jefferson and Adams Counties—depending, of course, on which side of the river they resided on—to complain to the authorities there.

Most were turned away post haste in either county, the officials there more than aware of the special nature of the town on the island. Each county had crossed the bridges to the island on numerous occasions in the past, arguing with Justice Payne over jurisdiction, taxation, deeds and titles, and other such legal concerns. His claim was so simple that it escaped him that the bureaucrats and civil servants and officials and pencil pushers and directors and commissioners and bean counters and managers and executives and supervisors and representatives sent to see him could not understand its straightforward clarity. Why could they not see that Jefferson County ended at the riverbank on one side of the stream, Adams County ended at the riverbank on the other side of the stream, and his island, contiguous to neither riverbank, separated from each by a channel of the river, was part of neither county? Simple!

Whether fully satisfied with his reasoning or not, whether content with his explanation or not, they left town castigated and cowed, more often than not with their tails between their legs, with a firm resolve never to return to the town on the island in the river, beyond the influence of their respective counties.

Whack!

And so no official delegation from either county came to complain on behalf of its citizens about the newly implemented ordinance in the independent town.

However.

One eager young attorney, new to the area, accepted a retainer from one disgruntled citizen with a promise to employ the finer points of the law to recover his fine, have the ordinance rescinded, and collect court costs and expenses from the offending town's government in the process.

When the misguided advocate rode into town one quiet morning, Justice Payne soon learned of his presence and was informed by the town marshal that the counselor claimed to have business before the court. The judge wandered out of his rooms at the back of the Cactus Thorn Saloon, big book and gavel in hand, Navajo blanket over his shoulders, and took his seat behind the table—bench, if you would rather—on the dancehall stage.

Whack!

The blow startled the few drinkers in the establishment at that early hour, causing one to slosh beer out of his mug into a puddle on the bar. Another choked on a swallow of whiskey gone astray at the shock, and coughed and hacked several times in recovery. Excited at the prospect of some excitement, the patrons adjusted their chairs or turned away from the bar so as to pay attention to the proceedings.

Justice declared court in session. Luther read from a card handed him by the judge, advising all who had business before the court to come forward. The lawyer stepped up. The judge told him to come closer so he would be sure to hear his complaint clearly. But the true reason for the gesture was to position the attorney so he had to crane his neck to look up at the judge, and the judge could look down his nose at the advocate from a superior position.

"State your business, Sonny."

The lawyer cleared his throat and handed up a thick sheaf of papers. "I have a petition to place before the court, your honor. A complaint concerning the illegal establishment of an ordinance forbidding parking on a public thoroughfare."

Justice riffled through the pages, pausing now and then to glance briefly at the words. He set the papers aside and leaned forward. "I have neither the inclination nor the disposition to waste the court's time reading all that tedious twaddle."

The attorney's eyebrows arched. "But Your Honor—"

"Save it," the judge said. "Just tell me—who the hell are you representing?"

The advocate cleared his throat. It took him a moment to find his voice. "It's . . . it's right there in the petition your honor."

"Like I said, counselor, I'm not interested in this stack of circumlocution and verbosity. Just tell me—who are you here to represent?"

The lawyer gave the name of his client, but said he intended to contact other injured parties and perhaps refile the claim as a class action suit on behalf of all who have been defrauded of funds by means of the patently unconstitutional ordinance forbidding parking on a public thoroughfare—with, of course, compensatory damages and court costs sought as well as punitive damages.

As the attorney made his argument, Justice Payne opened his big book and studied several pages. Then, he said, "Do you really think you have a chance with this ill-advised action, Sonny?"

"Most certainly, Your Honor."

"And you say that with full realization that I am the judge who instituted the law you're whining about, and this is the court that collected the fines in question?"

The attorney swallowed hard. "Yes, Your Honor. I am fully aware that you will likely rule against me. Should that prove to be the case, I am fully prepared to appeal your decision."

"To who?"

The perplexed counselor asked the judge to repeat the question.

"Who are you going to appeal to?"

"Why, the district court in Jefferson County, where the claimant resides."

Justice Payne smiled and shook his head.

"It sounds like you are well educated in matters of the law."

The attorney smiled and stretched to stand taller than his natural height. "Yes, Your Honor. I like to think so."

"Unfortunately, Sonny Boy, it seems like you shirked your geography lessons."

The attorney sagged. For a moment that stretched into a minute, then two, the bewildered lawyer wondered what the judge meant.

Finally, figuring the youngster had suffered enough, Justice spoke. "Tell me, Boy, how did you get to town?"

"Sir? I mean Your Honor?"

"How did you get here?"

"Horseback. I rode a horse rented from a Jefferson County livery stable."

The judge expelled a long breath. "How, for heaven's sake, did you get here, into this town?" he said, punching his pointer finger onto the tabletop.

After thinking for a time, the attorney said he had followed the road.

The judge, exasperated, stood and leaned across the table, further intimidating the attorney. "Do you remember crossing a bridge?" he said, in a voice forceful enough to riffle the sparse side whiskers on the lawyer's face.

"Bridge? Why, yes, Your Honor. I remember crossing the bridge. The horse I rode was a bit hesitant—I believe the hollow sound of it was unfamiliar—"

"Never mind that! What was under the bridge?"

"Why, water, Your Honor. A river."

Justice sat down. "Right. A river. Now for the geography lesson—which also has legal implications and ramifications as you shall see, so pay attention. That river represents the end of Jefferson County. Once you set foot on that bridge—or your horse did—you were no longer in Jefferson County. And once you stepped off that bridge, you were on an island. An island! An island that is no part of Jefferson County! Do you see what I am getting at, young man?"

In an instant, the blood drained from the lawyer's face, even as understanding filled his eyes.

The judge gave him a moment to absorb the newfound knowledge. Then, "Here's what it all comes down to. It is a matter of jurisdiction. Your client has no standing to challenge the laws and ordinances of this town. Nor can they be appealed to the district court in Jefferson County." The judge smiled. "So, you see, my decisions are final, and my rulings are law in this town, on this island."

The attorney bowed his head and tried to shrink into invisibility, or perhaps seep through the floorboards and disappear.

"Now, then, you have wasted a great deal of this court's time and caused me no small measure of aggravation. And, for that, you must be punished!"

Unable to decide between humility and protest, the counselor said nothing.

"I hereby sentence you to be chained to the whipping post in the town square, where you will receive ten lashes, to be administered by the town marshal." The judge nodded toward Luther, standing beside

Justice and Mercy

the dancehall stage with hands clasped behind his back, doing his best to look official in his duties as bailiff. "That's him, there. Luther. As you can see, he is a big, strong boy. And he is adept at handling the whip."

The attorney panicked. "But your honor!"

The judge studied him for a moment. "I'll tell you what, boy. Since you are young and unschooled in frontier justice, and since this is your first appearance before this court and hence your first time wasting our time, here's what I will do. Your sentence will be served over the course of two sessions at the whipping post."

"Your honor?"

"You will be taken from the courtroom henceforth by the town marshal and escorted to the town square, and at that appointed place he shall mete out half the sentence—administering on this day five lashes. Do you understand?"

The lawyer nodded.

"Furthermore, you are hereby ordered to return here seven days hence to receive another five lashes on that day, thereby completing your sentence. Do you understand?"

The attorney nodded.

A respectable, if not sizable, crowd witnessed the flogging. Luther spared the lash somewhat, but not enough that the judge would castigate him for leniency. His punishment complete, the young lawyer mounted his rented horse, rode down the street, crossed the bridge, urged the horse into a high lope, and disappeared behind a dust cloud of his own making.

"What'd you go and do that for, Judge?"

"Whatever do you mean, Luther?"

"Divide up his whippin' thataway. You said ten lashes, but he got off with only five."

"You were there—in court—weren't you?"

"Sure."

"So, you heard the part about me ordering him to come back next week for the other five lashes."

"Yeah, I heard it." Luther looked at the judge, took a deep breath, and said, "But, golly gee, I don't think he'll be comin' back to get them."

The judge smiled. "You don't?"

"Nope."

Justice laughed and slapped the marshal on the shoulder. "Neither do I, Luther. Neither do I. I don't suppose he'll ever come back to challenge our ordinances or try a case in my court, either."

A few Saturdays passed and the public grew accustomed to the no-parking ordinance. Luther spent less time writing tickets for illegal parking. He got back to his accustomed routine of ticketing riders and drivers for speeding, traveling on the street at a rate that endangered the public. It was all a matter of interpretation, and Luther's interpretation carried the weight of law. Not once did Justice Payne overrule one of his citations, no matter the excuses, complaints, explanations, or arguments offered by the offending parties.

Whack!

The penalties assessed by the judge were likewise arbitrary and capricious. More often than not, Justice ordered the defendant to empty his pockets. Then he would thumb through his big book, smack his gavel, and—lo and behold—the amount of the fine equaled the contents of the cash in the offender's pockets. The same was likely to be the case with other miscreants Luther dragged before the bench—drunk and disorderly, causing a ruction, kicking dogs, lewd behavior toward womenfolk, vagrancy, theft, skipping out on a bar tab, spitting on the sidewalk, engaging in fisticuffs that resulted in damage to persons or property, hoorawing and howling at the moon at an unreasonable hour, littering, stealing chickens, jaywalking, unnecessary abuse of Chinese or Mexicans or Indians, and anything else that Luther thought might offend the judge's sensibilities and his attitudes concerning acceptable behavior in his town and on his island.

Whack!

When necessary, in cases of serious violations, or when the guilty party lacked the means to pay a fine, Justice Payne reluctantly sentenced the criminal to some number of lashes. Or, rarely, to confinement. There was no jail in the town, no prison, no lockup or hoosegow or jug. The judge, you see, thought such distasteful—a blemish on the town. So, the whipping post in the town square served a dual purpose. Offenders found guilty were chained to the pillar and left to languish in embarrassment as they awaited the onset of the lash or release. For whatever reason, Justice found this somewhat primitive approach less offensive than the presence of heavy locks and iron bars in his town. At times, particularly after an especially celebratory weekend, there may be multiple men tethered to the post.

If public works were wanting—say the construction of a new commercial building to house a new rent-paying and taxpaying tenant, or improvements to streets or sidewalks—the judge may sentence likely looking arrestees to a period of hard labor. Remarkably, the length of the sentences most often coincided with the estimated time needed to complete the public works project, with as many convicts assigned to the task as needed to finish the job in a reasonable period of time.

Whack!

Chapter Eight

Mercy O'Malley left her suite on the upper floor of her House of Passion. With afternoon looming, she would soon make the rounds of the upper hallways, knocking on doors to awaken the girls in readiness for the coming night's work. But first, she would go downstairs to the kitchen, pour herself a cup of tea, toast a slice of bread, and spread it liberally with butter and red currant jelly. She stopped on the balcony landing to survey the parlor below to assure herself that the night before had been dusted, swept, mopped, and polished away in readiness for the evening's festivities to come.

There, in an overstuffed chair, sat Justice Payne.

It was a rare occurrence for the judge to darken the door of Mercy O'Malley's House of Passion. The town marshal usually stopped in to collect the rent and the town's—the judge's, really—share of her monthly take. Officially, it was a tax. In reality, at least to Mercy's mind, it was graft. A shakedown. Corruption. Extortion.

"Good morning, Mercy," the judge said as she started down the stairs.

"To what do I owe the pleasure of your company, Justice? Business, or pleasure?"

"Just business, I'm afraid. Here to collect what's due."

"Why you?"

"Why not?"

"It's just that Luther is usually the bearer of bad news."

"Oh. Yes. Well." The judge smiled. "You know that I take an interest in all the goings on in town. I like to stay close to my tenants. Just to assure myself—and them—that all is well."

Mercy snorted. "As well as can be expected, I guess, considering you always approach with your hand out."

"Mercy, Mercy, Mercy! How can you say such a thing? Why, with the unfair financial arrangement you forced me into, you have no complaint! Your rates are minuscule in comparison to those of my other tenants—both in terms of rent and taxes. You have a sweetheart deal, Mercy. You would do well to remember that."

Another snort. "Sweetheart deal! Lord above, Justice, after your payoff comes off the top, I've barely enough left to keep the candles lit and the doors open. Besides, rates aside, money from my business does more to support this town than all the rest—your businesses included! And you know it."

"Ah, Mercy—your understanding of the finances of the town is sorely misinformed."

"People talk. And I listen. I have my ways. Don't think for a minute that I could not come within a schilling of knowing your finances. Truth be told, my estimate would likely prove more accurate than yours, given the sorry state of your ledgers."

The judge gasped. "What do you know about my ledgers?"

Mercy smiled. "I won't be a minute." She went back up the stairs and opened the safe in her suite, then returned with an envelope full of cash for the judge.

Justice peeked into the envelope. "Is it all here?"

Mercy only smiled.

"How do I know you are not shortchanging me?"

Mercy leaned forward, put her hands on the arms of the chair the judge sat in, and leaned in until her nose nearly touched his. "Why, Justice!" she said in a voice barely above a whisper. "How could you think such a thing of sweet little ol' me?"

The judge squirmed. Mercy planted a kiss on his forehead, then backed away. "Anytime you'd care to take a closer look, you are surely welcome," she teased, fingering the ties on her robe.

Red in the face, the judge said that would not be necessary. He hurried out the door, cussing himself for always letting the woman get the best of him. What was worse, she enjoyed it so. Worse still, he had a sneaking feeling that he did not know the worst of it. What the hell did she mean about talking to other businesspeople in the town? And what did she know about his bookkeeping, and his finances?

Mercy stood at a front window at the House of Passion, parting the tasseled drapes and watching through lacy curtains as Justice Payne hurried down the street. She smiled at his discomfort in her presence, and vowed to crank it up a few notches.

Despite her complaints to the judge concerning the paucity of profits and a business teetering on the edge of insolvency, the House of Passion was, in matter of fact, a virtual money machine. So much money passed through her hands that she could barely dispose of it. She gave the girls hefty bonuses on top of a generous salary and a percentage of all the business they concluded. She tipped vendors and delivery drivers lavishly. The house staff—cleaners and cooks and handymen and bartenders and laundresses—earned wages well above the going rate in the town, or anywhere else in the known world where they might ply their trades.

As a result, résumés from working girls arrived in every post. Applications for work fell through the letter box with frequency. Requests for interviews were as regular as clockwork. As well, those on the payroll performed at the highest levels and beyond. Floors in the House of Passion were scrubbed and waxed until they sparkled. Rugs and carpets were continually cleaned and freed of dust. Walls always wiped clean of soot and smoke residue. Sconces, shades, and chimneys on lamps and lanterns buffed to a high gleam. Woodwork oiled to a high luster. Glassware glistened and glittered.

And, most of all, the working girls went about their business with enthusiasm. Repeat customers were routine, and fresh patrons arrived from far and wide in response to word-of-mouth praise for Mercy O'Malley's House of Passion that radiated like sunbeams. The place was universally regarded as a garden of delights tended by dainty, delicate, beautiful, aromatic, hand-picked, fragrant, and always fresh flower girls.

All of which presented problems for Mercy O'Malley. As mentioned, her House of Passion made money. Lots of it. The place was awash in coin, afloat in currency. The fireproof iron safe was overstuffed to near bursting at the seams. Cupboards, cabinets, cubbyholes, and other places of concealment held bundles, bales, bags, and stacks of cash. The backyard was littered with hidey-holes.

On the other hand, deposits at Justice Payne's bank in the town were minimal in order to keep the judge unaware of the House of Passion's actual financial performance. But wire transfers to banks in several cities kept the telegraph lines humming and the telegraph operator well paid for his silence. (And rewarded in other ways for his discretion.)

Shared animus and mutual animosity notwithstanding, Justice Payne and Mercy O'Malley were not opposed to cooperation when conditions required it in the best interests of the town.

For example.

While Adams and Jefferson Counties had abandoned all hope of cordial (and profitable) arrangements with the town on the island and its inhabitants, there were still governmental rabble-rousers abroad who found the situation intolerable and sought out ways to bring the island to heel. Among the instigators were certain officials at the state capital in appointed and patronage positions. Statutes and constitutional prohibitions allowed the state to deal solely with designated counties. Counties, in turn, dealt with the cities within their borders, collecting fees and taxes and the like, and passing the state's share of the revenue up the line.

But with the town on the island being independent of any relationship with a designated county, there existed no legal means for state government to get its hands in the pockets of the town.

This, they found unacceptable. Efforts at passing laws to "correct" the unique situation failed at every attempt, thanks to widespread attitudes among the electorate and the elected favorable to freedom from interference, against big government, supportive of sovereignty, and opposed to oppressive taxation. And, it should be said, owing in no small measure to intense lobbying efforts and the occasional bribe, financed by the town on the island, in order to ensure maintenance of the status quo.

But the bureaucrats were nothing if not patient and persistent. Their most recent attempt to subjugate the citizens of the town on the island involved an emissary in the person of Percival—"please don't call me Percy"—Van Buskirk of the state's Department of Revenue and Taxation.

He came to town in a coupé driven by a coachman and took rooms in the hotel. He signed the register with nothing more than his name, and throughout his visit told no one of his purpose or position. His driver, however, let it slip in convivial conversation with a local chatterbox after being stood to several drinks at the Cactus Thorn Saloon.

For his part, Percival Van Buskirk poked around in shops and stores, and observed comings and goings at offices and establishments, all the time taking notes in a pocket notebook. He asked no questions, offered no opinions, spoke only when spoken to, and confined his answers to as few words as possible. Perhaps he thought himself inconspicuous in his silence, but the opposite was true.

His appearance, too, stood out. His hair was parted so severely the job may have been accomplished with a meat cleaver or carving knife. His collar so starched and creased so acutely it could be used to slice bread. From there down, he wore a perfectly knotted necktie, boiled shirt under a five-button vest with matching suit coat and pleated and creased trousers, and shoes so shiny the sun glinting off their polished surfaces caused Percival to squint.

Unsure of his exact purpose, the judge had Luther keep the visitor under close observation. Not once did Percival commit anything that could be construed as even the slightest offense against any conceivable law or ordinance. And his polite refusal to engage in conversation and his oblique answers to questions left Justice Payne unsure how to deal with the government interloper who, he was sure, was up to no good.

In his quandary, he turned to Mercy O'Malley.

The madam herself turned out to take matters in hand. She ventured out into the main street dressed modestly, but with flair. She studied his movements for a time. She armed herself with an armful of packages wrapped in brown paper and tied with string from the dress shop and the grocer, and positioned herself to step into Percival's path as he rounded a corner (the collision assisted by a lookout and signal from Luther).

"Oh, my!" she said as she sat herself down on the board sidewalk, spewing wrapped bundles in every direction.

"I . . . I'm sorry," Percival said. "I didn't see you—I never . . . I mean—are you all right?"

Mercy fanned her face with a gloved hand. "Oh, dear! Oh . . . oh." She tipped her head upward and lifted the floppy brim of her hat to look at Percival. "Oh. I must have stumbled. So clumsy."

"Oh, no, Ma'am—Miss—it was all my fault, I assure you. Are you all right?"

Flexing a few joints and stretching a few muscles, Mercy added a few mild moans and groans for effect. "I don't know . . . I think so." She attempted to rise, but failed in the attempt and sat back down. "Oh, dear!"

"Here. Let me help you."

Mercy took the proffered hands in her own and allowed Percival to lift her to her feet, holding back just enough to test his strength. Once on her feet, she fanned her face some more, leaning against the man for support. "Oh, my. Dear me. I'm sure I shall be fine once I get home and lie down."

Percival did not respond. Mercy took a hesitant step away from him, bent over to retrieve a package, but stopped partway down with a sharp "ooh!" and placed a hand on the small of her back. "Oh, dear," she said as stood back up. "Would you mind helping me with my shopping?"

"Oh!" Percival said, jolted back to reality. "Of course. I'm sorry. I beg your pardon."

He picked up a couple of packages and handed them to Mercy. When he handed her a third one, she let the first one fall.

"Oh, my!"

"Here, let me get that," Percival said as he picked up the fallen package, then another one. He tried to help her arrange the bundles in her arms, but Mercy fumbled and fussed with them in near total incompetence.

"Oh, dear. I don't know how I shall ever get home!"

Percival looked stricken. Mercy batted her eyelashes and smiled through feigned pain. He said, "I . . . I guess I could escort you home. And carry the packages."

"Oh, no! I'm sure that won't be necessary." Mercy allowed her knees to sag slightly and reached out and held Percival's arm for support.

"Please. It is the least I can do." He placed a hand on her elbow.

"Oh, no, Sir. I won't hear of it." She sagged again, enough to cause him to grasp her elbow tighter to hold her up.

"I think I should. Yes. I must." He guided Mercy to a porch post and helped her lean against it for support. He gathered the spilled parcels, wrapped them in one arm, took Mercy again by the elbow and led her shaky self along the sidewalk in the direction of home.

Little more need be said of Percival Van Buskirk's visit to Mercy O'Malley's House of Passion on his mission of mercy. Suffice it to say that once inside its walls, he was treated to the grand tour and handed a bouquet of flowers. His knowledge of horticulture increased immensely. He was introduced to Posy and Hyacinth. He met Violet and Rose. Daisy, Camellia, and Iris contributed to his education.

The Percival Van Buskirk who staggered out of Mercy O'Malley's House of Passion two days later bore little resemblance to the man who had come to the town on the island. He was dissipated, dissolute, discombobulated, and disheveled. His once sharply parted hair was mussed. His shirt wrinkled, tie untied and draped around his neck, starched collar stuffed in the pocket of his suit coat, vest buttoned out of alignment, trousers sagging at the knees. His shoes retained their former polish and shine but had little effect on the man, as the eyes that usually squinted against the sun's gleam off their surfaces were already at half-mast.

One other big difference was evident in Percival's appearance and bearing. His mouth, normally a severe, straight slash across his visage, was today softer, mildly bruised, the lips looser and slightly turned up at the corners in a smile that may—or may not—be a permanent improvement.

Justice Payne watched the bureaucrat's coupé wheel out of town under the whip of a coachman suffering a hangover, the passenger sprawled in his seat, arms out flung, eyes staring into nothing save, perhaps, fond memories and mental images of his visit to the town on the island.

The judge was confident that the threat was eliminated.

For now.

But he was also aware that someday, some other functionary from the far-off capital city would come along, intent on upsetting the apple cart.

Chapter Nine

It was a busy night in the Cactus Thorn Saloon. Being a Saturday night, the normal crowd of townsmen was supplemented by the usual weekend influx of loggers, miners, ranch hands, and cowboys from around the valley and the surrounding mountains. Luther wandered from place to place, keeping his eyes peeled for any sign of trouble. He watched the card games, eyed the crowd around the stage where the dancing girls pranced and paraded, and observed the drinkers seated at tables and standing at the bar. Al did likewise from her post at the end of the bar closest to the doors, also keeping an eye on the comings and goings—mostly comings—through the batwing entry. As usual, Twah was stationed atop the end of the bar. However, given all the activity, rather than flopped and somnolent he stood alert and propped on his one front leg, ready to sniff out the slightest threat.

Hands encased in thin and tight black gloves rested for a time atop the swinging doors as the man who wore them studied over the doors the interior of the saloon. Then he pushed them open and stepped through, letting the doors swing shut behind him, and stood.

A low growl rumbled from Twah's throat. Al placed a hand on his head.

The man standing there looked like no one she had ever seen in the saloon—or anywhere else, for that matter. He bore no resemblance to the workmen, tradesmen, and businessmen who routinely populated the place. From head to toe, he was clad entirely in black. Black boots, pants, gunbelt, knife scabbard, vest, shirt, and string tie. His hat, also black, was a low-slung affair with a flat crown and a brim so straight and stiff Al thought it could slice through a sizable tree trunk if flung at one. His heavy eyebrows and sideburns were black. A narrow stripe of black beard stretched from his lower lip to the bottom of his chin. And his black mustache was waxed so sharp and straight it could put a partner's eye out should a passionate kiss go astray.

Al and Twah were not the only ones taken by his appearance. All the men standing at the bar turned as one to study him. Chairs scraped and skittered on the floor as their occupants turned to watch. Card games halted mid-hand. Dancing girls stopped mid-stride and the fingers of the accordion player to whose tune they danced froze above the keys and buttons, the bellows stopped mid squeeze.

The fascination lasted but a moment, and the chaotic cacophony, commotion, and clatter returned.

"Don't you worry none, Twah," Al said, patting the dog's head. "I'll keep an eye on him." She caught Luther's eye across the room, and he nodded once in understanding.

But the man did nothing untoward; only found and filled a vacant space at the bar and ordered a drink. He faced the room and sipped at the shot, resting his elbows on the bar behind him as he scrutinized the table games, watching cards slide across the felt, chips clatter into the pot, and decks shuffle. He kept up the vigil through three drinks. Then, having selected his game and identifying his marks, he slid into a seat at a poker table when the previous occupant left in disgust at his luck—or the lack of it.

He slid a gold half eagle and a stack of silver dollars toward the dealer, who pushed back a pile of chips.

"What is the game, *mes amis*?" he said with an accent seldom, if ever, heard in the town on the island.

"Poker. Five-card draw," came the answer from the dealer, and the game commenced.

Over the course of the next three or four hours, the new man won a few and lost a few, then won a few more and lost a few less, then won a lot more and lost hardly at all. The games drifted from draw to stud to straight poker and back again, with the man in black hauling in more pots than chance would suggest he should. He played his cards close to the vest, and his patterns of checking, betting, calling, folding, or raising were not discernible by anyone at the table or in the crowd that surrounded the table to increasing depths as the night progressed.

Luther watched the game from a position he established behind the right shoulder of the man but saw nothing unusual. (Which, of course, would not surprise anyone familiar with the marshal's understanding—lack of it, to be precise—of games of chance played with pasteboards.) Still suspicious, he elbowed his way through the ring of onlookers and made his way back to the judge's rooms in the rear.

"Judge, you oughta come out here."

"Oh? Why is that?"

"There's a feller what come in earlier. Odd-lookin' sort, he is—all dressed in black."

"So? Is there some dress code that has been established at the Cactus Thorn of which I am unaware?"

"Oh, no, Sir. That ain't it. It's just that he don't look—well, what I mean is, he's different. But mostly, it's his card playing. He's been playing a good long while and he's won a whole lot more than what he's lost."

Justice yawned. "Far as I know, Luther, that's what every player who is dealt a hand at one of the tables hopes for. They all think they will go home a winner. Otherwise, most men would not ante up. Oh, there are some who just cannot help themselves and would bet on damn near anything and lose, then offer up the same bet at double or nothing."

"Yessir. I know that. It's just that . . . well, it's hard to say . . . there's just something that don't seem right. Besides that, he talks funny. When he talks at all, which ain't much."

The judge laughed.

"Not only that," Luther said. "Al don't feel right about him neither."

Justice said nothing.

"Besides, Twah growled when he come in. And he's been watching that man with his hackles up all night."

"Twah!" the judge said, all but jumping out of his chair. "Why didn't you say so?" He lifted his suit coat from the rack and slid into it as he crossed the room and out the door.

Working his way through the observers, Justice stood behind the player and watched the game through several rounds of betting and several hands more. He could not see any sign of palming cards, holdouts, concealed cards, marked cards, or other forms of cheating. And since the deal stayed with the house dealer, there could be no stacking the deck, dealing from the bottom, or otherwise manipulating the pasteboards.

The judge had Luther fetch an experienced local cardsharp from his seat at another table. The man was on a winning streak and unhappy about cashing in, but the marshal made it clear his presence was required. Justice explained the situation and voiced his suspicions, although the gambler was aware of the man in black's success as was everyone else in the house.

"Keep an eye on him for a while. See if you can see what he is up to."

An hour later, the local man reported nothing unusual—except that the out-of-towner was unusually lucky and that the cards seemed to fall in his favor more often than they ought to by chance. Still and all, it came down to nothing more than luck so far as he could see.

The moon set in the west and dawn colored the sky to the east when the bartender hollered out, "Last call for alcohol!" Most of the patrons had long since gone home. The dancing girls had tucked into their beds hours ago, and the accordion player's instrument was locked in its case to rest up for the next entertainments. Only the game in which the man in black played was still in session, his opponents determined to win back their losses and continuing to fail in their attempts. As the out-of-towner pulled in a sizable pot, the dealer stacked the cards and declared the session at an end.

Justice told Luther to keep an eye on the gambler, then crawled into bed hoping the man would pocket his winnings and leave town.

But it was not to be.

Following a few hours' sleep at the hotel, the man in black reappeared. He ate a late lunch—or later breakfast—at the café, wandered the main street for a bit, then walked through the doors at the Cactus Thorn Saloon. Only a few habitual drinkers were on hand to witness his arrival, along with a bartender restocking the shelves, washing glasses, brewing coffee, and polishing the bar top.

The gambler sat at the table he had occupied the night before and took the same seat. He pretended not to notice when Luther eased into the saloon and made his way to Justice's rooms in the back.

"Judge!" He shook his boss's shoulder. "Judge!" He rocked the shoulder again.

Justice rolled over in his bed, propped himself on an elbow, and forced his eyes open. "Luther," he moaned. He fell onto his back and covered his face with a pillow.

"C'mon, Judge," the marshal said. "That tinhorn gambler is back. The one all in black."

Pulling the pillow away, Justice stared at Luther through bleary eyes. "Is he doing anything wrong?"

"Nosir."

"Is he breaking the law in some fashion?"

"No."

Justice groaned. "Well, what exactly is he doing?"

"He's sittin' out there at a card table all by hisself."

"That's all?"

"That's all."

The judge sat up and swung his legs off the side of the bed. "Why are you telling me this, Luther? Why did you wake me out of a sound sleep to tell me a man was sitting in my saloon?"

Luther stammered and stuttered as he formulated a response. "You . . . you told me to keep an eye on him. Last night, you said that. You said I was to keep an eye on him."

Scrubbing the sleep off his face with the palms of his hands, the judge acknowledged the order he had given and, to humor the lawman if for no other reason, asked for a full report. Luther told how the gambler had gone straight back to the hotel and stayed there (he neglected to mention he had fallen asleep in a chair in the lobby and would not have known if the man he was supposed to be watching had come and gone several times). Then, Luther told him how the gambler had eaten at the café (he neglected to mention that he was hungry himself and had lost track of his mark when he slipped into the backdoor of the café and cadged a snack from the cook).

Luther shrugged. "Then he come in here. That's all."

Shaking his sagging head, Justice asked if there was anything else. When Luther allowed there was not, the judge dismissed him and told him to go home and get some sleep. Then he washed his face and shaved, got dressed, and walked out into the Cactus Thorn, Twah tagging along behind. He stopped at the bar and fetched a cup of coffee, asked for a second one, and carried both over to the table where the man in black sat.

"Good morning to you," the judge said, and held a steaming mug out toward the gambler. "Coffee?"

"*Merci*."

"Mind if I sit?"

The man shook his head.

Justice sat and introduced himself. Twah sat down next to the judge's chair.

"Justice Payne," the gambler said. "I thought as much. It has been told to me that this your town."

"Aah, that's a bit of a stretch. Who told you that?"

The man shrugged. "A little here. A little there. It is not a matter of secrecy it would seem."

"Well, I suppose in a sense it is true that this is my town. When I first set foot on this island there wasn't a thing here but scrub trees and brush and bunchgrass. And that was all anyone else could see. But me, I saw possibilities."

The judge went on to tell how he had built the bridges, the town, the businesses, and a good life. Through it all, the gambler sat silent, but not quiet. His hands were never still, playing the whole time with a deck of cards and a stack of poker chips. He did tricks the like of which Justice had never seen before, and the ones he had seen were performed with a dexterity and finesse never before seen in his experience.

The gambler spread a deck in a fan across the table, then swept it back up as if in a single motion. He spread the fan again then lifted and rolled the cards over in a streaming wave. He walked a poker chip across the backs of his fingers, rolling it from one to the next. He rolled and flipped chips from one end of a short stack in his hand to the other end of the stack. He cut the deck and shuffled the cards adeptly in mid-air. He rolled a stack of chips one after the other across the felt to land stacked in the other hand. Cards flipped and twirled and danced in his fingers. Chips jumped from the palm of one hand to the other in all directions, including upward in defiance of gravity. And he kept it up, keeping his hands as busy as the judge's mouth as he told his story.

The judge asked about his background, and the gambler said little, only that he had learned and plied his trade as a riverboat gambler on the Mississippi.

Twah, who had watched it all, growled softly.

"Twah," the judge said, placing a hand atop the dog's head. "It is all right."

"That is a strange name for a dog, Twah. How came he by it?"

"Years back, I got this dog from an old Canuck fur trapper who drifted through here. Took him in lieu of a court fine the old man couldn't pay on a charge of vagrancy. The dog, as you have likely noticed, has not got but three legs—lost that one front one pawing at a beaver trap when he wasn't but a pup, that old trapper told me. So, he named him Twah. Said it meant 'three' in whatever language it was them Canucks speak."

The gambler laughed.

"What is so funny? I do not recall saying anything amusing."

"It is not 'twah' *mon ami*! It is *trois*. It is the French. I, you see, am Cajun. We speak the French, as they do in far Canada. So, it is *trois*. Three. *Trois*."

"That's what I said—Twah."

The dog's head swiveled back and forth from speaker to speaker, following the calling of his name.

"*Non, non, non, mon ami*! You merely open your mouth and let the word fall out! To speak it properly, to say it in the French, you must use your lips, the back of your mouth, your tongue, and your nose! Like this: *trois. Dis le comme ça*—say it like that—*trois*."

"Twah."

"*Non! Trois.*"

"Twah." The judge shook his head. "I cannot do it, I am afraid."

"*Non*, Justice Payne. Try again. *Lache pas la patate!*"

"What?"

The gambler shrugged. "*Lache pas la patate*. It is what we say in the bayous, in *L'Acadiane*, Cajun country. It says, do not let go of the potato. It means, do not give up."

The judge shook his head. "To hell with it. The dog comes when he is called, and that's all that matters. I guess he is not as fussy about proper French talk as you are. So, let's never mind all that and get down to what I came here for."

"Oh? And what might that be?"

"First off, I do not believe I ever got your name."

"You did not ask."

"Well?"

"Lucien LeBlanc."

"Well, Lucien—Mister LeBlanc—you took a lot of money out of a lot of pockets last night."

"It is my business. I am a gambler, as I have said."

"Your luck seems to be better than it ought to be."

"Ah, yes, *mon ami*. But luck is only a part of it. A small part. There is skill involved."

"I suppose. But skill does not determine what cards you are dealt."

"It is so," LeBlanc said with a shrug. "But it is not the cards I play. It is the men across the table."

The judge's brow wrinkled. "I don't know what you mean."

"Not many understand, *Monsieur* Payne. That is why those who played against me left here with empty pockets and I did not."

Justice studied the Cajun for a time. The gambler paid him no mind, picking up a stack of poker chips and manipulating them with his fingers.

"I had you watched, while you played."

"And what did you see, with all your watching?" LeBlanc asked with a smile.

"Not a damn thing. And that is what troubles me. I am pretty sure you are cheating, but I am damned if I can figure out how you are doing it."

LeBlanc said nothing, just stared at the judge and played with his poker chips.

"You had best be careful as long as you are in my town. Watch yourself."

"I will not have to, *mon ami*." The Cajun smiled. "It seems you will be watching me."

Chapter Ten

Al walked into the Cactus Thorn Saloon. She stopped just inside the swinging doors to look around. A few local alcoholists occupied the place, nursing the drinks they would top off throughout the afternoon and evening. The bartender, his bottles replenished, kegs tapped, and glasses polished, leaned against his hands on the bar top, towel slung over his shoulder, and stared into nowhere. Somehow sensing Al's presence, Twah trotted from out of the back. She squatted down, grasped the fur on both sides of the dog's head and pumped it back and forth, cooing sweet nothings as the mutt licked her face.

She ruffled the fur atop the dog's head then stood, again surveying the establishment. The black-clad gambler sat at a poker table alone, fiddling with a deck of cards. As she studied the Cajun, a low growl rumbled in Twah's throat.

Only then did she see Luther. He sat at a far table, tucked in beside the dancehall stage, head pillowed on arms folded atop the table, the brim of his hat bent at an odd angle against the side of his head. A coffee mug sat on the table, the coffee gone cold, Al discovered when she tested it upon arriving at the table. She dragged back a chair, but the noise did not rouse the sleeping marshal. She sat and watched him breathe, soft snores rattling each time he inhaled and exhaled. A string of drool stretched from his mouth to the tabletop.

After admiring the lawman for a few minutes, she stretched a leg under the table and poked his shin with the toe of her boot. His breathing altered, but otherwise there was no acknowledgement of her probe. She drew back her foot and, rather than a gentle poke, delivered a swift kick.

Luther bolted upright, wide but bleary eyes darting around in an attempt to identify the source of the attack or other threat.

Al laughed.

His eyes came into focus and settled on the girl. "Al."

"Hey, Luther. Startled you some, did I?"

"You sure did. Golly gosh—my stomach's trying to jump out my mouth, my heart's pounding, and I can't hardly get my breath." He swallowed hard, perhaps in an attempt to keep his stomach from escaping. "What'd you want to go and that for, Al?"

"Well, Luther, you was so far gone there wasn't no other way to wake you up. You was sleepin' like the dead."

Luther yawned, stretching his jaws as wide as they would go. He shook his head and ground at his eyes with his fists. "I guess I must've dozed off for a minute there."

With a smile, Al asked why he was sleeping in the saloon.

"I been keeping an eye on that card mechanic over yonder. The judge, he asked me to."

"Didn't you sleep last night?"

Luther shook his head. "Not much. Some in a chair over to the hotel lobby."

"Why?"

"Like I said, I'm watching that feller." He yawned. "Judge told me earlier on today to go home and get some sleep. But I figured I had best keep watch."

Al sighed. "I don't know 'bout you, Luther. Sleeping in chairs like you ain't got a bed to go to. Still, I reckon it's better to have you sleeping in the hotel lobby and here in the Cactus Thorn instead of crawling into them beds over at Miss Mercy's place, where you ain't likely to get much sleep at all."

Luther blushed, but offered no reply.

"I suppose you're still sweet on that girl Rose, over there."

Luther's face fell and he exhaled slowly. "Miss Rose ain't there no more. She's gone. Oh, there's still some woman they call Rose, but she ain't the same one."

Al felt a stab of excitement but dared not say anything for fear of betraying her feelings.

"I don't know, Al. I guess it just wasn't in the cards for me and her." He sighed again. "I don't guess I'll ever meet another girl like what Miss Rose was to me."

"I think you will, Luther." Al swallowed hard. "And I don't think you'll have to look too far to find someone to love you. I mean *really* love you. And maybe you'll learn to love them back."

"Whatever do you mean, Al? There ain't never going to be anyone like Miss Rose."

"I ain't saying there is. But just maybe there's somebody better. Somebody who cares for you truly, and ain't just in it for the money."

Luther's face reddened. "Don't you say that! Miss Rose wasn't only after my money. Me and her, we had something more than that. Something special!"

"Oh? Then why did she up and leave you?"

Luther thought for a long moment. "I don't know. She never said. Didn't say goodbye, neither. Never even said she was leaving, come to that. I asked Miss Mercy. She only said she likes to keep bringing in new girls. 'Keep the garden fresh' was how she put it." He sighed again, then perked up. "But she did say Miss Rose maybe will come back again sometime."

"And I suppose you'll just pine away after her till she does—if she ever does come back."

Luther nodded.

"Seems darn stupid to me. 'Specially when there's something better, looking right at you."

Luther's brow furrowed and he asked Al what she meant.

"Me, Luther! I mean me!"

Luther laughed. "You! You, Al?"

Al stared at him for a time. "Don't you like me, Luther?"

"Sure I like you, Al! But, good golly, you're more like one of the boys than a girl. I guess I sort of knowed you was sweet on me, but I ain't never thought of you like that."

"Not ever?"

"Gosh, no—you're . . . you're different, Al. Like I said, you ain't like no ordinary girl."

Al felt her eyes filling. "That's right, Luther. I ain't like no ordinary girl. And I ain't like no ten-dollar whore, neither." She stood and stomped off, wanting to be as far away from Luther as possible before the tears started falling.

Twah lifted himself off the floor where he had lain beside Al at the table, growled at Luther, then hobbled off on his three legs after the girl.

For his part, Luther sat so still in his chair you might think him a stuffed dummy. He pondered Al's words and wondered whatever on earth had made her feel for him as she did. Heck, he told himself, she ain't hardly a girl at all, what with the clothes she wears and the job she does. Oh, he knew she was a girl, all right. But there's girls, then there's girls.

Then there's Al.

It was too much to think about. And so Luther turned his attention to the gambler. The man still sat where Luther remembered seeing him before he had dozed off—alone at a poker table messing with a deck of cards and stack of chips. *I guess he's got to while away the time somehow,* Luther thought. *Me, I'd rather take a nap.*

Luther thought he might just as well brace the man. He walked across the room to the gambler's table and, without asking for or receiving an invitation, pulled back a chair and sat down across from him.

LeBlanc paid him no attention, as if he was unaware of the intrusion. Luther knew better, but said nothing. He sat and watched, mesmerized by the gambler's manipulative tricks with the tools of his trade.

After a time, LeBlanc spread the deck of cards in a fan across the table, flipped them into a roll that turned the cards face up, then rolled them back in a wave to turn them face down. He swept the deck into a stack and shuffled it several times, interlacing the cards by one corner, by the sides, and in a midair flight. Then he slid the deck to the center of the table.

"Care to cut the cards, *mon ami?*"

"Huh?" Luther said, still somewhat spellbound from the movement of the cards.

"Cut the deck. You know to cut the deck?"

"Sure. I lift off some, then you lift off some. Whoever's card on the bottom of his cut is higher wins."

"You are, of course, correct." LeBlanc nodded once toward Luther. *"Tu vas."*

"Huh?"

"You go."

"Hold on, there. What we cutting the cards for?"

LeBlanc smiled. "If you win, nothing changes. But if I win, you must no longer follow me around like *le chien.*"

"Like what?"

"*Le chien*—the dog."

Luther bristled. "You calling me a dog?"

"*Non, non, mon ami.* I only say that you have been following me as a dog follows its master's call. I have been told by your *Monsieur* Justice that he has told you to watch me. It is a waste of time. So, if I win the cut of the cards I will no longer be followed, and you will no longer have to sleep in chairs."

Luther mulled it over, thinking how good it would feel to roll up in a blanket on his bed and sleep. "All right. I guess it will be all right. The judge, he told me earlier to go home and get some sleep, so I guess he won't mind too much. But you got to promise not to get up to nothing while I ain't watching."

Le Blanc smiled. "*Tout à fait.* Absolutely. You have my word. Now, cut the cards."

Now Luther smiled. He shook his head. "Oh, no. I seen the way you handle them cards. Could be you know where every card is in that deck and how to get the one you want."

"But how can that be? I assure you such is not the case."

"How 'bout if I shuffle them?"

The gambler slid the deck from the middle of the table toward Luther. The marshal picked up the cards and attempted to riffle them together. The shuffle occurred in clumps and clusters, and a few cards flipped out of the deck to skid across the felt tabletop. Luther gathered them in and tried again, and then again.

"*Ça c'est bon,*" LeBlanc said. "*Ça va.* That is good. That is enough."

Luther evened up the edges of the deck with all the deftness of a bear cub wearing boxing gloves. He slid the deck to the middle of the table and nodded toward the gambler. "Seeing as how I did the shuffle, you go on ahead and go first."

LeBlanc reached out and lifted off a portion of the deck. He did not look at or reveal the bottom card, simply placed his cut on the tabletop.

The marshal lifted his cut, looked, and smiled. He turned the cards to face LeBlanc, then laid his stack on the table. The card showing was the queen of diamonds.

Luther stared at the gambler with a smile on his face, assuming that with a queen as his cut he was a sure winner, or very nearly so. LeBlanc stared back at him, his face as blank as a cloudless sky. He did not look at his cut. He reached out and turned over the stack. Still, he did not look. Luther did. His smile faded. His face sagged. He slapped the table.

"Son of a gun! How did you do that?"

The Cajun shrugged.

"The ace of hearts! There ain't no way!"

LeBlanc shrugged again. "It was your shuffle, *mon ami*."

"But I had a queen!"

"And I, I have the ace."

"You cheated! You must've cheated."

The gambler smiled. "Perhaps it is the magic. A *gris-gris*, as my *grand-mère*, God rest her soul, would say."

"I want to know how you did it."

"I did nothing. Only to cut the cards."

"Hmmph! I swear you're up to something."

LeBlanc shrugged and swept in the cards, stacking the deck in the center of the table. "And now, Marshal, it is time for you to go."

Luther's brow furrowed. "Go? Go where?"

"That is none of my concern, where you go. But go you must. It was the wager you made."

"But you cheated!"

"So you say. I say, *non*." LeBlanc shrugged. "It matters not. What matters is that now you must go."

Luther sighed. "I guess so. But don't think you can get away with anything. And I'll be back." The marshal stood and walked out of the saloon. He stole a glance at Al as he passed her station at the end of the bar. Twah raised his head from dangling over the edge of the bar and gave him a low growl. Al did not betray any knowledge or notice of Luther's passing.

Lucien LeBlanc sat at the table for a few minutes, then walked out of the Cactus Thorn Saloon and followed the sidewalk along the main street to the last building before the bridge, Mercy O'Malley's House of Passion.

"Well, well, well," Mercy said. "Sure and begorrah, it's Lucien LeBlanc. I heard you was in town and wondered when you would see fit to darken me door."

The cajun smiled. "Mercy O'Malley. The time has been too long since last we meet. And now, *mon cher, laissez les bons temps rouler!*"

Chapter Eleven

When, finally, Luther rolled out of bed he had slept away the remainder of the day and all of the night. He sat on his cot and yawned several times, his sleep-smeared face sagging and his mind foggy. How he could still be sleepy after so many hours abed occupied his sluggish thoughts for a time. When no answer came, he shook his head like a soggy dog and stood.

Two steps took him to the wash basin. He splashed tepid water from a pitcher into the bowl then laved it onto his face, scrubbing with his hands. Patting his palms dry on his scalp, he moved his head around and watched in the tiny mirror hanging on the wall as he raked fingers through his hair, attempting to bring order to the chaos.

Luther gave it up after a time, pulled his hat from its peg on the wall and plopped it on his head. He yawned, then picked up the pitcher and drank what was left in it in a series of long swallows. He dumped the wash water from the basin into the chamber pot by the bed and contemplated carrying it out to dump it in the backyard, or maybe even down the hole in the outhouse, but decided it would keep. He was hungry.

At the café, he did away with a half-pound of sausage, half a dozen fried eggs, and a stack of pancakes dripping with maple syrup, washing it all down with a quart of milk. Still not satisfied, he ordered up a beefsteak with fried onions and potatoes and a basket of yeast rolls still warm from the oven with a bowl of butter to slather them with. He put it all away as fast as he could work the knife and fork, keeping his throat lubricated with most of another quart of milk. Then he ordered up half a rhubarb pie for dessert, washing it down with the rest of the moo juice.

Stepping out the door onto the sidewalk, Luther yawned and stretched and expelled a long, rolling belch. He smiled at the memories of breakfast it carried with it. He studied the main street in both directions in the soft morning light. All looked in order, except the presence of a tall, narrow wagon parked down the street next to the town square. All he could see of the strange conveyance was the back end. It was painted in gaudy colors with words he could not read at this distance, framed with lots of swirls and flourishes.

Since it was not Saturday, he could do nothing about the wagon being parked on the street. Still, there was something about it that did not feel right. He hitched up his britches. *Well*, he thought, *I am the town marshal. I guess I had best see to it.*

He saw the wagon was of average width, only appearing narrow because of its above-average height. The felloes and hubs on the wheels were painted red, the spokes yellow. The box, from top to bottom, on every surface, was covered with words, so much and so many they nearly obscured the green paint underneath. Hanging from the front of the box, shading the spring seat, was a sunshade, faded blue and edged with yellow fringe and tassels. Two mules stood, heads down and hip-shot in harness, ears and tails lazily swishing and twitching to ward off flies.

Luther circled the wagon, reading and rereading the words. Most prominent, embellishing a painted-on banner at the top of both sides and the rear, were the words, *Dr. Maximiliano Morales*, and, in smaller letters beneath, *Healer, Medico, Physician, Professor*.

Listed from front to back on the sides as well as listed on the rear, the words read, *Elixirs, Potions, Tinctures, Tonics, Balms, Nostrums, Remedies, Ointments, Cures, Physics, and Medicaments for every ailment, illness, disorder, disease, malady, condition, complaint, and infirmity*. Painted beneath that were the words, *Specializing in remedies for female complaints and restoration of masculine vigor*.

On each side of the wagon, prominent in the center, a painted rectangle in contrasting colors, framed with frills and flourishes, advertised *Dr. Maximiliano Morales's Miracle Medicament, 25¢ the bottle*. And the invitation, *On Offer Every Evening at Sundown at This Location!*

The marshal looked around the square and up and down the street for any sign of the wagon's owners or occupants, but saw no one that aroused his suspicion. He circled the wagon again, and saw covered and almost hidden among the paint and pronouncements on the back a doorknob, then noticed a step hanging from the bottom of the wagon.

Luther took a deep breath and knocked on the door. He waited for an answer, a response, but there was none. He knocked again, harder. Still nothing. With the heel of his fist he pounded on the door, rattling it against its hinges.

The wagon rocked and creaked as someone, or something, moved around inside. Luther heard mumbling and grumbling, and the door rattled and opened. A woman's face appeared out of the dimness, framed by long dark hair standing out in every direction. She looked down her nose at Luther. "What do you want?"

Luther took off his hat. "Are you Doctor Morales?"

"No. Of course not."

Luther cleared his throat. "Is this your wagon?"

"The wagon belongs to Doctor Morales. He is my husband."

"Where is he?"

"What business is that of yours?"

"Well, Ma'am, I am the town marshal."

"So? Have we committed some infraction?"

"No, Ma'am." Luther shifted his weight from one foot to the other. "I'm just wanting to know what you're up to—you being strangers in town, and all. . . ." The woman only stared at Luther. Her gaze made him uncomfortable. "We ain't never had no outfit like this one here in town before."

"You come back later. The doctor is resting. Perhaps he will make time for you." She shrugged. "Perhaps not."

The door closed. Luther stood as if rooted to the spot. He was tempted to knock on the door again, but could not think of what he might say to the woman, or to the doctor, or what he might do if his knock went unanswered. He decided the best course of action—the only one he could think of—was to consult the judge.

Luther stopped at the Cactus Thorn Saloon's front doors and peeked over the tops to see if Al was at her post. Being early in the day, he hoped she was not at work yet, and his hope was realized. It would take some drumming up of courage to see her again and he was not ready. Try as he might to not think about their last meeting, he could not get it out of his mind. That Al was sweet on him had been no big surprise. Heck, he was something of a catch, if he did say so himself. But that she could even think he might have similar feelings for her was more than he could imagine. Like he had told her, he liked her just fine. But he liked her like a pal, a chum, a buddy. Heck, maybe even a good buddy.

He tried to put Al out of his mind as he walked to the judge's rooms in the rear of the saloon, but even when he wasn't thinking about her, thoughts of her were never far away—they seemed to swirl around his head like cigar smoke, or a swarm of mosquitos. He shook his head in an attempt to clear his mind. It was always good practice to be alert when visiting the judge, as Justice Payne did not suffer fools gladly and Luther had felt the sting of his tongue on many an occasion when unable to keep up with, or even understand, the judge's orders and instructions. And he had long since learned not to ask "why?" when the judge set him to some task.

Taking in a deep breath and letting it out again, swallowing hard, Luther knocked on the door. Unlike at the wagon, an invitation—order, more likely—to "come in" sounded even before the last knock.

"Luther. It is you. What are you up to this morning?"

"Oh, nothing much, Judge."

"Well, there must be something on your mind or you would not have tried to knock down my door with your ham-fisted pounding."

"Yessir." Luther cleared his throat. "I just thought you ought to know . . . it seemed like a good idea to tell you . . . see, there's this . . ."

"Good Lord, boy! Spit it out!"

"Down by the square, Judge. There's this wagon, see."

Justice waited for him to go on, but the marshal continued to stammer, his weight shifting from one foot to the other. He took off his hat and scratched his head, then put his hat back on.

"Luther! There is a wagon parked down at the square. As there is nothing unusual about that, there must be something else. What the hell is it?"

Luther sighed. "Gosh, Judge, I don't know how to explain it. Maybe you had best just come and have a look."

The judge cussed and muttered and complained under his breath as he tightened and straightened his necktie, then put on his hat and suit coat. He kept up the whispered tirade all the way through the Cactus Thorn and halfway down the street. Then he saw the wagon. Luther quick-stepped to keep up with Justice's hurried stride.

"This is it? This is what has taken away your ability to speak? This wagon is what has you worried beyond words?"

Luther bowed his head. "Yessir. It's just that I ain't never seen nothing like it before." He looked up at the judge and poured forth a torrent of words as if he had rediscovered his ability to form sentences. "This here doctor whose name is painted all over it, Doctor Maximiliano

Morales or however you say it, well, he wouldn't come out of the wagon to talk to me. Some woman in there—she says she's his wife—says the doctor is in there sleeping. Said if I come back later he might talk to me, but maybe not. I don't know, Judge. It just don't seem right. Like I said, I ain't never seen nothing like this here wagon and all before. Could be it's ag'in the law, I thought, maybe. So I come to get you."

Justice stared at Luther so long and hard the boy wished he could disappear. "It's a medicine show, Luther."

"A what?"

"A medicine show. These doctors—quacks, mostly—like Doctor Morales travel around the country selling their wares. Patent medicines, such as this 'medicament' as the doctor calls it on this advertisement on wheels. There may be some entertainment to start things off, but mostly it is the doctor pitching his wares. Most of them talk a blue streak, spouting all manner of fancy language most folks do not understand, but they make it sound good. They claim their particular brand of patent medicine is a miracle cure, and that the only way you can enjoy true health and happiness is to buy a bottle—hell, maybe a dozen bottles—and take it religiously."

"Is it legal?"

The judge shrugged. "As long as his so-called medicine does not cause widespread illness or outright kill folks, there is no law against it. Of course, the good doctor will be expected to pay the local tax on every bottle sold." The judge smiled. "And it may be in the law book somewhere that he purchase a temporary business license in order to conduct commerce in the town." The judge smiled again. "Yes, I believe there is such an ordinance."

"Ought I to knock on the door and get the doctor out here so's you can talk to him?"

"No. Let him sleep. The sign says the show starts at sundown. Come fetch me an hour or two before that, and we shall inform the good doctor of his financial obligations to the town."

"Sure thing, Judge. Which is it when you want me? An hour before sundown, or two hours before?"

"Oh for God's sake, Luther. It does not matter. Do you even know what time the sun will set?"

Luther pursed his lips and screwed up his face in thought. He decided he did not know the exact time the sun would set and so informed the judge.

"I thought as much. It is an approximation, Luther. The exact hour of our arrival relative to the setting of the sun—whether one or two prior, or somewhere in between, or even before, within reason—does not matter. It only matters that we have sufficient time to conduct our business with the doctor before he starts his show."

The marshal nodded.

"You understand?"

Luther nodded again.

"You are sure?"

Again, Luther nodded. For the rest of the day, he kept one eye on the position of the sun. He tried to gauge its passage as he went about his business—such as it was, what with the timekeeping occupying the better part of his mind—in order to arrive at a guesstimate of the proper time to summon the judge.

When, finally, at some measure of time in advance of the setting of the sun, the lawman escorted the judge to the town square.

Luther saw the woman he had encountered earlier, but hardly recognized her. The eruption of dark hair he had noted earlier was tamed, oiled and pulled tight against her head and knotted in a bun encased in a hairnet at the nape of her neck. A colorful dress with flaring skirts and ruffles of petticoats showing was hitched across her chest and arms, leaving bare shoulders and ample décolletage exposed.

The doctor, dressed in a ruffle-fronted white shirt with a string tie at the collar, a swallow-tail black coat, tan jodhpur-type trousers flared at the hips and tucked into knee-high black riding boots, worked with the woman in a ballet of labor performed with such precision and economy of motion that it suggested long practice and much repetition.

The entire side of the wagon box facing the town square was unfastened at the bottom and raised on hinges then propped up on painted posts built for the purpose, creating a sort of porch roof. The lifted lid exposed narrow shelves reaching from the base of the wagon box to the hinges, upon which were row after row of bottles and jars of Dr. Maximiliano Morales's Miracle Medicament. The doctor and his wife hung small lanterns from hooks along the rim of the porch roof, and larger lamps from pegs on the corner posts. They carried a box, as wide as the inside of the wagon box, half its length, and half a foot high, and placed it under the roof. It would later be revealed that the box, too, was hinged, the interior filled with various sizes of bottles and jars of the patent medicine. It would also serve as a speaker's rostrum.

Justice and Luther, along with a slowly gathering crowd of town folk, watched the couple go about their work. When it looked to be nearly complete, the judge buttonholed the doctor and asked for a moment of his time.

"Of course. But if you have questions, sir, all will be revealed during the show."

"I have no questions for you, Doctor—if, in fact, you are deserving of the appellation. I am here to apprise you of the legal niceties surrounding doing business in our fine community."

The doctor was taken aback. "Who, if you would be so kind as to say so, are you? Are you in some position of authority in this burg?"

Justice smiled a toothy smile and extended his hand. "That I am. I am Judge Justice Payne. I am also mayor of this 'burg' as well as a businessman, investor, property owner, landlord, and any number of other 'positions of authority' as you say."

Doctor Morales returned the smile. "I have a sneaking suspicion that you are about to put your hand in my pocket."

"One must obey the law, Doctor. We do have an ordinance requiring the issuance of a temporary license to those wishing to conduct business here. Also, there is the matter of taxes on goods and services sold within the town."

"So, not only do you intend to lighten my purse, you intend to take a double helping."

The judge assured the doctor that the costs of doing business in the town on a temporary basis were well established and longstanding, and fair and equal for one and all. The doctor offered a supply of his patent medicine to cover all or part of the expense, which the judge refused. The judge offered a reduction in the cost of the license in return for payment on the spot in cash, with the provision that the tax would be paid in full upon close of business. The doctor demurred, saying he intended to contest the license fee in court. The judge reminded the doctor who would be on the bench at any such legal proceeding and assured him that his action would be dismissed without a hearing. And he informed the doctor that the town marshal was standing by and that the show would not go on, nor would any business be conducted, unless and until the license fee was paid in full, the aforementioned offer of a discount now withdrawn.

The doctor huffed and puffed, grumbled and griped, bemoaned and bewailed, argued and groused and threatened to pull up stakes, fold his tent, hitch his wagon, and leave town posthaste. And he kept up his diatribe until his wife intervened with a slap upside his head, at which point Doctor Morales handed over the license fee.

And then, the lanterns were lit and the medicine show commenced.

Chapter Twelve

As the last curve of the circle of the setting sun dipped below the western horizon, the woman in the colorful dress stepped onto the small platform under the roof extending from the side of the medicine show wagon and rattled the tambourine in her hand. The rows of bottles and jars of Dr. Maximiliano Morales's Miracle Medicament on the shelves glinted and sparkled with light reflected from the flickering lanterns hanging roundabout. With much ceremony, accompanied by the jingle jangle of the shaking tambourine, the doctor stepped out the door of the wagon and around the corner to stand near the little stage upon which his wife stood.

With a sharp rap on the skin of the tambourine, she said, "Ladies and gentlemen, boys and girls, it is with great honor that I present Doctor Maximiliano Morales, physician, medico, and professor; educated and trained in the hallowed halls of the most famous European institutions; renowned in our own country, this great nation, from coast to coast and border to border; his accomplishments and acclaim envied by the profession and the public alike! I give you then, and please welcome to your fair city, DOCTOR MAXIMILIANO MORALES!"

With that, she rattled and pounded her instrument repeatedly. A few in the crowd applauded without enthusiasm while most of the gathered curiosity seekers only looked at one another.

The doctor stepped forward and bowed slightly. "Thank you! Thank you!" He held his hands aloft, needlessly asking for quiet. "Please! It is enough!"

Some in the audience chuckled, as the slight applause had long since faded. But the doctor's faux humility did silence the tambourine.

"Ladies and gentlemen," the doctor said, "Within minutes, a short time only, you shall hear of the miracle of my medicament, acclaimed the world around for its efficacy and curative powers. But first, allow me, please, to introduce the lovely Mariposa Morales, my dear wife, who shall favor you with a few tunes as performed in the past on the great stages of the Continent, as well as in concert halls here in America!" With a bow, he flung an arm toward his wife, who smiled and bowed and jingled her tambourine.

From its concealment lying behind the platform, the doctor picked up a guitar and strapped it around his neck. He strummed a brief flamenco *rasgueo* to limber his fingers, then a few introductory chords to launch Mariposa into "Habanera" from *Carmen*. After bowing to much applause at its conclusion, the songbird followed with a selection of popular hymns, folk songs, and patriotic numbers, finishing with a rousing version of "Columbia, the Gem of the Ocean," enlivening the audience to sing along.

And then the songstress stepped off the stage and faded into the background, replaced as the focus of attention by the doctor, his guitar since returned to its place of rest. He praised and applauded his wife, calling her back to take a bow, and joined the onlookers in frenzied applause. The doctor avowed that science and medicine concurred in a belief that music had curative powers, and that a song in the heart was essential to health and happiness.

But, he advised the audience in solemn tones, music alone was not enough.

"My friends, there are, no doubt, some among you suffering neuralgia. Perhaps you are afflicted with partial paralysis. Painful abscesses. Rheumatism. The common cold. Chronic complaints related to the liver or kidneys. Creeping hair loss, even baldness. Consumption. Ingrown toenails and toenail fungus. Bunions. Dropsy. Nosebleeds.

Cholera. Cancerous growths. Fatigue. Necrosis. Skin eruptions." Doctor Morales then leaned forward toward the audience and spoke in a hushed voice that, somehow, still spread to the farthest reaches of his audience. "Female complaints. Venereal diseases. Impotence. And, of course, the bane of your gentle babes—diaper rash."

He stood upright and waved an arm as if casting aside the named maladies and all others. "But fear not, my friends. Do not abandon hope. There is help!" As if by magic, a bottle of Dr. Maximiliano Morales's Miracle Medicament appeared in his hand. The doctor held it aloft in such a way that lantern light illuminated the liquid in the bottle, causing its honeyed amber shade to fairly glow. "I give you, ladies and gentlemen, Doctor Maximiliano Morales's Miracle Medicament!"

Mariposa broke into applause, stepping forward with clapping hands held high to encourage those assembled to join the ovation.

"The composition of this tincture," the doctor said, "is a closely held secret, its recipe of ingredients known only to myself and a few native healers ensconced in the jungles of Amazonia, some—a few—shamans in sub-Saharan Africa, a rare practitioner or two of traditional Asian healing in remote corners of Siam, and one—only one—medicine man of the Tarahumara tribe of the Chihuahuan desert!"

Doctor Morales paused, allowing tension to build. "But!" he said, punctuating the word with an upward pointing pointer finger, "No one of the aforementioned virtuosos of the curative powers knows the full story! Oh, no, my friends! For I have taken the knowledge provided by these practitioners of the healing arts and used those secrets to blend and brew, combine and concoct, refine and rarify, distill and concentrate centuries of healing power into a patented cure-all unrivaled in all the world!"

Justice and Mercy

A second bottle of the elixir, passed unseen into his hand by Mariposa, joined the other held aloft in the lantern light illuminating the medicine show, the elixir glowing in the island of light in the darkness.

"Yeah, sure," came a voice from the crowd. "But does it work?"

"Does it work?!" said the doctor. "Does it work?! My friends, I have, right here in this wagon, sheaves and stacks and bundles of testimonial letters of praise from satisfied customers! Users rave about the pain-relieving properties of my medicament, its curative powers, its calming qualities, its—"

"Hold on there!" came a voice from the depths of the crowd. "Just hold on a minute!" elbowing his way through the assemblage, the speaker broke through into the narrow arc of empty space between the speaker's platform and the crowd.

Doctor Morales looked skeptical, even a little worried at the intrusion. "What is it, Sir? Have you a question?"

"No, by jiminy!" He turned to face the people. "I just wanted to tell these fine folks that I have used this here potion of yours."

"And?" the doctor said.

"Folks! Every word he says it true! God's honest truth! Why, I, myself, was once laid low with the rheumatic fever, and the ministrations of physicians were worthless. Worthless, I say! But while in the depths of my misery, a package arrived by post. A bottle of this very medicine, sent to me by my long-lost brother, him having had a premonition or vision concerning my diminished health. I hadn't used more than half a bottle when the pain flowed from my body like water, and restored health filled my every pore. I say 'restored health' but that ain't the truth of it. In point of fact, I felt better than I had ever felt in all my years on God's earth!" The man jumped into the air and clicked his heels together.

Doctor Morales held the palms of his hands together as if in prayer and bowed slightly toward the man. "Thank you."

"Hogwash!" came another loud voice. An old man with a long white beard and hair walked into the light leaning on a crutch, dragging one leg. "I don't believe a word of it. I've tried patent medicines by the gallon from hucksters like yourself, every one of them spouting the same nonsense as that spewing out of your mouth! And there ain't a one of 'em has given me a minute of relief from the pain in my leg—the result of a wound received on the battlefields of the late unpleasantries!"

The doctor said, "But, sir—thank you for your service, by the way—have you tried Doctor Maximiliano Morales's Miracle Medicament?"

"Nah. But they's all the same, ain't they? All them patent medicines?"

"Not a bit, Sir! *Not a bit!* I can assure you that no other formula approaches the ingredients, the recipe, the prescription, the mixture, the dosage found in my medicament. It is the one and only of its kind, and I say without fear of contradiction, superior in all aspects to all other curatives!" As he spoke, Doctor Morales pulled the cork from one of the bottles in his hand and encouraged the old man to drink of it—no more than two swallows—to test its efficacy.

The old man drank from the bottle, and the doctor requested that he step aside and wait a few minutes for the elixir to take effect.

Morales then launched into an oration on the kinds and varieties of his medicine. The basic formula, he claimed, was efficacious as a general cure-all for most conditions. But there were also special preparations devised for specific purposes. One blend served as a liniment to be massaged into the muscles and joints to restore movement and relieve pain. Another jar offered an ointment for treating skin eruptions and healing lingering sores and ulcerations. A lotion relieved itching and swelling of the skin. Tiny bottles held a concentrated formula for treating female complaints. An unguent rubbed into the scalp restored hair growth and cured baldness. A mixture to add to bath water soothed tired muscles as well as smoothed and moisturized the skin. Another lotion wiped away wrinkles and tightened sagging skin.

The doctor went on and on, displaying the various bottles and jars on the shelves and reciting their uses. He answered questions, countered skeptical claims, and hyped his potions in every imaginable way.

Mariposa, meanwhile, collected the money from the few customers willing to part with their hard-earned money. Then, as if on cue to cure the waning enthusiasm, the white-bearded man let out a whoop and a holler.

"By jingers, I'm cured!" he hollered. He walked out of the shadows, crutch in hand. But rather than lean on it for support, he held it aloft like a drum major's scepter. His stride was swift and sure. He stepped onto the podium in a trice, jumped off again to land on both feet, then jumped up to land on the platform the same way. He shouted with glee, claiming to be free of pain, body and soul. The medicament had not only healed his wounded leg, it seemed, but also cured his contrary disposition and improved his mood.

Doctor Morales congratulated the patient, but urged caution. The relief was temporary, he advised, but would be made permanent with continued daily use of the medicament. A course of treatment lasting say, four to six months, should be sufficient to effectuate a permanent cure. The old man pulled his purse from a pocket and purchased several bottles of the potion, along with an equal number of bottles of the liniment mixture for topical use.

Members of the crowd crowded around, slapping him on the back with congratulations and shaking his hands with good wishes, as well as asking after the truth of his claimed relief, which he verified in no uncertain terms.

For their parts, Doctor Morales and Mariposa had cleared the shelves of their wares and cleared the platform, lifting its lid, and scooped out more containers of the medicament, passing them out as quickly as they could pocket the payments.

Judge Justice Payne had watched the whole thing from the shadows, from the first notes Mariposa's aria to the melee of money exchange then in progress. As the money changed hands, he calculated the amount of tax due him, but he could not keep up. Still, his wheels of thought started turning, grinding out a way to get his hands on even more of the money. "Luther," he said, "I want you to keep an eye on that old soldier. Follow him. And find someone to keep track of that other fellow who claimed this snake oil cured him. Don't let them out of your sight. Gather them up in the morning and bring them to see me at the saloon."

Luther agreed to the task and started off.

"No. Wait," the judge said. "Never mind that."

"You mean you don't want me to watch them?"

"Of course I do!"

"Then you don't want to see them come the morning?"

"Of course I do!"

"Then you don't want—"

"Luther! Shut your pie hole for a minute and listen. Here is what I want you to do. Keep an eye on them tonight. Collect them in the morning. But do not—do not—bring them to the Cactus Thorn. Take them to the blacksmith shop."

"The blacksmith shop?"

"Right, Luther, the blacksmith shop."

"Why—"

"Never mind, Luther. It does not matter why. Just do as you are told."

Luther shrugged, nodded his agreement, then went about his business.

The judge watched him go, wondering if his instructions were understood, let alone what part of them would be carried out.

Then Justice walked down the street to the Cactus Thorn. He stepped through the swinging doors to find Al at her accustomed place at the end of the bar. Twah reclined beside her as her hand stroked and ruffled the fur along his ribs, and occasionally dropped to his belly, scratching and tickling as he squirmed in delight. Twah lifted his head slightly at the approach of his master, but let it plop back down.

"I swear, Al, you are spoiling that dog. He will not be worth a damn if you keep coddling him. He is a working animal, keep in mind—not a lap dog."

Al smiled. "Ah, don't you worry none about Twah. He's doing his job right along. A little scratch now and again ain't goin' to hurt him none."

Justice snorted and turned his attention to the room. The medicine show on the town square had diminished attendance somewhat. Only serious drinkers lined the bar; a few others sat alone at tables. The accordion player sat on the edge of the dance hall stage squeezing out a mournful tune. A card game was in progress at a back table, the Cajun gambler, Lucien LeBlanc, among the players. The judge threaded his way through the tables to reach the game.

"I trust you are minding your manners, Mister LeBlanc."

"*Oui*. But of course," the Cajun said with a smile, tapping a forefinger to the flat brim of his low-crowned hat in greeting.

"It looks like the pasteboards are falling in your favor," Justice said, with a nod toward the stacks of chips in front of LeBlanc. "Surely you are not doing anything untoward to cause that."

Another player at the table snorted. "I think the Frenchie sonofabitch is cheating."

The Cajun bristled. "You had best watch what you say, *mon ami*. Repeat the accusation and I shall demand satisfaction, as a gentleman must."

"I can't see how you're doin' it, but that don't mean you ain't."

LeBlanc's eyes hardened and his lips tightened. "Listen to me, you *peeshwank*. You are not good at the cards. You cannot see what you yourself are doing with your cards, let alone understand my play. I suggest you leave the table immediately."

The other player refused. He vowed to keep playing until he won his money back.

LeBlanc shrugged, then smiled. "*Ça c'est bon*. It is good. Keep playing, by all means. Having your money in the pot is a *lagniappe* for me—an unexpected gift, so to say."

"I do not think so, LeBlanc," Justice said. You can forget your lanny-yap or whatever the hell you are talking about. Cash in your chips and leave. You are no longer welcome at the Cactus Thorn."

The Cajun eyed the judge and smiled without humor. "As you wish, *mon ami*. As you wish." He stood and swept in his chips. "You will not see me in your establishment again. But you have not seen the last of me, *Monsieur* Justice Payne."

As LeBlanc left the Cactus Thorn, he passed the town marshal coming in. Luther heard Twah's low growl but avoided looking at Al. He walked to the judge and told him the two men in question were bedded down for the night and under watch by a couple of men he recruited for the job.

"Good work, Luther. Now, don't forget what you are to do first thing in the morning."

"Sure thing, Judge. I ain't forgot. I'm to bring them two men here."

"No, Luther. That is not what I told you. Take them to the blacksmith shop."

"Oh! Right! Golly gosh, I nearly forgot. The blacksmith shop. I'm to take them to the smithy's place."

"That's it, Luther. Don't forget. And one more thing—make damn sure that quack Maximiliano Morales does not leave town."

Chapter Thirteen

The sun was well up by the time the town marshal roused the two medicine show testifiers from their beds and escorted them to the blacksmith shop.

"Here they are, Judge."

Justice Payne looked up from his work and nodded. He stood behind the anvil, hammer in hand. Shirtless, he wore a leather bib apron scarred with burn marks and stained with soot. A film of sweat shone on his bare skin. With a pair of tongs, the judge picked up a bar of iron from off the anvil and stabbed it into the forge as the smithy, reduced this morning to the role of assistant, worked the bellows.

"You two may as well have a seat," the judge said to the two men Luther had brought to see him. He nodded toward the spring seat of a wagon, sitting on the shop floor awaiting repairs.

"The hell you say," the old man with the long, disheveled white hair and beard said. "Just who the hell are you, anyhow, to be givin' orders?"

Luther shoved the old man toward the seat. "Sit down, like he said. You too," he said to the other man. "This here is the judge. He's the law around here, and you had best do what he says."

The other man laughed. "Judge?" He looked around the shop. "And I suppose this here is his courtroom."

Whack!

Justice smacked the anvil with the hammer, the sound ringing and echoing away. "Right you are, sir. As the marshal said, I am the law in this town, and I hold court wherever I see fit."

Whack!

"I advise you two to come to order, as court is now in session."

Whack!

The prisoners looked at each other. They looked at the marshal. They looked at the judge. One said, "You mean we are under arrest?" The other said, "Are we accused of a crime?"

Whack!

"Not in so many words," the judge said. "This is what you might call an informal hearing." He turned to Luther and told him to see that the medicine-show wagon and its occupants parked down at the town square stay put, as he intended to deal with them later. Then he turned to the forge and pulled the glowing bar from the coals, held it up with the tongs and studied its color. He laid it on the horn of the forge and proceeded to hammer and bend it into a three-quarter circle with flanges on each end. He studied it again, hammered it a few more strokes, then stuck it sizzling into a water barrel. He picked up another iron strip identical to the other and laid it on the coals. The smithy pumped the bellows and the coals flared up and flamed.

"Now," the judge said, "this is an unusual place to hold court, I will admit. As it happens, I own this shop. I also own several other businesses in our fair community. I own all the property. Not only am I the judge, I am the mayor, the town council, commissioner of roads and streets, building inspector . . . well, I suppose you get my meaning.

"And part of what I mean—the part that concerns you gentlemen—is that I *know* this town. I know it inside out, upside down, and backwards. I know, on a personal basis, most everyone who lives here. And I know, at least by sight, most of the people from the surrounding valley who visit our little island for one reason or another."

A word from the smithy halted the judge's discourse, and he fetched the nearly white-hot iron bar from the forge, laid it on the anvil and went to pounding. He bent it around the anvil to create a three-quarter circle and hammered an angle at each end to create the flanges. Even upon close inspection it would match the other in every curve and detail. Then it, too, went into the water barrel with a hiss.

He smiled at the detainees. "As I said, I own this shop. As I do with all my businesses, I like to keep my hand in when it comes to the work involved. My skill as a smith would by no means qualify me as an expert, like the fellow there at the forge surely is, but I get by. And that, gentlemen, is why we are holding this informal hearing in the blacksmith shop.

"But I digress. As I was saying, I know on sight most of the folks who inhabit and visit this town." He pointed at the pair, waggling his pointer finger back and forth from one to the other. "And I know neither of you has ever graced us with your presence before. In fact, the first time I ever laid eyes on you was at last evening's medicine show. I did some asking around, and I am told that you arrived about the same time as that so-called doctor did—one of you an hour or so before, the other a short while after."

"So what?" the bearded man said. "It's a free county, ain't it? We can come and go as we damn well please."

The anvil rang again.

Whack!

"If I want you to speak I will let you know. Otherwise, remain silent or you will be found in contempt of this court." The judge-turned-smithy laid the hammer on the anvil, took up the tongs, and pulled one of his metal straps from the water barrel. He held it up and examined it with a smile. "Would either of you gentlemen care to venture a guess as to what this is—or, rather, what it is to become?"

The men shook their heads in unison.

"You may have noticed, during your time on the town square last evening, a whipping post. You see, our generally law-abiding town has no need of a jail. From time to time, however, we are forced to confine

Justice and Mercy

a scofflaw of one kind or another as he awaits a hearing before this court. So, he is shackled to the whipping post, most often with leg irons.

"As it happens, gentlemen, we have a limited supply of shackles. And I am convinced the demand may soon outstrip the supply. So, what you see here is the first step in assembling a new set of leg irons. Smithy, here, will handle the rest." He set the ankle-cuff-to-be aside, took off his leather gloves with their high gauntlets, and stepped out from behind the anvil to tower over the seated prisoners. "Now, what I want to know is how you two came to be in my town, and what, exactly, is the nature of your relationship with Doctor Maximiliano Morales and his medicine show."

"We ain't tellin' you a damn thing," the bearded man said.

The other man stayed silent, but started quivering.

Justice turned around and picked up his hammer.

Whack!

The anvil rang with the resounding blow.

"Rest assured, gentlemen, that despite my saying our supply of shackles is limited, we have a sufficient quantity to chain the two of you to the post right now. "And, need I remind you, we call the post the whipping post—and it is not by chance that it carries the name. You remember Luther, the town marshal who brought you here? You will have noticed that Luther is a big, strong boy. He is well-practiced and accomplished at laying on the whip to administer the punishments meted out by this court."

The frightened man poured forth a torrent of words, despite the bearded one's repeated admonitions for him to shut up. He confessed that they were, in fact, in the employ of Doctor Morales and traveled with the show from town to town, acting their parts as plants to promote sales of Dr. Maximiliano Morales's Medicament. With the cat well out of the bag, the white-haired old man confessed his guilt in the sham as well. Both, as it turned out, were the picture of health and owed none of that good fortune to the patent medicine they promoted to the public in the guise of satisfied customers.

"As I thought," the judge said with a nod.

"What are you goin' to do with us?"

The judge leaned his backside against the anvil and thought. The detainees twitched and fiddled as they watched him and wondered. The judge stood. "Here is what I will do," he said as he stepped around the anvil and picked up the hammer as if he were, again, in the legal sense, at bench and bar. "Upon payment of a fine, I am inclined to dismiss the charges against the two of you and release you on your own recognizance."

The men looked at each other. They looked at the judge. They looked at each other. They shrugged in unison. "Pardon me, Your Honor, but just what the hell does that mean?"

"It means you pay your fine and you can go—and by 'go' I mean leave town. And you must promise—although I have no means to enforce the order, and will have to rely on your solemn word—that you will have nothing more to do with Doctor Morales and his medicine show."

The frightened man nodded. The old man asked how much the fine would be.

"How much does the doctor pay you?"

Again the old man's hackles went up. "What business is that of yours?"

Whack!

"One more outburst and you will be found in contempt! Answer the question!"

Five dollars a show, came the answer. And both men claimed their work was worth much more, but that Morales was a tightwad and refused to up their wages no matter how successful their contribution to sales of the medicament.

"Fork it over," the judge said. "I declare punishment in the form of a fine in the amount of five dollars from each of you, payable on the spot."

Whack!

The men grumbled, but paid the fine.

"Now, get out of town and do not come back. And I remind you that you are to have no further dealings with Doctor Morales and his medicine show." He smiled. "But I am of the belief that it will be quite some time, if ever, that the so-called doctor will be back in business. He shall be dealt with by this court in due time. This very afternoon, perhaps."

Whack!

The ringing of the anvil followed the now-chastened accomplices out into the street.

For the remainder of the morning, the judge went about his business as if nothing were amiss in the town. Luther did not have so easy a time of it. Maximiliano and Mariposa Morales were determined to leave town as quickly as possible. The marshal reminded them that taxes were due on the previous evening's sales of Dr. Maximiliano Morales's Miracle Medicament, and they would not be permitted to cross the bridge off the island until the tax was paid in full. And no one, he told the couple, could declare the fullness of the payment save Justice Payne, who would be along in due time.

The doctor and his wife had other ideas, and allowed that they would leave anyway, as soon as the mules were harnessed and hitched, then lit into the task.

For his part, Luther was having none of it. While the Moraleses were preparing to leave, he was preparing to make them stay, and he chained the back wheels of the wagon together with links brought along for the purpose. Then, just to be sure, he chained each back wheel to the front wheel it followed. The gaudily painted wagon was going nowhere, much to the chagrin of its owners and occupants. They steamed and stewed and fussed and flapped throughout the morning, their demands alternating between being allowed to leave and being allowed to see the judge. Luther encouraged calm, and assured them all would be taken care of—according to the judge's clock and calendar, not their own.

After whiling away the morning and indulging in a filling dinner at midday, Justice Payne sent word to Luther to bring the offenders to the Cactus Thorn Saloon. He then went about seeing to the setting up of the courtroom—the table and chair placed on the dancehall stage to serve as his bench, his wooden gavel and block in their proper positions on the tabletop, his big black book at hand, Twah perched on his pillow on a stool next to the bench, and Justice draped in the woolen Navajo blanket that served as his judicial robes.

Sensing something important about to happen, saloon patrons rearranged their seats to observe the goings-on, and made sure the beverage of their choice was topped off.

The judge retired to the shadows at the back of the room. Luther opened one of the batwing doors and waved the Moraleses through, then escorted them to seats arranged below the judge's bench.

Then, assuming his duties as bailiff, he read from the card provided by the judge. "Hear ye hear ye! Court is now in session, the Honorable Justice Payne presiding. All rise!" The sound of chairs scraping across the floor and the stir of people rising accompanied the entry of the judge. He took his seat behind the table.

Whack!

"Be seated," he said, as the rap of his gavel faded. "Bailiff, call the first case."

Chapter Fourteen

The judge ordered those assembled to remain silent while court was in session. He advised the barmaids to go about their business quietly in order to avoid noise and confusion, likewise the bartenders. Anyone causing a ruckus in the courtroom would be escorted from the premises by the bailiff, who may well arrest them in keeping with his double duty on the occasion as town marshal. The patrons stayed as quiet as possible, but noise continued as other townspeople filed into the saloon, word of the trial having spread and curiosity running rampant. Soon, the room was filled to capacity and overcrowded, with people—women of the town included—occupying the seats and standees lining the walls. Even the surface of the bar served as bleacher seats, its extent lined with backsides.

Whack!

"Now, then," the judge said, "we are here today to try these defendants you see here before me, known only to the court as Mister Maximiliano Morales and the woman imputed to be his wife, Missus Mariposa Morales. The defendants will please rise. Bailiff, swear them in."

The Moraleses stood, their necks craned and eyes still glaring upward at the judge. From atop his pillow on the barstool, Twah emitted a low, rumbling growl. Luther read the oath from the card provided him by the judge and the Moraleses swore to tell the truth.

"Maximiliano Morales, we shall start these proceedings by examining your case. First of all, are you represented by counsel?"

"No, I am not. I was offered no opportunity to retain a lawyer. According to the marshal there, there is not a practicing attorney in this town."

"I assume, then, that you will be representing yourself in this matter. Is that correct, Mister Morales?"

"Listen, you old blowhard! It's not like I have any choice is it! And it is *Doctor* Morales, not Mister."

Whack!

Morales continued, uninterrupted by the gavel.

"Besides, I don't suppose it would make any difference in this kangaroo court of yours whether I was represented by a lawyer or not."

Whack!

"Mister Morales! First of all, this court will not address you as 'Doctor Morales' as I have no confidence in your right to the title. Secondly, I would remind you to watch your tone. Now then, if it is your wish to retain counsel, this court will be happy to order you confined until such time as an attorney willing to represent you before this bar can be located and brought here to defend you." The judge smiled. "When I say 'confinement,' I speak, of course, of our usual method in this town of chaining you to the whipping post at the town square. You are, of course, familiar with the whipping post, what with that garish medicine-show wagon of yours being parked near it. So, what is it going to be, Mister Morales? Do you wish to be represented by counsel, or appear before this court *pro se*?"

"*Pro se?*"

"In your own behalf, Mister Morales. I apologize for the confusion." He tapped the cover of the big black book on the table. "Much legal jargon comes from the Latin. And while I, myself, am conversant in the language of ancient Rome, I tend to forget that such knowledge is not widely shared." The judge leaned forward over the table. "Do you wish to be chained up, Mister Morales, or represent yourself?"

The doctor said he would appear *pro se*, and upon questioning by the judge, Mariposa Morales said the same. The judge was asked if they could confer together and contribute to one another's defense, and Justice Payne assented to their wish.

"Now, then, Mister Morales, let us—"

Morales interrupted the judge and asked again to be addressed as "Doctor" rather than "Mister" Morales.

"I will be pleased to do so, sir, upon your showing the court your diploma from a medical college, a valid license to practice medicine, or other official document showing you are entitled to be so addressed. Have you any such paperwork to present to the court?"

Morales flushed. "No, I do not, Mister Payne. But I can offer you my personal assurance that—"

Whack!

"Your 'personal assurance' is not worth one damn thing in this courtroom, *Mister* Morales. And, by the way, you are to address me as 'Judge Payne' or 'Your Honor' when you speak."

Morales smiled. "May I ask, *Your Honor*, to see your diploma from a law school, papers appointing you to the bench, or other official documents showing you are entitled to be so addressed?"

Whack!

"Enough of your nonsense, Mister Morales. This gavel in my hand is all the 'official' that matters. Do not waste any more of this court's time with such fiddle-faddle, or you will be found in contempt.

"Now then, Mister Morales, as I was saying before being so rudely interrupted, what is it you do for a living?"

Morales stood tall and cleared his throat. "I am a physician. A pharmacist, of sorts. A healer. A medico, in the language of my parentage. I prepare and sell a medicament to treat and heal a variety of medical conditions, ailments, illnesses, and maladies."

"And how, exactly, do you accomplish this?"

"We—Missus Morales and I—travel from town to town distributing our wares. Mariposa—Missus Morales—entertains for a short time with vocal renditions to attract a crowd, then I inform those assembled of my preparations and their uses."

The judge thought for a time, then asked what, exactly, was in the so-called medicament he sold.

"That, I am afraid I cannot answer, *Your Honor*. 'Doctor Maximiliano Morales's Miracle Medicament' is a patent medicine. Its ingredients and formulation are proprietary, carefully protected, and not to be disclosed."

"Hmmph. I must say, Mister Morales, that I have sampled your tonic. It tastes strangely like alcohol to me—bad whiskey, at that. Since it will not divulge any 'secret' tell the court if your mixture contains alcohol."

Morales nodded in the affirmative.

"I detected a hint of molasses. A touch of tobacco. Are these substances present?"

"Your Honor! I—"

Whack!

"Come along, Mister Morales! No one of these ingredients could be considered by any measure to be medicines. At best, they could be viewed as extenders or flavorings. Surely you will not contend before this court that tobacco, alcohol, and molasses are the source of your so-called medicine's healing properties. I remind you, sir, you are under oath!"

Mariposa leaned over and whispered something in Maximiliano's ear. They conversed in hushed tones for a long minute, then the man spoke. "I suppose there is no harm in agreeing to what you say. Those ingredients are present. But, I hasten to add, they are not the source of the medicament's healing power."

"I see. Now, to another question. You sell this stuff in a whole host of containers and forms. You advertise lotions, creams, unguents, salves, and the like, under the guise of healing countless conditions. How is this accomplished?"

"Again, Your Hon—"

Whack!

"Answer the question!"

Again, Mariposa whispered something in his ear. Morales cleared his throat. "Those concoctions are created by introducing the medicament into an inert medium suited for topical applications."

"I am not sure I understand, Mister Morales. What, exactly, do you use? I ask only to ascertain if there are any harmful substances involved."

"I assure you there are not. We use *paraffinum perliquidum* in some mixtures, *paraffinum subliquidum* for others, depending on the desired viscosity. You may know those substances as mineral oil. We also use pure petroleum jelly as a base for salves and balms."

"I see. Now, to get to the crux of the matter," the judge said. He furrowed his eyebrows and intensified his gaze, staring into the defendant's eyes for a moment before speaking. "Does this stuff work? Any of it?"

Maximiliano puffed up like a fighting cock ready to do battle. He huffed, he wheezed, he flushed, he tensed, beads of perspiration dampened his forehead. Mariposa took him by the arm and whispered in his ear. He tried to pull away. She tightened her grip. She whispered again, this time the hiss of it could be heard at some distance. He sagged.

"Your Honor, may I speak?"

"Yes, Missus Morales, you certainly may. By the way, I enjoyed your singing immensely. You have a voice that is powerful, yet has the ability to interpret the most subtle of musical moods and feelings."

"Thank you, Judge. Since you were in attendance at our show last evening, you no doubt heard the doctor refer to the many testimonial letters in our possession from many, many custome—patients—praising our medicament and its usefulness."

"I did hear that. However, I am sorry to say, without verification of the authenticity of said letters, they cannot be admitted as evidence. They could be manufactured—forgeries, every one."

"But, Your Ho—"

Whack!

"You have my ruling, Missus Morales. Move on."

Mariposa swallowed hard. "Yes, Your Honor. I direct your attention to the gentlemen who stepped out of the crowd—strictly on a volunteer basis, with no collusion or collaboration on our part, I might add—to testify of personal experience in one case, and a live demonstration in the other, of the curative powers of Doctor Maximiliano Morales's Miracle Medicament."

Justice smiled. "Indeed, Mister and Missus Morales. I know the gentlemen to whom you refer and of whom you speak. As a matter of fact, I spoke to them myself, only this morning. They confessed—with very little prompting, I might add—that the whole thing was a sham. That their claims were bogus. Fabrications cut from whole cloth. Falsehoods. Lies. Not only that, they revealed that this dishonesty and these deceptions were performed—and that is just what they were, performances—at your behest, in your employ, for payment received!"

The judge spent a long minute or two staring down at the defendants. "I suspect that the both of you are guilty—at the very least—of fraud, deceit, deception, artifice, chicanery, running a confidence game, dupery, flimflam, and a host of other crimes against the citizens of this community." Justice shook his head and looked askance at the alleged criminals. Then he slid his big black book with its scuffed leather binding in front of himself and flipped it open. He thumbed through the pages, flipping back and forth until he found what he was looking for. He ran a finger up and down the columns, pausing now and then and then moving on. He turned page after page and repeated the process. Flipped to another part of the book and did the same. Then again. After considerable consultation, he closed the book and pushed it aside. He fixed his eyes on the miscreants.

Before the judge could speak, Maximiliano cleared his throat. "Your Honor, might I ask as to the nature of that book?"

"What do you mean?"

"What is it? What are its contents? What is its relevance to myself and Missus Morales and our appearance here in this . . . this court of law?"

Justice sat up tall in his chair and leaned forward. "Quite simple, Mister Morales. It is a law book. A volume I consult from time to time as occasion requires to discern the exact nature of crimes and misdeeds, determine if they are misdemeanors or rise to the level of felonies, and for guidance in meting out the appropriate sentence and proper punishment."

"And what did it tell you? Right now, today, concerning our 'case' as you call it."

"You will hear the gist of it soon enough."

Maximiliano stepped up close to the table. "Might I see it, Your Honor?"

"See it? Why on earth would you want to see it?"

The defendant shrugged. "Only curiosity, I suppose."

"Request denied. Now, step back."

"Your Honor! Surely it is a matter of fairness. It is a simple request. Surely it can do no harm."

"Surely not, Mister Morales. Nor can it do any good."

"Please, Judge."

"The book is written in Latin. Are you, as am I, conversant in the language of ancient Rome?"

"No. But that is all the more reason that satisfying my curiosity is harmless."

Justice Payne sighed, long and slow. He slid the book across the table. Morales reached out and picked it up, surprised at its heft. He cradled it on one arm and used the other to lift the cover and turn the pages. He examined the title page, the Table of Contents, and flipped through the pages, examining chapter headings, subheads, and blocks of text here and there.

He looked up at the judge and smiled. He grasped the book with both hands and held it aloft. "Your Honor, if there is a fraud in this courtroom, I submit it is you!"

Justice's eyes widened.

"Latin!" Maximiliano said. "This book is not written in Latin! Its language is Spanish—an old-fashioned kind of Spanish, to be sure, a Galician dialect, I suspect, but most certainly Spanish—the language of my birth and with which I remain adept."

Whack!

Still holding the book aloft, Morales turned to face the spectators. "Not only is this book not in Latin as this man claims, it is not a law book! No! It is a catechism of *Iglesia Católica Romana*—the Roman Catholic Church! A book of religious instruction, my friends." He tucked the book under one arm and turned to face the judge, his pointer finger taking dead aim at the jurist. "You are a fraud, sir! A fraud!"

Murmuring and muttering spread through the crowd in a wave of disbelief.

Whack!

"Silence! Come to order!" the judge said, pounding his gavel repeatedly. "There will be order in this court!"

Twah propped himself up on his front leg on the stool and started barking, his effort to aid his master only adding to the confusion. The judge hushed the dog and kept pounding the gavel in an attempt to hush the crowd. It took a minute or three, but surprise and shock faded, and the room quieted.

"Mister Morales, give me back my book."

Morales stepped up to the table, lifted the book, and dropped it with a resounding thump onto the tabletop.

"I suppose some explanation is in order," Justice said. "Mister Morales is correct. The book you see here before me is not a law book. It is merely a prop. I consult it from time to time with no notion whatsoever of the meaning of the words on its pages."

The crowd stirred.

Whack!

"However!" the judge said with a raised voice. "However, the time thus spent offers me an uninterrupted period of contemplation. During that time, I consider the nature of the crime and criminal before me and come up with what seems fair in the way of punishment. And the implied authority of a hefty tome such as this book diminishes, if not eliminates, dissent or disagreement. A harmless—but helpful—object to suggest codification. My rulings, law book or no, are beyond reproach and that is the crux of the matter!"

Whack!

"Now, ladies and gentlemen, there can be no doubt that this man and woman before me have committed crimes. They have fleeced you and your neighbors out of hard-earned money for a potion whose effects on health are questionable at best, and most likely nonexistent.

And they perpetrate their crimes from town to town and city to city all across this fair land!

"Given the unique nature of the situation before us, specifically Mister Morales here questioning my authority, *I* will not decide the guilt or innocence of these people."

Maximiliano and Mariposa Morales locked eyes, smiled, and embraced. Disbelief spread through the crowd.

Whack!

"Instead, ladies and gentlemen, I direct you all, each and every one of you, to serve as jurors. *You* will render the verdict in this case!"

The Morales's faces fell. The crowd again voiced disbelief. Never before, in all the history of the town on the island, had Justice Payne called a jury. As the law in the town, Justice Payne, himself, had decided all cases. And, it should be noted, the decision had always been, "Guilty as charged."

Whack!

"You have all heard the evidence. By voice vote, how do you find? Those finding this pair of confidence artists and fraudsters guilty say, 'Aye.' "

The word, loud and long, shook the chandeliers and rattled the rafters.

"Those of you who find these perpetrators of crimes against the community innocent, sound off with a 'Nay.' "

Silence. Interrupted only by a weak chorus of "nays" from the mouths of the Moraleses, followed by a low growl from Twah.

Whack!

"Maximiliano and Mariposa Morales, the jury having found you guilty of the crimes for which you are charged, the finding of this court is one of guilt!"

Whack!

Justice and Mercy

"Thank you, jurors, for your valuable service. Bartender, set them up, one and all, with a drink on the house!"

When the hubbub died down and a good share of the crowd had decamped for home or work, Luther escorted the convicted couple into the judge's office where he would pronounce sentence.

First, Justice demanded the applicable tax on their sales be handed over.

He assessed a punitive fine equal to the amount of money the Moraleses had taken from the community at the medicine show.

He fined them court costs equaling twenty-five per cent of the punitive fine.

He ordered that the entire inventory of Dr. Maximiliano Morales's Miracle Medicament be destroyed, dumped off the bridge into the river.

However, that order was rescinded when his honor realized the medicament might harm the fish and taint the water, and told Luther to instead dump it into a pit, throw in the empty bottles and jars, and bury the whole mess—and to do it across one of the bridges in Adams County or Jefferson County, as convenience dictated.

He ordered the Moraleses to purchase sufficient paint to paint over every surface of the medicine-show wagon, from axel hubs to the rooftop, including every bolt and screw. The color was to be plain and nondescript—gunmetal, slate, cream, buff, tan, taupe, beige or the like, depending on the availability of paint.

Finally, he told the Moraleses to hit the road and never, ever again show their faces in his town on his island.

As for the big black book, it would continue to appear on the bench at every trial conducted by Judge Justice Payne henceforth.

Chapter Fifteen

Mercy O'Malley walked down the main street of the town, her destination the milliner's shop. But there was more on her mind than covering it with a new hat.

The hatmaker was a middle-aged widow woman, an Italian immigrant who learned her trade as an apprentice in the old country. She had fashioned several hats for Mercy, as well as a good many for the girls who worked at Mercy O'Malley's House of Passion.

Like Mercy, the milliner owned her business, independent of Justice Payne. Independent, that is, save for a cut of every sale he took as a tax, and the rent he charged for occupying the building, which he owned. Mercy found the proprietor leaning over a cutting table, measuring out fabric.

"How's tricks, Francesca?"

Francesca lifted her eyes from her work and smiled at Mercy. Talking around the pins held in her lips she said, "That seems a question more appropriate for your business, Miss O'Malley."

Mercy laughed at her own unintended joke and plopped her reticule on the counter. "It is time we had a talk, Francesca."

The hatmaker laid down her shears, pulled the pins from her mouth and stabbed them into the pin cushion. "Sounds like refreshments may be in order. Would you care for a coffee?"

"Thank you, no." Mercy smiled. "But if you've a bottle of wine on hand, I wouldn't turn my nose up at a wee dram."

Just as Mercy suspected she would, Francesca reached under the counter and produced a pair of drinking glasses and a jug—not a bottle—of wine.

The women sampled the drink and passed several minutes in small talk. Then, after the second glass of wine was poured, Mercy got down to business.

"Tell me, friend, how are you getting along with Justice these days?"

Francesca threw her hands up. "Ach, the judge! That man is the bane of my existence. Always sticking his snoot through my door wanting an accounting of this, that, and the other. Always questioning my ledgers. Always implying I do business—how do you say it?—under the table. Thank the Lord it is the marshal he sends around most often." Francesca glanced from side to side as if assuring herself no one would overhear. "He is a handsome lad, though, isn't he, that marshal."

"That he is," Mercy said. "But the boy is as thick as a plum pudding."

Francesca sighed. "So big and strong, though." She sighed again. "But Justice Payne. As I have said before, his name fits like one of my hats—he is a pain! Not that my hats are painful, you understand. They fit perfectly, just as the name Payne fits the judge, you see, as he is a pain, if you get my meaning, so, you see—"

Mercy interrupted, saying she understood perfectly what Francesca meant. Then, "I suppose you've heard what he did to them medicine show people."

"So I did. If you ask me, they had it coming. Sharpies and swindlers, they are."

"I wouldn't disagree. But setting that aside, it is the judge declaring himself arbiter of all things that gets my goat. In Ireland we was under the thumb of them sassenach bastards across Saint George's Channel. It irks me to have Justice lording it over us like he was Queen bloody Victoria! Worse, even! He makes up the rules as he goes along, and they always seem to benefit his judgeship." Mercy snorted.

"What you say is true. But what can be done? It is, after all, his town—as he does not hesitate to point out at every opportunity."

"True that may be, my Francesca. But we live here. We do business here. We line his pockets. By rights, we ought to have a say in things. And I propose we go about getting our say!"

"How do you intend to do it?"

Mercy sighed. "I don't know. It will not be easy. But we must figure it out. Are you with me?"

Francesca shrugged, then nodded. "I am all for the idea. It will come down to what must be done."

"I intend to have a chin wag with other shopkeepers in the town—them that ain't on the judge's payroll, that is. There may be enough of us to get up Justice Payne's nose if we work together."

Mercy and Francesca poured more wine then went about the business of the ordering of a new hat. With brim style, crown shape, colors, embellishments, fabric, and ribbons decided, the madam bid the milliner farewell.

But a fashionable hat was not the only thing that would come out of their meeting.

Meanwhile, Luther had been sitting in the parlor at Mercy O'Malley's House of Passion. He was there on business, not pleasure. Taxes were due—overdue, at that—and this was Luther's second attempt at an audience with Mercy. He had a funny feeling she was avoiding him.

Hat in hand, he sat in an overstuffed chair. He had sat in that chair often, whether waiting to do business or do pleasure, and was well familiar with its contours. Being early in the afternoon, he seemed to be the only visitor. That there were three horses at the hitch rail and a buckboard and a buggy parked out front troubled him, as there was no sign of life upstairs. There was a bartender at his little station against the far wall. Every now and then he would duck through the door in the corner with a tray of drinks, and come back out a bit later with empty glasses and beer bottles. Luther knew that particular room was not open to the public—it was reserved for the working girls, a place where they could take a break from their duties in peace and quiet on a busy evening.

It took a while, but curiosity got the best of him and Luther moved to a chair near the bar, from which he could maybe learn something about what was going on behind that door. He ordered a beer, and the bartender opened a bottle and handed it to him, along with a pasteboard coaster printed with the name of the establishment to protect the finish on the side table.

Halfway down the bottle, the cook came along carrying a tray of sandwiches. Luther admired them as they went by, thinking a sandwich or two would be just the thing for an afternoon snack.

The cook opened the door and Luther leaned forward for a better look. Smoke hung heavy in the room. He could not see anyone other than a glimpse of a seated man leaning forward in a chair so his face was out of view. But everything the marshal could see of him was covered in black—polished leather boots, sharply creased trousers, and a dressy jacket. The black hat with its low crown and flat brim completed the picture. *Damned if that ain't that Cajun fellow. I thought he had gone and left town.*

Luther perked up at the recognition. He could hear voices, but they were quiet and muffled. And he heard what he swore was the click of poker chips landing in the pot.

The cook came back through the door empty handed and closed the door behind her.

Golly gosh darn sakes alive, Luther thought. He got up from the chair, put on his hat and snugged it into position, then swallowed the last of the beer in the bottle. His business with Mercy O'Malley could wait. For now, he had business with the judge.

"He is doing what?!" Justice Payne said, shortly after Luther burst through the door and interrupted his train of thought.

"Playin' cards, Judge."

Justice leaned back in his chair. "You are sure it is Lucien LeBlanc?"

"Couldn't see his face. But I swear it was him."

"Well, was he playing solitaire, or what?"

The marshal shrugged. "Don't know. But for sure there was others in there. I could hear voices."

The judge laced his fingers together and let his hands rest on his chest. The chair squeaked as he turned it a bit in one direction, then the other as he thought. He sat upright and lifted himself out of the chair, then took his suit coat from the coat rack and put it on, followed by his hat.

"What've you got in mind, Judge?"

"Well, Luther, we will just go on down there and see what the hell is going on." He snapped the lapels of his jacket with a tug. "Whatever it is, it is sure as hell illegal. Or if not, it is as of now!"

The pair, propped up by law and order, did not stop to knock on the door of Mercy O'Malley's House of Passion, nor wait to be invited in. Without hesitation, the men walked directly to the door that had earlier roused Luther's curiosity, opened it, and walked through into the room.

Five men sat around a table topped with green felt. A pile of chips lay scattered in the center. Each man held cards in his hand. A drinking glass or beer bottle sat on the table near each player, next to stacks of chips of various colors. The tallest and most stacks stood in front of Lucien LeBlanc.

LeBlanc turned in his chair when the door rattled open and Justice and Luther rushed through. He watched them as they studied the table, the players, and the room. He smiled. "*Ça va, monsieur* Payne. And you, Marshal." He extended a hand toward the table. "I am afraid our little game is at its limit of players just now. But if you care to wait, *mes amis*, I am sure a seat will become available at some time."

"I thought I told you to get the hell out of town, Lucien."

"*Non, non,* Judge. You told to me to get out of the Cactus Thorn Saloon. And to never come back, or words to that effect. And so I have not come back. But I enjoy a friendly game of the cards, *mon ami*, and so I play here, as you can see."

As LeBlanc talked, the judge studied the players around the table. All were townsmen, save one, and Justice recognized him as a ranchman, owner of one of the valley's biggest spreads. The men withered at his glare, some ducking their heads, other faces flushing.

"Hmmph," the judge said. "I wondered why I had not seen some of you at the Cactus Thorn lately. I am surprised you would come here to play and be fleeced by this riverboat gambler."

The men shuffled and stirred a bit in their seats but said nothing. The thick silence thinned out in a hurry when Mercy O'Malley swished into the room.

"What in the bloody hell is going on here?"

"That is precisely what I am here to find out, Mercy O'Malley," the judge said.

"You ain't got no right to be coming into my establishment without so much as a howdy-do and upsetting my guests!"

The judge smiled, but there was no humor in it. "I have every right, Mercy. As you damn well know, I own this building and the land it stands on."

"Be that as it may, this is my business. I run it as I see fit, and as long as I pay me rent and pay your damn taxes, I have every right to do so!"

"Need I remind you, my dear, that your tax payment is overdue, and has been for some time. I could evict you on the spot, should I so desire."

As Justice and Mercy argued, the men at the table slid out of their seats, gathered their stakes, and slipped out of the room as unobtrusively as possible.

All except Lucien LeBlanc. The Cajun stayed seated, watching the debate with a smile on his face, his gaze shifting from speaker to speaker. The discussion went on, each party parrying the thrusts of the other, neither seeming to gain an advantage. He decided to intervene, pushed back from the table and stood, turning to face the judge.

"*Excusez-moi, monsieur* Payne. If I may be so bold as to ask, what is the purpose of your visit?"

"This!" Justice said, waving an arm at the poker table. "You are running an illegal poker game."

"Illegal, you say? It is but a friendly card game. Why is that against the law?"

"Because you," the judge said, pointing at Mercy O'Malley, "do not have a license to operate a gambling establishment."

"Me?" Mercy said. "Me? I ain't got nothin' to do with this."

"But it is under your roof! In your place of business!"

Mercy smiled. "Why Justice—you have only just now made a big show of the fact that this is your building and that I am a mere tenant! So, I suppose it is *your* game." She shrugged. "All the same, whose ever card game it is, it ain't mine. I ain't got nothin' to do with it."

The judge snorted and smirked. "You mean to tell me the house does not get a rake from this game?"

"Certainly not! Not a schilling! Nary a ha'penny! All I do is let Lucien here use the room. He invites his friends over and they play cards. Poker, canasta, pinochle, gin rummy, hearts—it's all the same to me. I don't know and I don't care. As long as they pay for their drinks and whatever food they eat, it's all right with me. They can play to their little hearts' content."

"Hmmph!"

"Besides, what's all this about a license? There ain't nobody ever heard nothing about needing no license to run a gambling outfit. Who says you need a license?"

Justice Payne puffed up like a game cock. "Why, I do, that is who!"

Mercy laughed. "You! What did you do, find it in that phony-baloney law book of yours?"

"You would do well to remember, Mercy O'Malley, that I am the law in this town. We will speak another time concerning your gambling license—or lack of one, I should say. For now, I shall take you at your word that this is none of your affair—but I warn you, you have not heard the last of it!

"But you, Lucien LeBlanc," the judge said, turning his attention to the Cajun. "You have just purchased yourself a peck of trouble. Consider yourself under arrest. Marshal," he said, turning to Luther, "put the cuffs on him. Trial starts a half hour from now at the Cactus Thorn Saloon." Then, to Mercy, "You will want to join us, Miss O'Malley. You may well be called as a witness."

Chapter Sixteen

Twah raised up and propped himself on his front leg when the batwing doors at the Cactus Thorn Saloon swung wide. Lucien LeBlanc came through, encouraged by a shove to his back by the town marshal. A low growl rumbled deep down in Twah's throat. Al placed a hand on his neck and gave him a pat. She wondered if the dog was growling at Luther or if the lawman had been forgiven for his slight to Al. Maybe. Maybe not. It could be the growl was inspired by the entrance of the Cajun. Or, perhaps, both Luther and Lucien. Al could not say.

She watched the lawman shove the gambler repeatedly—unnecessarily, she thought—all the way back to the dancehall stage. Luther dragged out a chair and sat his prisoner down on it, then fetched the table and chair that served as the judge's bench and placed them on the platform. He followed that with a barstool. Twah trotted through the room, hopped onto the stage, and lay down next to the stool he knew was his, but would not hop onto it until his pillow cushioned the seat.

Soon, Justice Payne came in. He nodded to Al and told her that court business was pending and to so inform the few patrons and the barmaids and bartender. On the way back to his rooms, the judge instructed Luther to relieve the gambler of everything on his person, make an inventory of it, and have LeBlanc verify its accuracy and put his signature to it. Then he went into his office and returned, wrapped in his woolen Navajo blanket, gavel and block in one hand, big black book in the other, and Twah's cushion tucked under an elbow.

Already on the bench when he sat down was Luther's list and the items found on LeBlanc—a black-handled Bowie knife and black tooled-leather scabbard, a matching holster holding a black metal Colt's revolver with black gutta percha grips, a black leather billfold holding a variety of papers and stuffed with currency amounting to three hundred and twenty-three dollars, poker chips from a pocket with a total value of two hundred and fifty-one dollars, one half eagle and one gold eagle coin totaling thirty dollars, and two dollars and seventeen cents in assorted coins. Justice studied the list before he sat down and asked the defendant if it was correct, to which the Cajun answered in the affirmative.

Twah hopped onto his stool, the judge took his seat. Justice looked around the room taking note of the scant crowd. This hearing lacked the publicity or public interest of the trial of the medicine show people, and that was fine with him. The judge nodded toward Luther, and he stood and read from the card provided by the judge, calling the court to order and reminding the saloon patrons and employees to maintain decorum.

Whack!

"Lucien LeBlanc, you have been charged with running an illegal card game, operating a gambling establishment without a license, conspiring in a tax avoidance scheme, malfeasance, misconduct, hooliganism, outlawry, immorality, depravity, corruption, and malefaction. How do you plead?"

"Not guilty, *mon ami*."

"None of this monamee nonsense. You are to address the court as 'Your Honor.'"

LeBlanc nodded once. "As you wish—*Your Honor*."

Justice sat back in his chair. "Now, then, let me understand this. You are pleading not guilty to all charges?"

"*Oui.*"

"What do you mean with this 'we' malarkey?"

"Pardon, Your Honor. It is to say, 'yes' in my native tongue, the Cajun French."

"Well, then, let us stick to the English language here. Although there may be a word or two of Latin here and there when we get down to the legal niceties. So, then—not guilty?"

"Yes."

"Yes?"

LeBlanc looked blank, then smiled. "Yes, Your Honor."

Justice smiled. "Keep in mind, Mister LeBlanc, that you were caught red-handed in the midst of a card game."

"Yes, Your Honor."

"And yet you plead not guilty to gambling?"

The Cajun shrugged. "It was but a game among friends. No gambling was taking place, I can assure you."

"How do you explain all those poker chips on the table? And the ones here on the bench, taken from your person?"

"Merely a means of keeping score, Your Honor. They represent points in a tally, not money. For example, the token there with the numerals for fifty means fifty points, the twenty represents twenty points, and so on."

"Are you employed, Mister LeBlanc?"

"Your Honor?"

"Do you have a job?"

"No."

Justice waggled his finger over the wallet and coins on the bench. "You seem to be carrying a lot of cash money for someone with no visible means of support."

LeBlanc shrugged.

"Where did you get it?"

"The money?"

"Yes, the money, dammit! Stop wasting the court's time."

"The money, it comes from my people. A bequest, left to me by *Nonc* and *Tante* Doucet—an uncle and aunt who, sad to say, passed from this world without issue. I was something of a favorite nephew, I suppose." Lucien shrugged with a slight smile. "*C'est tout*—that is all."

"Then you won none of this money playing cards?"

"It is impossible to say, Your Honor. Perhaps some—a dollar or two—remains from the days when I was allowed a place at the gambling tables here in this saloon, this Cactus Thorn place. But I have been forbidden to play the cards here, as well you know. Perhaps some of the money in question has been in my possession from before here I arrived, from the card playing on the riverboats." He shrugged. "*Qui peut dire?* Who can say?"

The judge asked if the defendant had any witnesses who could substantiate his claims, and LeBlanc said no. He asked if there were any documents that could attest to the veracity of his claims. LeBlanc said no.

Justice Payne spent several moments thumbing through his big black book, despite the fact that everyone in the place, including the defendant, knew the volume had nothing to do with the law. Still, they allowed the judge his deceit. He closed the book with a thud.

"The court finds your explanation untenable, Mister LeBlanc. It cannot be checked or verified. It will not hold water and it won't wash. It is fishy, flimsy, and farfetched. This court, having witnessed with our own eyes your card game in the back room of Mercy O'Malley's House of Passion, and having seen poker chips and cash on the table clearly indicating the exchange of money in a game of chance—gambling, in other words—I have no alternative but to find you guilty of all charges."

Whack!

"Furthermore, as punishment for your many crimes, this court assesses a fine, payable in cash or other legal tender, in the amount of three hundred and fifty-five dollars and seventeen cents."

Whack!

"Further still, the court recommends that you avail yourself of the next stagecoach to pass through here in order to leave this town, and to arrange your future travels to avoid coming here ever again."

Whack!

The judge raked in the wallet from among LeBlanc's goods on the bench and relieved it of the currency within, then retrieved the coins from the pile. He counted the cash money and expressed surprise that it amounted to precisely three hundred and fifty-five dollars and seventeen cents, an amount equal to the assessed fine. Then Justice slid the empty wallet, poker chips, knife, and pistol across the table toward the convicted gambler. The judge felt a twinge at returning the poker chips but knew his chances of ever redeeming them were nonexistent. Luther stepped up and removed the hand cuffs.

Lucien LeBlanc's feelings about the whole business could not be discerned, his poker face expressionless and manner unrevealing. It could be that he was comforted by the knowledge that several thousands of dollars lay concealed in a money belt at his waist, and several hundreds more were tucked into pockets inside the shafts of his boots. And who can say how much money was hidden in the luggage awaiting him at Mercy O'Malley's House of Passion?

As for Mercy O'Malley, she was not nearly so sanguine about the state of affairs in the barroom-cum-courtroom. The madam had sat quietly throughout the proceedings, nursing a drink. Several drinks, come to that. But it was not the alcohol that was responsible for the flush coloring her face and neck, or the trembling, or the clenched jaws and tight lips.

Justice and Mercy

No, it was not the alcohol. Mercy O'Malley had her Irish up.

The first words out of Mercy O'Malley's mouth on entering the office at the wagon yard were, "Otto, we have to put a stop to it!"

Otto Gunderson owned the wagon yard. Justice Payne, of course, owned the land and the buildings. But Otto ran his own business, operating the shop where horse-drawn conveyances of various kinds were built and repaired, as well as wagons stored for people of the town. Mercy, herself, owned a one-horse shay stored at the wagon yard, and Otto saw to its maintenance and upkeep.

"Pray tell, Miss O'Malley, what are you talking about? Put a stop to what?"

"Justice Payne, that's what! The man has gone beyond the pale."

Otto smiled. "Sit down, Miss. Take a load off. Would you care for a drink—I have a bottle of rye whiskey, and we will toast to the demise of our common enemy. And then you can tell me how you plan to dispose of him."

"Rye, you say? Well, it ain't Irish whiskey but it'll have to do. Lord knows a drink is what I need as of now."

Gunderson poured the drinks, taking time to wipe out Mercy's glass with a rag that looked to be more soiled when it started than when it finished the job. Otto was accustomed to sharing drinks with men, who made up the bulk of his customers, and they were not so fussy about the presence of a little film tainting a glass. But, with a lady present, he opted to show some couth and clean, so to speak, the container from which Mercy would drink.

Mercy did not care.

"I tell you he has gone too far, Otto. 'Judge' my eye! The man knows no more about the law than that box and skein sitting there in the corner," Mercy said, gesturing with her glass toward the wheel and axle parts.

"What has he gone and done that's upset you so, Mercy?"

"You heard about what he did to those patent medicine people."

"No more than they deserved, I'd have to say. I purchased a bottle of their potion myself, and it hasn't done a thing for my lumbago."

"Sure, and they was charlatans, Otto! But that is not the point."

"What is the point, then?"

"The point is, Justice just took it all upon himself. He acted as prosecutor, judge, and—in spite of that bit of showmanship there at the end—as jury! Not only that, he made up the very laws he convicted them of—that law book of his is as phony as a Confederate ten-dollar bill! The man declares the law and decides who's broke it, and then pulls the punishment out of thin air—which is all he's got between his ears!

"And now he's gone and ruined Lucien LeBlanc on account of he was afraid Lucien might make a dollar that he didn't get a piece of."

"You mean that Cajun card sharp that's been around town?"

"The very one! Lucien is a friend of mine. An old friend. I know him from when I was in New Orleans."

Otto shook his head. "I hear tell he's a cheater, Miss O'Malley."

Mercy shrugged. "Me myself, I could not say one way or t'other. Don't know a thing about cards, me. I know he's been accused of such, by the judge and by others, but there ain't never been nobody ever catch him at it. Not here, not in New Orleans, and not on the riverboats where he gambled for a good many years."

Again, Otto shook his head. "Even so, playing cards ain't no honest way to make a living."

"Maybe not. But we've all got to do what we can to get by. Besides, that ain't the point."

"What is the point, Miss Mercy?"

"Again, it's that that damn Justice wraps himself in that damn blanket and declares himself the law! He ain't got no more right to it than you or me or that flop-eared mule hitched to the rail out there. Just like he did with those medicine show folks, with Lucien he just made up all kinds of offenses Lucien committed, declared him guilty, and took every cent Lucien had on him as a fine! Funny how that works out, ain't it, Otto?"

The wagon yard man agreed that Justice Payne did get above his raising on occasion. Then talk moved on to the way he treated them, and the other business owners in the town who were forced to portion out a large share of their income to pay his taxes, and pay exorbitant rents besides.

"I tell you, Otto, we must act!"

"What is it you intend to do, young lady?"

Mercy sagged in her seat. "I do not know yet, Otto. But I am thinking on it. What I need to know now is, are you with me?"

Otto was noncommittal. He did not give Mercy his blessing, nor did he deny his interest in what might be done. He was not against action, but he would wait and see.

Otto Gunderson was not a man to act on impulse. Let him wait and see.

Mercy O'Malley marked him down in her mental tally as a definite maybe. But she knew he would come around once he could see which way the wind was blowing. And she fully intended to stir up a tornado if that is what it would take. She left the wagon yard and tromped down the street in the direction of her next intended conquest—Earl and Clara Carlson down at the feed and seed. Then she would see the proprietor at the barber shop, the dentist, the sign painter, and so on down the list of "independent" businesses in the town.

According to her calculations, if they all stuck together they might just have the numbers to make things difficult for Justice Payne.

Chapter Seventeen

After the trial, the judge advised Luther to get down to Mercy O'Malley's House of Passion and collect her past-due taxes. The marshal went about his business of disassembling the courtroom in the saloon, then moseyed down the street to see if he could catch the madam unaware.

Alas, as had been the case more often than not of late, she was not in the house, and no one there claimed to know where she was or when she might be back. Luther took a seat in his favorite easy chair and nursed a bottle of beer until it turned flat and tepid. Giving up the cause as lost, he wandered back down the main street, keeping a sharp eye on the side streets and through the shop windows in hopes of catching a glimpse of his quarry. He gave up the half-hearted search and wandered back to the Cactus Thorn Saloon.

Twah propped himself up and grumbled at his arrival, but Al spoke softly to him and the dog flopped back down on the bar, head dangling over one side and tail the other, as was his wont to do. Al ruffled the fur lining his ribs and avoided looking at Luther, doing her best to ignore his presence. She wondered if the heat she felt in her cheeks was visible, betraying her feigned lack of interest in the marshal's presence. Her ire and anger at him, unfortunately, did nothing to allay her feelings for him.

Much to her chagrin, Luther dragged back the barstool nearest her and the dog and sat down. He looked down the length of the bar and held up a finger. The bartender nodded and brought the marshal a bottle of beer. He sipped at if for several minutes, finished it and called for another. To all appearances, he was deep in thought. But those who knew Luther, including Al—and Twah, for that matter—knew that was not the case. More likely, the man had something he wanted to say and was trying to string together words that meant what he meant to say.

It took a while.

"Say, Al," he said after taking a deep breath and clearing his throat.

"Don't bother, Luther."

Her response threw into chaos all he intended to say, jumbling the words beyond retrieval. "Wha . . . what, Al?"

"I said don't bother."

"Don't bother what?"

"Don't bother talking to me. I ain't got nothing to say to you. And I don't care to hear anything you've got to say to me."

"But Al!"

"Don't 'but' me, Luther! You said all you needed to say about me back yonder at that table the other day. Far as I can see, there ain't no more to say."

"Golly sakes, Al, I never meant it to come out the way it did. Gosh, you're my best friend!"

Al let loose a long sigh and shook her head slowly. "That's just it, Luther. To you, I ain't nothing but a friend. Not even like a girlfriend, neither. More like a boy friend!"

"But gosh, Al! Look at you! You wear them—"

"Don't say it! I know damn good and well what I wear, and that ain't got nothing to do with it. I swear, you're so blind that I could be buck naked and you still wouldn't see what you're missing!"

Luther blushed.

"One of these days, maybe, you'll wake up, Luther. Till then, you'd do best to just keep your mouth shut and stay away from me."

With that, Al clicked her tongue and said "c'mon" to Twah and she pushed through the batwing doors with the dog at her heels.

Luther had a flash of panic at her abandoning her post. He looked around the barroom and saw there were only a few patrons in the middle of the afternoon, and that those in attendance looked to be a quiet bunch. He decided—him being the town marshal and all—that he could keep an eye on things till Al came to her senses and got back to work.

Twah, the tri-shanked tail wagger, wandered and sniffed his way down the main street, his tongue wagging as much as his tail, and with what looked for all the world to be a smile on his face. Getting out for an airing was always a treat, and a welcome respite from the fetid air of the Cactus Thorn. Even in his bliss, Twah kept an eye on the people they passed on the wooden sidewalks fronting the shops and those in the street, but no one aroused his suspicion or raised his hackles.

Al had no place to go and was in no hurry to get there. She wandered aimlessly, moving from one side of the street to the other, gazing into shop windows and unaware, as often as not, of what she was seeing. The bright colors in Francesca's hat shop caught her eye, and she studied the fancy, frilly, floppy head coverings, wondering how she might look under one. Next door was a dressmaker, and again she examined the frocks in the show window, noting their fabrics, patterns, prints, colors, and cuts. The variety overwhelmed her. She could not imagine how any woman would go about choosing a style that suited her.

A little way down the street she stopped for no particular reason and stared off into the distance, looking at something no one else could see, probably seeing nothing outside her own mind. Mercy O'Malley stepped out of a shop and almost bumped into her.

"Alice! What on earth are you doing here?"

It took a moment for the girl to regain her senses, lost as she had been in her reverie. She shook her head like Twah might do, and looked at Mercy, recognition finally arriving. "Oh! Miss Mercy! Sorry—I didn't see you."

"Good gracious, girly, you wasn't seeing a thing! Not anything of this world, anyways."

Al mumbled something nonsensical.

"I swan, Alice! You have been crying!" Mercy dabbed at the girl's reddened eyes with a lacy hanky. "What is the matter?"

Al sniffled, and her downcast face belied her response. "Oh, it ain't nothing. Just the dust in the air, I guess."

"Nonsense! I've been drying the eyes of girls and ladies longer than I care to remember, and these ain't tears caused by no dust." She dabbed at Al's eyes again. "Now, out with it, girl. What is it that's troubling you?"

That was all it took. All it took for the floodgates to open and the tears and words to pour forth. Mercy led the girl to a bench in the shade on the town square and listened to her tale of woe. Al revealed that she was sweet on Luther, which was a complete waste of time. She made her living tossing drunks out of a saloon—a job that suited her just fine but caused everyone else in the world to think her a sideshow freak. She was ignorant of the ways of women and had no clue how to solve the problem, or even if she wanted to. She was lonely in the company of many acquaintances but few friends.

Mercy listened to it all without interrupting, wiping away tears as needed. When Al wound down, Mercy asked her about her plans for the afternoon and evening.

Al sniffled. "I reckon I ought to be getting back down to the Cactus Thorn. Things'll be livening up about now, and I had best be on duty."

At the mention of the saloon, Twah, who had been lying next to the bench with his jaw nestled on his front paw, stood.

"All right then, Alice. Here's what you are to do, and I'll brook no disagreement. When you get to the saloon, you look up that worthless waster of good air, Justice Payne, and tell him you've other business to attend to tomorrow and will be unable to report for work."

Al's forehead furrowed and her eyes squinted. "Whyever for?"

"Just you do it. Then, first thing tomorrow morning, you are to come and see me at my place."

This time, the girl's eyebrows arched and her eyes widened. "Oh, no, Miss Mercy! I couldn't do that!"

"Nonsense. It ain't like I'm hiring you on to work for me."

"Still, if Pa or my brothers found out I was in a place like that—beggin' your forgiveness, but you know what I mean—why, they'd tan my hide good and proper!"

"Not to worry, Alice. If anything untoward should happen with your father I shall tend to it. Your brothers, as well."

Al's eyes widened even more. "You know my Pa? My brothers?"

Mercy reached out and patted Al on the arm. "Let's not discuss that just now. We've more important fish to fry." She stood and handed Al her hanky. "Now, be gone with you. I shall see you in the morning."

Early the next afternoon, just after the sun had reached its high point, Mercy O'Malley sent her houseman out to find the town marshal and tell him "to get his sorry butt down here."

The man looked hither and yon, searched from Dan to Beersheba, without success. Then, on a whim, he walked down to the river on the Jefferson County side of the island and found Luther sitting on the bank gathering handfuls of pebbles and tossing them one by one into the stream.

"Marshal . . . sir . . ." Mercy's man said.

Luther did not respond. The messenger stepped up and tapped him on the shoulder. Luther jumped up as if lifted by a dynamite blast, pulling his pistol from the holster as he rose. The houseman stepped back, raising his hands in the air.

"Don't shoot! I ain't armed!"

Luther blushed at being surprised. He stuffed his revolver into its sheath, missing the mark on the first two tries. "Golly gosh darn it! You like to've scared me plumb out of my boots!" He looked at the man standing there with his arms raised. "Go on ahead and put your hands down. I'm sorry if I scared you. You're one of them that works for Miss Mercy, ain't you."

"Yessir. Yes I am, Marshal. She sent me to fetch you."

"Sent you to fetch me! Gee whiz, I been down there looking to see her for days and she ain't never been there. I thought she didn't want to see me."

"Well, Miss Mercy is a busy woman. She's got lots of things goin' on."

"Either that or she don't want to pay her taxes."

The man shrugged. "I wouldn't know anything about that. All I know is she wants to see you and sent me to fetch you."

Luther lifted his hat and raked his fingers through his hair. "Well, shucks. I guess we might had just as well get going then."

A few minutes later, Mercy came down the stairs to find Luther sitting in his favorite overstuffed chair in the parlor, holding his hat by the brim and rotating it around and around in his fingers. "Marshal. I'm glad you could make it."

"Gosh, Miss Mercy. I been here lots of times the last little while looking for you. I was surprised when your man come to get me." Luther stood, holding his hat against his chest. "The judge, he's awful upset at me on account of I ain't collected your tax money as yet. I'd be obliged if you could hand it over so he'll get off my back about it."

Mercy smiled. "Not to worry, Luther. We'll deal with that later."

"Gosh, Miss Mercy—why did you get me down here, then?"

"I have something I want to show you—some*one*, I should say." Mercy turned and extended an arm toward the staircase.

Luther looked up and saw a young woman at the top of the stairs. Slowly, with a gloved hand—the cuffs on the gloves reached to her elbows—on the banister, the girl came down the steps. She tried to smile, but was unsuccessful in the attempt and held her lips tight. A ribbon with a flower attached to the side wreathed the top of her head, holding softly swept-back hair in place. Dark lashes framed her eyes. A faint shade of red glowed from her cheeks, a darker shade colored her lips.

Unlike the customary attire worn by the flower girls at Miss Mercy's House of Passion, the dress she wore did not have a plunging neckline to display skin and reveal cleavage. But from the cut and fit of it there was no doubt there was a woman underneath.

"Who . . . who's this, Miss Mercy?" Luther managed to say, between hard swallows and rapid intakes of breath. "This a new girl come to work for you?"

"Good Lordy, no, Luther! Does she look like one of my girls?"

"No . . . no, I suppose not." Luther managed to look away from the woman, who had stopped two-thirds of the way down the staircase to stand, holding the rail, looking down at him.

"Well, boyo, what do you think?"

The question perplexed Luther.

"About the girl, you big lump! How does she look to you?"

Luther looked back at the young woman, who had since come on down the stairs and stood on the bottom step, only a few feet from the marshal. He took a deep breath as he contemplated the question and attempted to form an opinion, then searched his mind for words to describe it. He sensed the heady aromas of bergamot and lemon oil, although he could not have named them. But he knew he liked the scent. He swallowed hard. He again managed to avert his gaze to answer the question.

"Why, she's right pretty, I guess." He swallowed hard and glanced again at the woman. "More than that. Darn pretty. Why, I guess you'd have to say she's prettier than a speckled pup. Gosh . . . ." Luther swallowed hard, regretting the canine reference. "Golly, Miss Mercy—she's even prettier than what Miss Rose was! You know, the Rose I was sweet on, not them other Roses that's been here. Maybe even she's the prettiest girl I ever seen . . ."

Luther stopped talking. Whether flustered by his words, or having run out of them, no one can say. He fixed his gaze on the girl, eyes all but popping out of their sockets, a blush on his face and a smile on his lips, both fascinated and intimidated by her presence.

Then, she spoke.

"Don't you know who I am, Luther?"

Luther tipped back. Wrinkles lined his forehead and created a bridge between his eyebrows. His eyes squinted. He could not speak, and barely managed to shake his head.

"Why, it's me, Luther! It's Al!"

It is a good thing the marshal had not stepped away from his chair, or his backside would have landed on the floor when his knees gave way and he sat. He swallowed hard. "Al? From over to the Cactus Thorn?" He stood and leaned toward the young woman, studying every detail. "Nah. Can't be. You two are funnin' with me. This is some kind of trick."

Al's skirts swished as she turned and dashed back up the stairs, taking them two at a time in a most unladylike fashion, but in keeping with her normal locomotion.

Mercy stepped up to Luther and put a hand in the middle his chest and shoved, forcing him back down into the overstuffed chair. She leaned in toward him, her hands on the arms of the chair. He leaned back as far as the seatback would allow, then a bit farther, his bulk threatening to disassemble the chair.

"Luther, all told you are good boy. You are a fine figure of a man and a worthy representative of the handiwork of God. The very look of you can take a woman's breath away, just as that girl just took your breath away."

She snorted. "But I swear by all the saints that you are as dumb as a day-old mule turd." She sniffed and snorted again, pushed herself upright, and followed Al's path up the staircase.

Luther sat, his mind reeling for reasons he did not understand. He sat for several minutes. He stood and put on his hat. *Gosh darn it,* he thought. *The judge ain't goin' to be happy that I never got Miss Mercy's tax money while I was here.*

Chapter Eighteen

Justice Payne sat at the desk in his office at the Cactus Thorn Saloon, staring at the jumble of ledgers and notebooks and loose sheets of paper. The amount of money going out the door troubled him. Sometimes he thought the businesses he owned were bleeding him dry. There was a never-ending supply of flour and sugar and eggs and lard for the bakery, iron and steel and coal for the blacksmith shop, groceries to stock the grocery store, and groceries to supply the café. Cattle and hogs and sheep for the butcher shop. Beer and whiskey and wine and lunch counter food for the Cactus Thorn Saloon. The manager of the hotel always had his hand out. As did the man who ran the newspaper and the print shop. Oats and hay for the livery stable. And on and on and on, all the way down the list of his many holdings in the town.

He wondered if the independent business owners in the town were taking advantage of him and enriching themselves at his expense. He wondered if the rents he charged them for occupying his buildings were high enough. If tax rates could be higher. If their financial reports—scattered among the papers scattered on his desk—were accurate, or fudged in their favor and against him. None of his tenants appeared to be flush with excess cash, and there was some comfort in that.

All, that is, except Mercy O'Malley and her House of Passion. He was convinced she was taking in more than she claimed, and keeping more of what ought to be his than she ought to. But he could not prove it, or even imagine how she was doing it. Then he remembered her past-due taxes and his ire flared up at the thought of Luther and his inability to collect from her. When the marshal had last come back from the House of Passion empty-handed—he claimed to have been distracted by some woman—the judge told him not to bother going back, that he would see to it himself.

If there weren't so many things he had to see to himself, he might have more time to figure out all this money business. He knew he had more money than he could ever spend squirreled away in various places. But he shook his head in despair of ever understanding in any detail how, where, and from whom it came, what his profit margins were, and, for that matter, where all his money was.

As he had often done in the past, the judge gave some thought to hiring an accountant, or at least a bookkeeper or a clerk, to sort it all out and bring some order to his finances. But he was slow to trust anyone but himself, and where money was involved, he even questioned his own incorruptibility. But, he thought, if *he* was cheating someone somewhere, at least his misdeeds would figure in his favor, as opposed to taking a chance on being cheated by others.

After several more minutes—that seemed like hours—of frustration with his finances, he threw up his hands and walked out into the Cactus Thorn. He stood by the dance hall stage, hooked his thumbs in his braces, smiled, rocked back a bit on his heels, and surveyed the single most favorite of all his holdings.

He knew, at first glance, that something was out of order. It was unusually quiet. There were no patrons lining the bar. No players at the card tables.

Then he saw Luther. He sat in a chair pulled away from one of the tables with his hat in his lap. Standing behind him was a man with his fingers in the marshal's hair.

Sitting on the table atop the case that carried it was a plaster model of a human head. It was hairless, white, and bright. The surface of the skull was inscribed with a network of black lines, and inside each section was a word.

Most of the patrons of the saloon stood in a circle around the man with his hands in Luther's hair. There stood the accordion player, his instrument hanging from his shoulder by a strap. Even Al was there, with Twah at her side. All along the ridge of the dog's back the hair stood on end and intermittent low growls rolled through his throat. No one else made a sound.

"What the hell is going on here?" Justice said after walking near to the gathering.

All eyes turned to him in surprise. So intense was their concentration on the man who had brought the white head into the saloon that no one noticed the judge's entry or his presence, even though he had stood nearby and watched for several minutes.

The judge said, "Who the hell are you?"

The man with his fingers in Luther's hair stood without moving, even his hands still. "I might ask the same question of you."

The crowd stirred at the impertinence of the statement.

The judge stared at the man for a moment that stretched well into discomfort for everyone in the room. Then, "I am Justice Payne. Owner of this establishment. I will not bother to inform you of my other credentials. Be advised, however, that I am confident they will far outweigh the attainments in your portfolio, whatever they may be, at least within the confines of this town."

Stepping back from the task at hand, the man placed his hands on his thighs and bowed at the waist. "Begging your pardon, Sir."

"Luther, you have work to do. The rest of you, go on about your business." He told the stranger to have a seat, and the man sat down in the chair abandoned by the marshal.

Despite their dispersal to various parts of the saloon, the attention of the onlookers remained riveted on the table holding the white head and the two men seated near it. If they expected fireworks—which a good many of them did—they would be disappointed.

"Now then, how about you tell me who you are and why you are in my town."

"Your town?"

The judge nodded. "And I am not speaking figuratively." He swept the words away with a wave of his hand. "But we won't go into that just now. Answer my question."

"I am Anton Gruber. I am a traveling phrenologist. At present, I am on my way to San Francisco and other California cities. But I travel at a leisurely pace and ply my trade in communities along the way."

"A phrenologist."

The man nodded. "You are familiar with the practice?"

"Only in passing. I have, of course, heard of it. I have not seen it done." Justice smiled. "You say you are on your way to San Francisco. I recall reading something Ambrose Bierce of that city said about your work. Of phrenology itself, I should say. Bierce wrote that it is 'The science of picking the pocket through the scalp,' or something to that effect."

Gruber smiled. "We have our critics and our doubters. Of that there can be no question. But allow me, if you will Mister Payne, to familiarize you with the origins of the practice and its present application."

The judge sat through a lecture that opened in Austria with a Viennese physician named Franz Joseph Gall, who invented—discovered, to hear Gruber tell it—the modern practice of an ancient art. He had a student, Johann Kaspar Spurzheim, who brought the art—science, to hear Gruber tell it—to America. Here, it fell into the hands of a pair of evangelistic brothers, Orson and Lorenzo Fowler, who spread it across the land so far and wide it put John Chapman and his apple seeds to shame. The Fowlers also manufactured and sold mapped phrenology heads, Gruber said, and the white head with its lines and writing that he had unpacked for display was the real thing, a Fowler original, not one of the cheap imitations some practitioners used.

Gruber attempted to heighten the appeal of phrenology with a list of celebrities who had succumbed to a skull reading and swore to its reliability—or so Gruber said. Among adherents to the science were such luminaries as Ralph Waldo Emerson, Horace Greely, Edgar Allan Poe, Horace Mann, Walt Whitman, Brigham Young, and—saving what must be the most, or least, credible endorser for last—P.T. Barnum, famous for saying in another context that "There's a sucker born every minute."

Suspecting Gruber had more to say and would continue to say it until stopped, the judge interrupted. "What is it you plan to do here in my town?"

Gruber smiled. "Read the skulls of those among your citizenry who might seek the knowledge needed to magnify their strengths and compensate for their weaknesses, of course."

"Hmmph. And I suppose there is a price for this. Or do you do it as a service to the public, given its usefulness?"

Again, Gruber smiled. "No more so than a dentist extracts a decayed tooth as a public service, or a physician lances an inflamed boil, or a restaurateur provides a healthful meal. All benefit the citizenry and serve the public interest. Would you expect those who provide these helpful services to do so without recompense?" He did not wait for an answer. "I suspect not. Nor do I expect you are serious in asking if I perform my service without pay."

Justice attempted to speak, but the phrenologist's monologue allowed no gap into which he could wedge his words.

"Of course there is a fee for service—for the phrenologist, as there is with the dentist, the doctor, the midwife, the veterinarian, the surgeon, the nurse. One must, after all, make a living."

The phrenologist launched another salvo.

As the kind of man who did not care to engage in a discussion in which he was not the major contributor, the judge decided his only alternative was to retreat and survive to fight another day. He stood in mid-sentence of the phrenologist's talk and tipped his hat. "I am sorry, Mister Gruber, but I have other matters to attend to." He snapped the lapels of his suit coat. "I will allow you to go about your business—for the time being. But fair warning—should I learn from the citizenry that you are bilking them of a scandalous amount of their hard-earned money for your sorcery, I will have you arrested and brought to trial. Or, in the alternative, ridden out of town on a rail."

With that, Justice hurried out of the saloon with the urgency of a man with a destination to reach and a purpose to realize.

Neither was the case.

On the sidewalk, he stepped beyond the view through the saloon doors and windows and stood. He looked up the main street. He looked down the main street. He looked to the sky to check the weather. He consulted his pocket watch. He reset the angle his hat sat on his head.

And then a thought occurred. He would visit Mercy O'Malley's House of Passion and demand the past-due taxes the town marshal seemed incapable of collecting.

But, as had been the case on numerous recent occasions when Luther went calling, the judge would be unsuccessful and frustrated in the effort.

Mercy O'Malley was not at home. Nor did she return during a longer period than Justice had the patience to sit through in her parlor—

even though the overstuffed chairs there were the most comfortable seats the town had to offer.

The madam was, at the time, out and about in the streets of the town calling on her fellow business owners. Some welcomed her for the first time, others invited her in for a repeat visit. All listened to her appeal for support to, if not overthrow, at least bring to heel Justice Payne and his one-man rule over the town. With each of her implorings, Mercy had developed more and better counters to the usual objections. Of course the judge claimed the island as his personal property, and not without reason. Of course the judge had built the town from the ground up. Of course the judge had had a hand in setting them up in business. Of course the judge owned the very walls about them, the ceilings overhead, and the floors beneath their feet.

But none of that, Mercy insisted, gave him the right to rule like a king. This was, after all, the United States of America where the divine right of kings was not recognized, and the very notion of royalty was itself eschewed.

And could there be any doubt that Justice Payne acted as a monarch on the island?

Could there be any argument that he routinely trod upon their rights as individuals and as business owners? That he inhibited free enterprise? That he manipulated, even controlled, markets to enrich himself at their expense? That he committed the sin of taxation without representation? That he constrained growth? That he shirked his responsibilities as a landlord? That he conceived crimes and improvised punishments at will, and to suit his own purposes? That he denied them—and every other citizen of the town—a voice or vote in originating or enacting public policy?

No one could fault Mercy O'Malley's logic or disagree with her assertions, but . . .

But it's not like the judge is all that bad.

But it's not like the judge couldn't be worse.

But it's not like the judge hasn't contributed to our success in some ways.

But it's not like the judge hasn't kept the peace and maintained order.

But it's not like the judge . . .

Mercy sat through all the buts, all the what ifs, all the if onlys, all the questions, all the fears, all the timidity, all the apathy, all the passivity. She countered their claims, refuted their protests, and encouraged their umbrage and irritation with the state of affairs on the island.

In the end, it always came down to one simple question: But what can we do?

Mercy confessed to one and all that she had no answer. Not yet. But if they would commit their support, if they would vow to stand together, she would find an answer. She would hatch a plan. She would right the wrongs.

But, she repeated and reminded and reiterated ad infinitum, she could not do it alone. It must be a joint effort, a unanimous undertaking, or it would fail.

And if it failed, so would they.

Chapter Nineteen

Justice Payne spent a long night and part of the next morning frustrated over his finances, fretting and throwing fits. But the fouled-up figures foiled him at every turn. He was not aware of the fact, but in the dark of the night, in the wee hours of the morning, the houseman from Mercy O'Malley's House of Passion had ferreted out the town marshal to report an altercation at the brothel.

Luther, half awake, took into custody a logger recently given the sack. The woodcutter invested the bulk of his backpay in booze at the bar at Mercy's place, holding back just enough for entertainments among the flowers. But he drank too much and his calculations went astray and he came up short in his negotiation with a girl in the bloom of youth called Lily. When she refused his demands, the lumberman's anger got the best of him, and Lily found it necessary to bonk him on the noggin with an empty wine bottle and tie him to a bedrail with half a pair of thigh-high silk hosiery.

The marshal fought through the fog in his head long enough to haul the offender to the town square and shackle him to the whipping post. Thinking the judge asleep, Luther scrawled a nearly illegible note and slid it under his door.

Justice discovered the missive when forced by time and circumstance to abandon his books and visit the backhouse. As he sat, he studied Luther's scribbles, wondering if the boy had taken up writing in code. But he finally made sense of it all and after his late morning ablutions he sent Al, already on duty in the Cactus Thorn despite the earliness of the hour—according to saloon standard time—to fetch Luther. She was to tell him to set up the courtroom and then bring the prisoner before the bar.

The only activity in the saloon at the hour—other than a few local lushes maintaining a perpetual buzz—was at a table tucked into a corner beside, and nearly behind, the dancehall stage. There, Anton Gruber plied his trade. The judge had decided to allow him to practice in the town for a time, and he designated the saloon as the place for the phrenology sessions, a decision arrived at for two reasons: first, Gruber was to pay a tax equivalent to twenty-five percent of his fee from each reading, and second, people waiting to have their heads examined may well need refreshment from the bar, further lining Justice's pockets. The phrenologist bartered and bargained for better terms but made no headway, and finally decided that three-quarters of something was better than one hundred percent of nothing.

Trade was slow but steady, and curiosity attracted onlookers and prospects. Some "patients" preferred privacy and Gruber would shoo the spectators away, but most folks sitting for the phrenologist figured it all a lark and did not object to having others aware of what the hills and valleys, bumps and bowls, ebbs and flows of their crania implied.

Luther stumbled into the Cactus Thorn, his back and backside bruised from Al's persistent prodding with pointer finger and the toe of her boot. The marshal, face still smeared from sleep—or lack of it—placed the judge's table and chair and Twah's stool on the dancehall stage and arranged a few chairs to face it. He then took the initiative—which brought a smile to Al's face, owing to the rarity of the occasion—to instruct the phrenologist to box up his map of the mind and take a break from his work while court was in session.

By the time the marshal returned with his prisoner in tow, the judge was already on the bench wrapped in his Navajo robes, lawbook near at hand on the table, gavel lying in readiness next to the block, and Twah standing guard atop his cushioned stool.

There was a stir in the sleepy saloon when the batwing doors burst open and Mercy O'Malley marched in. Lily, expecting to be called as a witness, followed in her wake, and a handful of other flowers followed behind.

"Mercy O'Malley, what are you doing here?" the judge called out.

Mercy stopped in her tracks, causing a bit of bumping and bustling among the blossoms behind her. "Why, Your Honor, we are here for the court! Why else would I set foot in this pestiferous establishment of yours?"

Whack!

"Mind your mouth, Miss O'Malley, or I shall find you in contempt of this court."

Mercy snorted. "Well, you won't have to look far if it's contempt you're looking for! I've a heap of it stored up where you're concerned!"

Whack!

"Be silent!" Justice opted not to push it any further where Mercy was concerned. Encounters with her always brought to mind the paradoxical question about what happens when an unstoppable force meets an immovable object. One day, one day soon, he would get the best of the Irish upstart. But today would not be the day.

The judge instructed the town marshal, now become bailiff of the court, to call the room to order and declare the court in session. Luther mumbled his way through the words on the card and Justice whacked the gavel. He asked Luther to read the charges against the prisoner.

Luther cleared his throat. "Gosh, Judge, I don't rightly know what all he got up to last night on account of I was roused out of a sound sleep and never really woke up much. But, as I recall, he attempted to abuse and assault one of the girls over at Miss Mercy's place. It was a dispute over money, I think. Anyhow, the girl—that's her over there,"

Luther said, pointing out Lily, "she whonked him on the head and tied him up, so it was all over 'fore I even got there."

The judge stared at the prisoner before him for a time, then turned to his big black book, thumbing through the pages and studying the text. After several minutes, he slammed the book shut.

"First of all, despite her taking the law into her own hands and battering the miscreant, the young lady will not be charged as it is the finding of this court that she acted in self-defense."

Mercy O'Malley, surprised that the judge had even considered any wrongdoing on the part of Lily, laughed aloud.

Whack!

"There will be order in the courtroom!" Justice said. He turned his attention to the prisoner, standing before him with cuffed hands and bowed head, slowly swaying back and forth as if remaining upright was an unanswered question.

"As for you—" Justice looked at Luther and asked the accused's name.

"Don't rightly know, Judge. Never come up. I know he used to work up at one of the lumber camps till he got fired yesterday."

Justice asked the man his name and was answered in an unintelligible mumble.

"It looks to me, young man, that what we have here is a clear case of assault on the person of the young woman yonder. Theft of services, as well. Drunk and disorderly. Causing a ruction. Violent conduct. Showing disrespect toward a member the fairer sex. Resisting arrest. And, since you are unemployed and appear to have no visible means of support or any money in your pockets, there is the matter of vagrancy. Do you have anything to say for yourself?"

The accused said nothing.

The judge asked him how he pled to the charges—guilty or not guilty—and, still, the hungover young man said nothing. Raising his gavel, Justice said he saw no alternative to declaring him guilty. But before the gavel fell, a voice rang out.

"I object!"

Justice sat upright and sucked in a big breath of air. Still holding the gavel aloft, he said, "Mercy O'Malley, what the hell are you doing? You have no standing in this business before the court! You cannot enter an objection! Just what in hell's name are you up to?"

Mercy smiled. "Permission to speak, Your Honor."

Laying the gavel down and waving a hand as if to brush everything away, the judge told her to go ahead.

"First off, Judge, since all these crimes you're laying on this gent took place at my establishment, it seems I ought to have some say in the matter."

"Not from a legal standpoint. But, what the hell—go ahead. Speak your piece." The judge sighed. "I doubt there will be any peace otherwise."

"Here's the thing, Justice—you don't mind if I call you Justice—even though it is a contradiction to what's going on here—do you?" She did not wait for a reply. "This here young man ain't no different than hundreds, hell, thousands, of boyos who frequent my establishment. He had a bad day and needed to blow off a little steam."

"Hold on! Do all those thousands of others expect the services of girls like Lily when they haven't the means to pay? I assume, Miss O'Malley, that it is the norm for men to pay for the privilege."

Mercy chuckled. "You know damn well it is, on account of you demand an exorbitant cut of every transaction. It's highway robbery, is what it is. But that ain't neither here nor there in the present situation. Sure, the young feller there miscalculated and drank up more of what he had in his purse than what he should have. And sure, he got his undies in a bunch when it was pointed out to him by Miss Lily that he lacked the means to pay her price.

"But land sakes, Judge—he was drunk and didn't know no better and couldn't hardly stand upright besides. Had he been sober, he might've been able to do Lily a damage, but as it was, she got him subdued before he could do anything more than bust a washbowl and tear loose the seam of a gown." Mercy smiled. "I've seen more things busted up when a young man and one of my flowers is havin' fun!"

There was applause and laughter among the crowd, which had grown considerably as the trial progressed.

Whack!

"Order! Order in the court!"

Justice sat for several minutes. He stared at Mercy O'Malley. He stared at the accused. He stared at Miss Lily. He stared at the ceiling. He reached out and ran his fingers through the fur on Twah's neck. He realized, then, that the dog had paid no attention to the accused, and that meant he posed no threat and was most likely a decent enough fellow.

Still, this was a court of law, and the technicalities of the law meant something. He sighed. "Miss O'Malley, it is clear that this man committed the offenses for which he is accused. In a word, he is guilty. Guilty as hell. To find him otherwise would be a miscarriage of justice." He sighed again. "So what do you propose we do, Mercy? We cannot simply turn him loose."

Mercy grinned. "Glad you asked, Your Honor. What say you find him guilty and sentence him to time served. It couldn't have been too comfy, you know, him sleepin' on the ground in the town square chained up to a post whilst you was all tucked up in your blankets."

Justice laughed. "Oh, hell, Mercy! He was drunk as a skunk! He never had the least idea whether he was asleep or awake, or where he was. Look at him! He's still so saturated with liquor he doesn't know even now where he is or what is going on."

"So much the better, Judge! That bein' the case, he could not have been responsible for committing the acts of which he is accused, on account of him bein' too drunk to know better!"

The judge sagged in his seat, elbows on the bench, head bowed into his hands. He sat there for some time, then shook his head back and forth and looked up. He picked up the gavel.

Whack!

"Guilty of all charges. Sentenced to time served."

Whack!

"Court is adjourned."

Mercy let out a whoop and a holler. "Drinks is on me!"

The crowd cheered and made its way to the bar.

The bar bill would cost Mercy O'Malley a pretty penny, but she did not mind lining the judge's pockets in this case, as getting the best of him was certainly cause for celebration on her part. And, she believed, cause for embarrassment on the part of Justice Payne.

But Justice knew as he hurried back to his quarters that victory in a battle did not equate to winning the war.

Mercy knew it just as well. But she had not yet begun to fight.

Chapter Twenty

Mercy O'Malley's round of drinks set the Cactus Thorn alight, even given the earliness of the hour. And no one benefited from the celebration more than Anton Gruber the phrenologist.

As soon as the gavel fell to declare the court adjourned, the bright white head with its inscribed phrenology map was out of and sitting atop its packing box in the middle of the table. Gruber convinced the accordion player to perch on a stool near his corner table and play a few tunes to attract attention. Between the lure of the music and the curious hairless statue, people gathered round, some wondering about the head and others, who had seen the man in action earlier, attempting to explain what it meant.

With interest aroused, Gruber stilled the accordion and begged the crowd for attention. Then, in a manner similar to what he had told the judge, he started lecturing those gathered on the "science" of phrenology and its value to mankind. With a pointer, he touched the various divisions on the white head and explained their meanings—that the part of the brain underlying each division may be strong from exercise and force a bump or bulge on the skull, while those characteristics in which a subject was deficient would leave a shallow dip, due to that part of the brain suffering weakness from lack of use.

But interest, once aroused, will wane if not continuously engaged. The phrenologist's lecture went on too long and the listeners started drifting away, the lure of libations at the bar outdrawing lumps and bumps on a theoretical head.

Now comes Mercy O'Malley to the rescue, if only out of curiosity.

"Sure, and it's all well and good on a head with nothing in it but plaster and no person attached to it. What about real people?"

Gruber assured her the head was only for demonstration, and that the very nature of phrenology was the reading of real heads in which the real brains of real people resided. "Would you care to sit for a reading? On the house, of course."

"Oh, why not," Mercy said, unpinning the hat from her head and pulling hairpins to let her copper-colored tresses fall free.

"Sit, please," Gruber said, positioning a chair for her. "All I ask of you is to remain as still as possible."

Mercy sat. The phrenologist stood behind her, hands on her shoulders, eyes closed. Then, after drawing a deep breath and releasing it slowly, he pushed his fingers through her luxuriant locks and proceeded to probe her pate. He kept at it for several minutes, his fingers sometimes sliding some distance and at other times pausing and shifting only slightly. Now and then, Gruber would pause at the certain feel of something and smile slightly. At other times he might flex his fingers and furrow his brow, then touch again to read the troubling—or misunderstood—message the bone was sending. A time or two he held his hands steady and looked aside at the white head and its map as if to get his bearings.

All the while, the people who had left the circle drifted back, like ocean waves returning from the beach to the sea.

Gruber withdrew his fingers from Mercy's hair and lay them on her shoulders. He looked around at the assembled crowd and smiled. He stepped around the chair to face Mercy, placed the palms of his hands on his thighs, and bowed from the waist. "It has been a pleasure to feel of your cranium, Miss. I have learned much."

"Well, what of it? What've you got to say?"

The phrenologist pointed a finger upward. "Of course, of course. May I know your name, please? Only for purposes of conversation."

"Sure. It's Mercy. Mercy O'Malley."

Gruber cleared his throat and picked up his pointer, then turned to the crowd. "Do these people know you, Miss O'Malley? Know you well, I mean?"

"Not so's you'd notice. I'd say that in the town I am well known, but not known well. In personal matters, I keep myself to myself."

Gruber nodded. "Perhaps I can enlighten them—perhaps yourself, as well." Again, the phrenologist cleared his throat. "First, if I may, there is something of a surprise. Not a surprise so much, I suppose, but something unusual."

He employed the pointer and tapped a section on the white head map at the base of the skull. "Here, inside the skull, of course, is the cerebellum—the 'little brain' we call it. Therein lies the propensity for *amativeness*. Now, in children this propensity is undeveloped. Most often, almost always, it is in the male brain that we find it most fully developed. Which is why what I find in you is unusual—seldom is the propensity for amativeness so strong in a woman as it is with you. I can safely say that I have never—never—seen the like!"

Mercy said, "Well, what is it? This 'amativeness' or whatever you call it? What is it?"

"It is . . . how should I say it? It is, some would say, a delicate subject. Amativeness is the desire for, shall we say, physical love. *Physical* love, if you catch my meaning."

Mercy O'Malley, bless her soul, blushed. Chuckles and giggles rippled through those assembled, cresting in outright laughter from the flower girls in Mercy's employ. Anton Gruber looked around wide-eyed, as if seeking the reason for the mirth.

"Get on with it!" Mercy said.

"As you wish." Gruber leaned close to Mercy. "I apologize if I have caused embarrassment, Miss O'Malley."

She waved him off, and he stood and tapped his pointer at a spot between the eyes and at the top of the statue's nose. "At this place, we find a subject's sense of *individuality*—the strength of your understanding of your place in the world, shall we say, your appreciation of your individuality among those around you."

Mercy nodded her agreement. The pointer moved to a section about midway between the eye and the ear, but a bit higher on the skull.

"Here lies *constructiveness*. And here you show strength. I suspect you are adept at devising plans and carrying out those schemes, say the design of a house, or decorating a room, even planning and building a complex machine such as a locomotive, should it come to that.

"And here," Gruber said, pointing out a section on the white head slightly behind the orbit of the eye, "is *coloring*—a propensity for appreciation of and understanding of color. Those with this propensity tend to be skilled at matching colors in a wardrobe, say, or in room décor. And, I suppose we could say, a heightened appreciation for the beauty of a flower garden."

Again, those assembled found the phrenologist's words amusing and laughter punctuated his statement. For his part, Gruber knotted his face and forehead, glanced from face to face in the crowd as if an explanation would reveal itself, finally landing on Mercy's flower girls. The painted ladies in their colorful finery chortled and giggled and hooted, some behind gloved hands, others with slaps on the backs of their companions, others with heads thrown back and mouths stretched wide in mirth.

When, finally, the laughter subsided, Gruber tapped his pointer above the forehead, about halfway to the top of the head. "*Benevolence*," he said.

He laid the pointer aside and stepped behind Mercy, placing his finger on the corresponding spot on her head. "Ah, I feel it now! Miss

Mercy has a well-developed bump for benevolence, or generosity. With such prominence displayed for this propensity, I suspect this woman is uncommonly kind. That she actively pursues fairness and equity, that charity is evident in her dealings with her fellow creatures.

"As I said, benevolence is a particularly well-developed characteristic in this woman, and I am confident that hearing this surprises no one." The phrenologist stepped back from Mercy, extended a hand in her direction, and said, "Ladies and gentlemen, Mercy O'Malley!" He again bowed from the waist to the sound of lively applause.

Mercy stood, gave her head a shake, and plopped her hat on her head, giving it a sharp tug. "What the hell," she said. "Another round for the house!"

The applause burst forth again, and many of the onlookers headed for the bar. But others stayed put, forming an orderly line and waiting their turn to have Anton Gruber, phrenologist, handle their heads.

For a price, of course.

As the day wore on, the demand slackened. For his part, Gruber did not mind. He had probed and palpated enough scalps for one day.

With one exception.

He ordered up a flourish on the accordion, tapped a spoon to the side of a decanter, stood upon a chair, and asked for attention.

"Is the town marshal on the premises? He looked around for an answer but heard none. "I had begun a reading on the marshal—Luther, I believe is his name—but was interrupted in the process. I sensed something unusual, and would like the opportunity to complete my investigation of the marshal's cranium."

A shout came from across the room. Luther had been spotted in a far corner, sagging in a chair with his feet propped on another, catching up on his sleep. Two men awakened him, and each taking an arm, half

Justice and Mercy

guided and half carried the somnolent lawman into the phrenologist's lair.

Luther plopped down onto the chair with a yawn. "Not this again," he mumbled. "You like to have rubbed my head as bald as that statue of yours there the last time you did this."

Gruber did not speak. He set the marshal's hat aside and got his fingers into Luther's hair, still thick despite the complaint. He stroked and poked. He felt and fondled. He groped and explored. He stepped away and wiped his hands on a towel and went at it again. He muttered and mumbled. He asked for a washbasin with soap and water and scrubbed his hands thoroughly and tried again.

Luther slept through it all. Or at least most of it.

After several more attempts, the phrenologist threw his hands in the air. "I cannot believe it!" he said. "It is uncanny. I would have denied the very possibility of such an occurrence. I have never heard of this, nor read of it in the literature. It is remarkable, I say!"

The onlookers knew not what to say, staying silent in respect for Gruber's obvious pain and frustration.

"It cannot be! It simply cannot be!"

One man—Giacomo Moretti, as it happened, whose near continuous state of inebriation often interfered with his grasp of social niceties—stepped forward. "What the 'ell are you talking about? Spit it out, man!"

"It is his head! There is nothing there! Absolutely nothing. He hasn't a bump for any propensity. I swear, this man's head is as smooth as a billiard ball! As featureless as a glass marble! I don't believe it—I don't believe my own hands!"

Anton Gruber lifted the white head off its packing box, deposited it within and snapped the latches shut.

He sat down at the table.

He crossed his arms on the tabletop.

He lay his head on his arms.

And he wept.

The phrenologist was still at the table as Al stacked chairs at closing time, which occurred not by the clock but when no one was left in the Cactus Thorn save Giacomo Moretti and his fellow dipsomaniacs. The bouncer and bartender escorted them out, reminding them the door would open again in but a few hours, and then they could then pursue their inebriation afresh.

Al went about dousing most of the lanterns and lamps, leaving a few aglow in case the judge might care to leave his quarters and wander the premises, as he often did.

Anton Gruber had not moved from the time he laid his head on his hands hours earlier. Whether from fatigue or frustration, his energy was sapped and sleep was the only cure, no matter the comfort of the accommodations. With a gentle shake of his shoulder, Al roused him. Gruber came instantly awake, wide-eyed and refreshed.

"My goodness! How long have I slept? It was the sleep of the dead, I tell you—so deep in the arms of Morpheus have I been that I have no awareness of the passage of time. But now—now I am fully refreshed and ready. What is the time, if you would be so kind?"

Al yawned. "I don't know about you Mister, but far as I'm concerned it's near about bedtime."

"I see. I note the saloon is closed, so the hour must be late. I hope I shall be able to sleep some more in my hotel bed, but I fear that is out of the question. As I said, I am fully refreshed!"

"Say, Mister . . . I don't suppose you'd . . ." Al shook her head. "Nah—never mind."

Justice and Mercy

Gruber smiled. "I sense you desire a reading but are hesitant to ask. Not to worry, my friend—sit! I shall be pleased to accommodate."

Al, the color rising in her cheeks, sat in the chair and removed her hat. She had let her hair grow longer than she was accustomed to wearing it, but it was still rather short in comparison to the current fashion among young women.

The phrenologist stepped behind her and placed his hands on her shoulders. "What is your name, Miss?"

"Alice—but you can call me Al."

"I shan't. Alice it is."

With that, Gruber's fingers went into Al's—Alice's—hair. He gave her cranium the once over, then the twice over, then went at it again. Sitting in her chair, silenced by nerves and timidity, Al listened to his *hmms*, his *aaahs*, his *ooohs*, and other utterances.

He dragged a chair around and placed it facing Al and sat, their knees touching.

He smiled. "I must say, Alice, you are a most interesting specimen."

Al blushed. "Sorry, I, well, I . . ."

"No, no, no, young lady! I say 'interesting' in the best sense of the word—your skull reveals the presence of a brain that has developed in most unusual, but wonderful, ways! You have many prominent propensities common among females, and yet others more commonly found among the better males of the species. Most unusual, and I confess I have no explanation for it."

Al asked, with much stuttering and stammering, if being raised in a house full of men and boys in the absence of any female influence might be the reason. Gruber allowed that being raised that way may well be the reason.

"You, Alice, are blessed with a brain that equips you for a happy and productive life—a rare and precious thing, it is."

"I ain't sure what you mean."

"I shall explain."

Unbeknownst to the phrenologist and his patient, Justice Payne had wandered from his bed and, hearing their voices, had slipped nearby, carefully lifted a chair from a table, and sat down to listen in.

"First of all, young lady, you have a strong propensity in the area we call *conscientiousness*. This means you have a firm and forceful sense of duty, of justice, of truthfulness. Without a doubt, this propensity is much to be desired as it shows strength of character.

"Moving on. You have a dominant bump for *adhesiveness*, which reveals a desire—and an ability—to form friendships, to build bonds with others. It is a trait not uncommon among women, and essential in building communities and society as a whole.

"At the same time, you reveal another propensity especially valuable to making the world a better place. And that is *philoprogenitiveness*, which leads to a stronger than average propensity for parental love. It shows a sincere desire to raise children, and to love them, and to help them develop into productive members of society."

Al sighed. "What you're a-sayin' is true, far as it goes. I would surely enjoy having me a family—but look at me! There ain't many a man who'd take up with the likes of me."

"What you say surprises me, Miss Alice. Perhaps you have suffered a disappointment of late—some event or incident that has dashed your hopes."

"Oh? Why do you say that?"

"Only because *hope* is among your most highly developed propensities. It is a prominent bump, one that—most of the time, I suspect—leads you to imagine that a happy, prosperous future is possible, well within your grasp. Whatever has caused you to lose hope is a temporary condition, and will soon pass, overcome by your natural faculty for hopefulness."

Al shrugged.

"Now, here is where it gets interesting, Alice."

The judge left his seat and crept to a nearer table and set a chair from atop it onto the floor. A slight bump when it hit the floorboards left him frozen, but so intent were Gruber and Alice in their conversation they did not hear it.

"You have, right here," Gruber said, reaching out and touching a place a bit behind Al's ear, "a bump most unusual to find among women, at least one so prominent. *Combativeness*. It reveals a propensity for fighting—physical combat—supported by the presence of courage." He shook his head. "Most unusual among the fairer sex, as I said. It could be explained, I believe, by your being raised among brothers and men. Could this be so?"

Al laughed. "I reckon so. We fought like cats and dogs—grappling, wrestling, fisticuffs, mostly just for fun—and they never treated me no different than how they treated each other. I was just one of the boys, so far as they was concerned."

"I see. That could help explain another anomaly." Gruber touched a place below and slightly beside the orbit of Alice's eye. Here is a bump for *weight*. It is somewhat difficult to explain. It does not allow one to, say, guess the weight of an individual at the county fair, or the heft of a beef steer. Nor would it prevent such. But it shows a propensity to understand resistance as it applies to weight—an ability to determine how to shift a load, how to move an object from one place to another. I suspect you developed this trait in conjunction with combativeness."

Again, Alice laughed. "I'd say so. Folks is always surprised when I toss some big bruiser out of here if he's causing trouble. I never have no problem handling men twice my size when we get into a clinch.

'Course it don't hurt none that they're usually so drunk they can't hardly stand up nohow. Between rasslin' my brothers and throwin' calves at branding time, it's something I learned to do."

Justice Payne coughed. He immediately stood and stepped into the island of light in the phrenologist's corner, hoping to create the impression he had just walked in. A dose of bluster might further the illusion, he thought. "What the hell is going on here? The saloon is closed!" Then, "Oh, Al. It's you. What on earth are you doing here with this charlatan?"

"Just talkin' is all."

"Well, you had best get on home and get some sleep. It is late."

Al retrieved her hat and headed for the back door.

"What about you, Gruber? What are you doing here?"

"I'm afraid I dozed off earlier and slept the sleep of the dead. Miss Alice only just awakened me. Then, bless her heart, she asked if I would read her skull. A most remarkable young woman, your Alice is."

The judge scoffed. "Hell, she does not hardly realize she is a woman. That girl is mightily confused, I fear. But she has a good heart and is useful around here. A female bouncer is something of a novelty."

"For now. I suspect there are better things in store for her." Gruber stared at Justice, an implied challenge in the gaze. "What do you say, Judge—care for a reading?"

"What the hell for? I have long ascribed to the ancient Delphic maxim to 'know thyself.' I doubt there is anything you can say that would contribute to my knowledge."

Gruber shrugged. "As you wish. But I'll bet a dollar against a dime that I can read you like a book."

"You have a bet."

The phrenologist held up a finger. "You must commit to be honest. Even if you do not like what I find, if it is true of you, you must not deny it."

"You have my word."

"For what it's worth," Gruber said with a smile.

Justice snorted and sat down. The phrenologist went at his head with a purpose. When the prodding and palpating were complete, he sat facing his patient, but pulled the chair back a fair distance, not wanting to bump knees with the judge as he had with Al.

"Let me get a few characteristics out of the way right off. They require little explanation, and will not, I suspect, surprise you—if you are honest."

"Fire away."

"Mister Payne, your cranium tells me you are stubborn and obstinate to a fault. This bump for *firmness* is extremely prominent. You lack nothing in the way of *self-esteem*. Again, that is evident from the ridges in your skull. And it is intensified by your propensity for, your desire for, *approbation*—you have an over-active concern that people respect you, even glorify you. A less odious characteristic, perhaps, is *causality*. You have a strong concern for cause and effect, for knowing the outcome of your decisions."

Justice laughed. "So far, Gruber, you have said nothing that would surprise anyone who has known me for more than five minutes. I know all of this. And, I must say, these 'bumps' or 'propensities' as you call them, have served me well. They have aided me in building something of an empire—a small empire, I will grant you, confined as it is to this island, but something of my own making nevertheless. I see nothing wrong with any of it."

"Perhaps not. But now we get to the nub of it. The characteristics that make you, *you*. The parts of your brain that you have exercised the most, that you have trained to dominate your behavior."

Gruber slid his chair forward a bit and cleared his throat. "These, then, are your most prominent propensities, Mister Payne. The 'bumps' you are so eager to vilify. First, *secretiveness*. You conceal your thoughts. You hide your deeds. Even your language is guarded. Such a propensity, if overused, as yours appears to be, leads to lying and dishonesty."

The judge rose to object, but Gruber held up a hand to still him, and Justice sat back down.

Finally, *acquisitiveness*. The most prominent protrusion of all. You are overwhelmed with the need to covet, to crave, to acquire. The objects of your desire are probably of little concern to you—you want only to have them. Nor do you care what it takes to get them, including resorting to dishonesty. It all comes down to selfishness, to love gain over all else."

This time, Gruber did not attempt to stop Justice when he stood. The judge's face was florid, the intensity of the flush enhanced in the shadowy low light of the lanterns. He quivered and trembled. He doubled up his fists. He clenched his jaws.

"Get the hell out of here. Out of my saloon. Out of my town. Off my island. The rising sun had better not find you here."

Gruber reached out and opened a shallow drawer in the base of the case that carried his white head map. Inside was a jumble of coins and currency. "I believe I owe you, what, Judge—a quarter of what's here?"

"Forget it!" Justice hollered. "Keep you damn money! Just leave!"

The phrenologist smiled. "Well, Justice, I guess was wrong. You can look at money without wanting it for your own." He pulled out a silver dollar. "I guess I lose our bet for not reading you as well as I should have. So, you keep your dime and I lose my dollar. Here it is."

Gruber flipped the coin into the air. Justice watched it rise, sparkling as it flipped through the lantern light. He turned on a heel and walked away, with considerably more noise than when he came.

The silver dollar hit the floor with a ringing ding and wobbled and wiggled and spun till it lay flat on the floor. Gruber shrugged, leaned down and picked it up, and put it back in the drawer. He slid the drawer shut until its latch clicked, picked up the case and walked out the back door of the Cactus Thorn, tipping his hat to the door of the judge's quarters as he passed.

Chapter Twenty-One

The phrenologist was gone. Just gone. Anton Gruber had disappeared in the night as if he had never been there, with memories the only evidence of his visit to the town between the bridges that led to—and away from—the island.

His hotel bed had not been slept in. The night clerk, who dozed off while reading the latest issue of the *Police Gazette*, had, when he stirred, found an envelope with cash on the counter covering the room charges. The hostler at the livery stable did not see Anton Gruber either—he was likewise asleep, aided, in his case, by a jug of wine gone down to the dregs. He, too, upon awakening, found an amount of money sufficient for the boarding of the phrenologist's horse, the envelope with the cash tucked into the bib of his overalls.

Perhaps Gruber considered his services no longer in demand among the citizenry. Maybe he had pressing business elsewhere. Or it could be that he had a bump for *locality* and was simply overwhelmed by his propensity to travel and had to be on his way.

More likely, having read the ridges, having handled the head, having caressed the cranium, having identified and understood the bumps on Justice Payne's skull, he took seriously the judge's insistence that he leave town.

In any event, the phrenologist was gone.

Some town folks were pleased with his visit, having learned from his readings that they were not as bad as they thought they were. Others were disappointed to learn that they may well be worse than they imagined themselves.

But it was only a matter of days until talk of the tapper of skullcaps dissipated and life in the town on the island returned to what passed for

Justice and Mercy

normal. Unbeknownst to most, however, was an undercurrent for change that had grown and continued to grow. For some, the phrenologist's findings encouraged them to make more of themselves.

For Mercy O'Malley's part, the ousting of the phrenologist from the town—for she knew to near certainty that the ire of Justice Payne must be, for one reason or another, behind the man's sudden departure—only hardened her resolve. She determined to double and redouble her efforts to organize the town to rise up in revolt and overthrow the judge's autocratic rule over their lives.

The judge knew nothing of it, nor did he suspect. Mercy O'Malley had always been a bur under his saddle blanket, and only the money she put in his pockets from her House of Passion kept him from ousting her from the island.

Still, the frustration of his misunderstood finances, coupled by lingering anger from the phrenologist's revelations concerning his odious motivations, drove him to distraction.

More from sport than necessity, he clamped down on those who ran afoul of the law—laws known and unknown, laws of long-standing, and laws made up on the spot.

He kept Luther busy bringing in miscreants for trial. He assigned punishments that seemed far removed from the seriousness of the supposed crime. For instance, he sentenced a boy caught stealing eggs from a backyard henhouse to spend a hundred hours in community service gathering trash from the streets, swamping out the Cactus Thorn Saloon, and hauling offal from the butcher shop to dump in the river. But a man found guilty of abusing his wife and beating his children, and drinking up the grocery money and leaving them sick from hunger, paid a fine of two dollars and seventy-three cents, that amount being the sum total of the cash he had on his person when brought before the bar of justice—or Justice, if you prefer.

Some chalked up such behavior on the part of the judge as nothing out of the ordinary. Others entered it into the debit column in ledgers attempting to balance the books of his behavior. But, as is often the case, most people in the town—like people elsewhere and everywhere—went about their daily lives paying little attention to the whys and wherefores of the world.

Saturday nights at the Cactus Thorn were usually rowdy. But on one Saturday night in particular the rowdiness cranked up to an unusually high reading on the pressure gauge. For some unknown reason, cowboys and loggers and miners from the surrounding valley and mountains showed up in town in numbers higher than the norm to blow off steam and empty their pockets of payday pelf.

Twah sensed something in the air and the circumstances prompted him to abandon his lazing pose across the bar top. Instead, he sat, propped on his front leg, eyes locked on the batwing doors. Low growls rumbled in his throat almost every time they sprung open then flapped shut behind the entrant or entrants.

Al stood by his side at her usual station, fingers entwined in the fur of his neck, wondering at the danger he sensed. Other than their numbers, the men seemed to her no different than any other Saturday night crowd. But, trusting the dog's instincts and to be on the safe side, she sent one of the barmaids to fetch the judge.

Justice was in a foul mood but, again, Al did not find that unusual. She told him that Twah was upset by something in the air, and that she was worried.

Justice snorted. "You and that damn dog. I have told you and told you not to spoil him. He is just a dog, for heaven's sake. A good judge of character, granted—but still a dog! Look around, Al! Do you see anything amiss?"

The girl confessed that she did not. But she reiterated her fear that all hell was about to break loose, despite all evidence to the contrary.

"Well, if it will make you feel better, I will send someone to find Luther. He is out patrolling the streets for illegally parked conveyances and hitched horses, but I am willing to forego the fines the town would collect from those lawbreakers just to scratch whatever itch is bothering you and that damn dog."

With that, he huffed and walked away. But, Al noticed, he did not return to his quarters in the rear. Rather, after sending a flunky out to find the town marshal, Justice took up residence at a table near the dancehall stage, from which he could keep an eye on the place.

After a time, Luther pushed through the doors. Out of breath and sweating, he asked Al what was wrong.

"Nothin' yet," Al said. She shushed Twah's growl, who still held a grudge against the marshal. "I just got a bad feeling, is all."

"Darn! I near busted a gut gettin' here on account of being told there was trouble." He shoved a drunken Giacomo Moretti off the barstool where he sat next to Al, and took the seat himself. Moretti mumbled and moseyed off to find a new accommodation, where perhaps someone would buy him a drink.

Across the way, the judge castigated the flunky he had sent after Luther. Owing to the errand—on which the judge had sent him—the boy was late firing up the footlights on the dancehall stage. As the lights came up, the accordion player climbed onto his high stool beside the stage and limbered up his fingers with a few flourishes on the keyboard and buttons, squeezing the stale notes out of the bellows and readying the instrument for a fresh tune.

The card players at their games paid no attention, but at other tables chairs scraped and stuttered across the floorboards as patrons shifted seats around to see the stage. They hurried up their drink orders, knowing that three of the barmaids would be taking to the stage to perform double and triple duties on the boards, hoofing it and singing songs, leaving a shortened supply of barmaids on drinks duty to keep the patrons lubricated.

The trio of drink servers made it to the stage, later than usual owing to the demands of the oversized crowd for drinks. The lateness of the entertainment raised the temperature of some in the room, including Justice Payne, although he was torn between lost money for drinks while they were on stage, and the possibility of increased drink sales spurred by their song and dance act.

The three barmaids performed something resembling a can-can dance, kicking high to the accordion player's rendition of something resembling Offenbach's "Galop Infernal." Once the applause died down, they followed up with a rousing three-part harmony rendition of the popular hit drinking song, "Little Brown Jug." Again, the applause was enthusiastic.

Following a long string of curtsies, two of the girls stepped to the rear of the stage to provide backing vocals to the third girl, who stepped forward and launched into "Banks of the Ohio." The sad ballad moistened the eyes of many in the audience.

But, for some reason, a miner took offense. He turned away from the bar, where he had been huddled over his drink—the latest in a long line, as it happens—and hollered "Cut out that caterwauling!"

The music continued, soon fighting for attention with the continuing complaints of the man at the bar, interspersed with angry orders from others telling him to shut up, put a sock in it, pipe down, button his lip, shut his trap, hold his tongue, dummy up, cut the cackle, and other ignored entreaties.

After a time, a drunken logger, angered at the interruption of the ennui of the song, stood up from his chair at a table front and center from the stage, pulled a pistol from his pocket, and—in direct violation of the town ordinance against firing a gun—unleashed a shot at the loud and obnoxious miner.

He missed.

But the big mirror on the backbar exploded when the wayward slug slammed into it, shooting shards of reflective glass in all possible directions and rendering the saloon silent. The barmaids stopped singing, The accordion player's fingers stopped moving and the drone of the reeds died a wheezy death as the bellows sagged. The patrons in the overcrowded bar were speechless, mouths hanging open.

The shocked silence seemed to last a long time, but in reality, no more than thirteen seconds passed before all hell broke loose. It started when someone sitting next to the shooter at the table, and someone standing at the bar beside his intended victim, as if on cue, threw punches. Others objected and slugged them, and soon the melee was general. Fists and feet flew. Bottles shattered. Tables overturned. Chairs crashed. Noses bled. Eyes blackened. Goosebumps erupted. Lips swelled.

Al, at her station, grabbed every man who came within arm's reach and gave him the old heave-ho out through the doors, including a few hardy souls who came back for a second helping. Luther waded into the fray, using the butt of his gun to knock heads, suffering more than a few blows himself for his trouble. The bartender performed similar duties with a sap he kept handy for just such a purpose. Even Justice Payne lent a hand, using his judge's gavel—why it happened to be in his pocket is anybody's guess—to call to order any head he could whack.

Fortunately, no one else in the Cactus Thorn, in keeping with the local ordinance, fired a weapon.

The efforts of Al, Luther, the bartender, and the judge to end the affray may have been helpful but the fact is, they were outnumbered. The ruction continued for some time until, almost as suddenly as it started, it stopped. Men sat on the floor in puddles of spilled beer nursing their injuries. Others lay beside them in whiskey slicks, out cold or so enveloped in fog they could not rise. Some huddled under the few tables that were still upright, having sought shelter to lick their wounds or to avoid the altercation altogether.

The three barmaids-cum-canaries still stood on the stage, equally astonished and amused by the big bar fight. The one out front turned to the girls behind her. "I'll be damned if I ever sing that song again."

The judge ordered Luther to arrest the loudmouthed miner who had started it all, as well as the trigger-happy logger who shattered his mirrored backbar. Luther marched them off to be chained to the whipping post. The other patrons dusted themselves off, staunched the flow and seepage of blood, and limped out the doors under orders from the judge, Al, and a growling, barking, and snapping three-legged dog.

Neither Al nor Justice Payne showed any damage to their persons from the fracas. Twah, too, was unhurt. The bartender suffered a few minor cuts and scratches from flying glass but was otherwise unscathed.

Luther, on the other hand, was another story.

He limped back into the Cactus Thorn after locking up the originators of the uproar and collapsed onto a chair. "Jumpin' Jehoshaphat! That was some slugfest! My head's a-poundin' like the judge was playin' a tune on it with his little hammer!"

Al slipped behind the bar, found a fresh bar towel and moistened it with cool water. She tugged at Luther's hat to pry it loose from his swollen head, initiating a stream of moans and groans and pretend profanity pouring forth from the lawman's lips. She daubed and mopped and sponged and washed his hammered head. No blow had broken the skin of his scalp, but the hide was stretched tight on knots and knobs raised by blows from boisterous brawlers.

The judge had long since retired to his quarters. The barman, too, called it a night. Tomorrow would come soon enough, and the cleanup would wait until then.

That left Luther and Al—and Twah—alone in the bar.

The bouncer wrung out and refreshed the water in the towel, folded it into a square, and placed it gently atop the marshal's head. She pulled up a chair and sat facing him. He watched her through eyes at half-mast.

"How is it you never got hurt in all that maulin' and brawlin'?"

Al smiled. "Why, it's simple—I just got out of the way whenever anybody looked to do me a damage."

"It must've been a whole bunch quieter where you was—golly gosh, I couldn't hardly even turn around there was so many men tryin' to get at me."

"Oh, there was plenty of them where I was, too. Thing is, I never invited them to hang around. Soon as they'd show up, I'd just show them the door. The way I see it, there ain't no sense in standing around trading punches when you can just toss them out onto the street where they can't bother you no more."

Luther shook his head, and hissed through gritted teeth at the pain it caused.

"You know, Luther, it's a damn shame that there phrenologist feller left town."

The comment confused the lawman. "Why's that?"

"Well, you'll recollect how aggravated he was that he couldn't find none of them bumps he likes on your noggin." Al smiled while Luther wondered and pondered. She saw the light come on his eyes and her smile widened. "If he was to stick his fingers in your hair tonight, he wouldn't find nothing but bumps!"

It took a long moment, but if finally dawned on him what she meant. He laughed, but cut the hilarity short with a hard intake of breath when he felt the hurt.

"Dagnabit, Al, you're about as funny as a barrel of skunks."

Al laughed. "I think you mean *monkeys*, Luther. As funny as a barrel of *monkeys*."

"Oh."

Luther, sitting on a chair in the Cactus Thorn with a towel on his head, looked at Al as if it was the first time he had ever seen her. "Y'know, Al, when you smile like that you look right pretty."

Chapter Twenty-Two

Justice Payne sat across a desk in the bank—his bank—huddled with the manager over a report of his finances. Despite the disorder of the judge's personal bookkeeping, the banker assured him his financial position was solid—more than solid, in fact. The money man showed him the record of his credits, which outweighed by a considerable and growing amount the withdrawals and debits against his funds on deposit. And that margin of profitability did not take into account money invested elsewhere and in accounts at other banks, the balances of which increased steadily with the transfer of funds from the island.

"You've nothing to worry about, Judge Payne. If you were to shut down everything and walk away, you could live the rest of your life in luxury. In fact, it is unlikely you could spend all your money if you tried."

Not that he disbelieved the man, but Justice still fretted.

The banker said, "Why not step away for a time? Your people here can keep all your enterprises going. You could travel, see the world! Climb the Alps. Explore the Amazon. Visit the Antilles. Take an Africa safari. See the sights in Asia. Hunt polar bears in Alaska. Hike up the Acropolis in Athens. Go down under to Australia. There's no end to the places you could go!"

Justice sighed. "I suppose. But I do not think I would enjoy myself. Worries about my little island paradise would likely interfere with any possibility of pleasure."

"But that's just the thing, Judge! You have nothing to worry about!"

The judge shook his head. He would never admit it, but his concern was that someone, anyone, might make a dollar and he would not get a piece of it. Never mind that he did not need the money. Never mind that he would never need the money. Never mind that he would not live long enough to spend whatever piece of that dollar he got.

It was not so much that he wanted money as that the thought of anyone else having money made him shudder.

"Besides, if I were to leave the island, it would not be three days before that damned Mercy O'Malley would be running things."

The banker could not help but smile, but he made out to wipe his mouth and massage his chin to hide it. "I think you misjudge the lady, Judge."

"Lady! That woman is as far removed from being a lady as I am from being a Knight Errant!"

"Hmmm," the banker said, still stroking his chin. "Given her line of work, I suppose you have a point." He cleared his throat. "Sir, while it would be a violation of my fiduciary responsibilities to open the books on another client's accounts, I can safely reveal without betraying any confidences that Miss Mercy's financial position, while far from tenuous, is not nearly so substantial as I believe you imagine."

Justice laughed, without humor. "That's what you know. That woman is coining money in that place. I know it!"

The banker allowed that it was possible but denied knowing where that money—if "that money" even existed—was going. He assured the judge that he had supervised no transfers to other banks, nor did he know of any other transactions that would serve to conceal or cache funds from the House of Passion.

What the banker did not know—nor did Justice Payne know—was that the Western Union telegrapher and the shipping agent at the Wells Fargo express office were well aware of the movement of Miss Mercy's money, and were well paid for their discretion.

Also beyond the judge's awareness was that, at that very moment, Mercy O'Malley was mere yards away. Next door to the bank was a

Justice and Mercy

narrow building that served as a photographer's studio and gallery. As it happens, Mercy and the photographer were just then ensconced in the sitting room of the photographer's second-story living quarters.

Mercy was on a mission—a mission that utilized a good deal of her time and most of her energy. As had happened with other business owners in the town, and as would happen with yet others, she was on an errand to recruit the shutterbug to join her quest to oust Justice Payne from his position of ultimate authority in the town.

It was a quest she often thought quixotic. For while the judge used his power to exploit his tenants, he also used it to protect them. Since he determined who engaged in trade in the town through his control of real estate on the island, competition in any line of business ranged from minor to nonexistent. So, while the judge dipped deeply into the pockets of the independent businesses, they pocketed enough profit to keep them satisfied—satisfied enough, at least, to avoid outright rebellion.

Mercy O'Malley sought to convince her cohorts they could do better. Her recruitment efforts, while sometimes frustrating, were successful enough to keep her in harness. And with each new recruit to the cause, convincing the next became easier and the hope of attaining her goal grew. At the same time, as her support grew the possibility of discovery increased right along with it. Time was limited, she feared. And that was the reason Mercy decided to engage the judge's empire on another front—one that did not involve the people of the island.

Still, she did not know how much longer she would be able to keep the cat in the bag.

But the next big blow up in Justice Payne's town had nothing to do with cats and bags—it involved an inebriated cowboy and an irate longhorn steer.

It was the custom in the town for one or another of the ranches in the valley to sell a small herd of cattle to the judge from time to time to supply his businesses on the island. Then the beeves, usually numbering from a dozen to maybe twenty head, would be driven to town where they would be penned and fed until their assistance was required at the local butcher shop and meat market. On one otherwise uneventful Tuesday, one such herd clip-clopped across one bridge or the other and into the town.

The cattle were accompanied by an oversized crew of ten cowhands—well more than the job required. But it was a quiet time at the ranch and the cowboys were restless. A trip to town would be just the thing to alleviate boredom and provide a distraction. With the cattle corralled and the gate closed, the drovers enjoyed a meal at the café—a welcome respite from beans, bacon, and biscuits at the bunkhouse—then jingled their way into the Cactus Thorn Saloon to test the tonsil varnish on offer over the bar.

The celebration started off civil enough. As cowboys will, they shared stories of wrecks and jackpots and come-aparts involving recalcitrant cattle and unruly horses. They recounted roundups and cattle drives in which they played a starring role. They boasted of their abilities as ropers and riders. And as will happen where cowboys congregate, the brags and boasts turned to debates, dares, and challenges.

One particularly boastful cowboy, a burly black man recently arrived from wandering the cattle country from Texas to Montana, allowed that he could ride anything with four legs and hair if he could get his saddle on it. His saddle pals had heard the same boast many a time from many a mouth, it being a not uncommon claim around campfires, in bunkhouses, and in barrooms around the West. They brushed it off as mere braggadocio. But as the level of intoxication raised and

Justice and Mercy

inhibitions lowered, they decided to put the newcomer and his boast to the test.

"You know that red roan steer we brung in today—the one with the antlers that kind of turn down?" one cowboy said.

"You mean that bunch-quittin' sonofabitch that never got branded or cut till he was three years old?" said another.

"Yeah, that's the one. I ain't never been so tickled as when the boss said to ship him. I've chased that surly ol' mossy horn from one end of the ranch to the other more times than I can count. I'm damn glad to be rid of him."

"We all are. But what about him?"

"You think ol' Red here could ride him?"

The black cowboy went by the name of Red. Now, most who carried that appellation did so owing to the color of their hair and the freckles splashed across their face. But, in this case, it came from the man's habit of always wearing a bright red bandana around his neck. The hands in the bunkhouse had looked on in amazement when he arrived and unpacked from his war bag no fewer than thirteen of the voluminous throat wraps, all the same intense shade of red.

One cowboy after another in the Cactus Thorn that day offered an opinion on the cowboy's chances of topping out the roan steer. Red, being a relatively new hand at the ranch, had already established himself as a good hand. But beyond that, his abilities were unknown and so opinions were divided, with the fraction in favor of him besting the steer considerably smaller than those in the majority, who believed he would buck off.

Red listened to the give-and-take, heard them discuss the pros and cons, looked on as they debated the ups and downs. Finally, he spoke up. "Boys," he said. "I've heard enough of all you-all's chin music. I know the steer you-all's talkin' about and if all you-all can get him saddled, I can get him rode. When I say I can ride anything with hair on it I ain't lying. You-all get that cow critter roped and snubbed to a post and we'll get him saddled and if I ain't got him broke to ride and gentle as kid's horse before the dust settles, you-all can call me a gunsel or a greenhorn and I won't argue the point!"

The parade of punchers walked out of the Cactus Thorn and, being well oiled with whiskey, weaved and wobbled their way to the hitch rail. They snugged their saddle cinches, untracked their horses, stepped into the stirrups, and rode down the main street, around the corner, up the side street, and into the alley to the cattle pens.

Red tied his horse to a corral rail and pulled his hull. He eyed the roan steer with the downturned horns as his compadres ran it around the pen trying to get it roped. He estimated the animal's girth and adjusted his saddle cinches to the proper fit. It took more loops than the cowboy crew would ever admit they threw to get the mossy horn caught and snubbed to the post. Red swung his saddle onto the steer's back and the ornery creature bellowed and bawled, hooked with his horns, and lashed out with his hind hooves as the hands got the cinches ringed to the latigos and snugged up tight. The hands fought to hang a halter on the steer's head so the rider would have a pair of reins to help his balance and perhaps—although no one believed it—allow him to control the bovine's direction. They let the steer blow while they opened a gate and pushed the other cattle into an adjacent pen.

Draining the last of the firewater from the bottle he carried, Red hitched up his britches, tucked his pants legs into his boot tops, checked the buckles on his woolly chaps, pulled his hat down tight, and adjusted the position of his red bandana. "Well, boys," he said. "Stand back and let's see if this here steer can buck, or if he'll sull up like a old milk cow."

The cowboys lined up along the top rail of the fence. One stayed behind to free the steer from the snubbing post. Rather than attempt to pull the loop off the oversized horns, he would cut it loose. Red gave the man a nod and leapt into the saddle as the cowboy reached around the post with his pocketknife and sliced through the lariat.

The steer lowered his head and gave it a shake, slinging snot and slobber. He bellered and stepped backward but did not buck. Red took off his hat and slapped the steer on the rump, then on the head, but to no avail. He put his hat back on and tugged it tight. He eased into a deeper seat in the saddle. He adjusted his grip on the reins. He wormed his feet farther into the stirrups. Then he turned his toes out and jabbed the steer in the belly with his spurs.

There was so much dust stirred up in the corral once the roan steer cut loose that the cowboys on the fence could only wonder at what was going on. The confusion got more chaotic when the two cow dogs they brought along to help herd the cattle darted under the fence and went after the steer. The railbirds could see nothing more than an occasional antler break out of the dust cloud then duck back in. Red's hat surfaced from time to time, and now and then a particularly high jump on the part of the steer allowed enough of the cowboy to see the light that the spectators could see his red bandana flapping and waving in the hurricane. Sometimes it was a cloven hoof they saw. Sometimes the snapping jaws of a dog rising and falling through the dust. A switching, swatting, tail switch. A shirtsleeve. A patch of roan hide. A leg wrapped in woolly chaps. The glint of the sun on a spur rowel.

Then the dust got so thick the cowboys did not see it happen. But they all heard it. Fence posts shattered. Fence rails snapped. Dust settled.

"There he goes, boys!" one of the cowboys yelled.

The cowboys turned in time to see the steer round the corner out of the alley and onto the side street, Red still aboard and riding high. They jumped off the fence and ran, arriving in time to see the jumping, twisting, spinning steer, harried by a pair of barking dogs, turn the corner onto the main street. They hoofed it after them, following the trail of dust, the sound of the bawling steer, the yapping of the dogs, and the whoops and hollers of the rider.

People going about their business in the town watched in wonder as an oversized red roan steer with downturned horns stormed onto the main street, a cowboy wearing a red bandana sitting in a saddle on the cow critter's back. They hid behind porch posts, ducked through doorways, or whipped up whatever was hitched to their wagons to get out of the way, then watched in awe as the steer jumped high, rolled to one side or the other till his belly could see the sun, landed like a pile driver, then leaped again. The agile steer could turn a full circle in midair, stand on his front legs and kick so high his tail thumped Red's hat, then twist and turn as if hinged in the middle.

The steer broke through a hitchrail, turning it into toothpicks with his sweeping antlers. He leapt onto the boardwalk and hooked three porch posts out of the way, bringing the porch roofs down in his wake. The destruction continued as the angry bovine bellered its way along the sidewalk. At the Cactus Thorn, he horned his way through the batwing doors, breaking out the door posts to make room for the spread of his rack.

Twah jumped up from where he lay on the bar, barked three times at the intruder, then plopped down and did his best to cover his head with his one paw. Al grabbed the dog and ducked behind the bar.

Fortunately, the wild steer turned the other way. Red let loose a loud holler as his mount leapt onto a table, collapsing the legs. The steer did the same to another table, hooking chairs with the tips of his horns and tossing them away. The few drinkers in the place scurried for cover. All, that is, except Giacomo Moretti, who sat on his stool nursing a glass of jug wine, watching the commotion of a cowboy riding a saddled steer through the saloon as if it were a common occurrence.

The ruction brought Justice Payne out of his quarters, and he came into the barroom from the rear at the same time Red's cowboy pals came in the front through the unhinged batwing doors. They watched the steer bull its way through the card tables, then jump onto the dancehall stage. It paused for a moment to strike a pose, pawing the boards with a front hoof, nose in the air and blowing, with Red firm in the saddle, reins in hand, and a smile on his face.

"You got to admit," one of the cowboys said, "that makes a right purty picture."

Red poked the roan with his spurs and it leapt off the stage. The steer, tiring from all the activity, headed for the door. He kept up the game with an occasional kick of his hind legs, or horning a table or chair out of his path. But by the time he jumped off the boardwalk and back onto the main street he was spent. Front legs splayed, head down, tail sagging, the steer sucked in air as the smiling cowboy sat in the saddle.

When the roan steer caught its breath, Red prodded it with his spurs and reined the critter down the center of the main street, smiling and tipping his hat to the spectators lining the sidewalks. He made a lap from one end of the town to the other, pausing to wave at the flower girls at Mercy O'Malley's House of Passion as they leaned out of open upstairs windows to cheer the cowboy on.

Back up the street, Red turned into the side street, then the alley whence he came, and into the broken corral. He dismounted and hitched the steer to the snubbing post. By the time he stripped his kack his cowboy friends had arrived, laughing and cheering and waving the latest round of whiskey bottles.

Right behind them came Justice Payne, with Luther the town marshal at his heels.

Chapter Twenty-Three

Red spent an uncomfortable night chained to the whipping post in the town square—not that the accommodations were all that different than many another night spent under the stars. But once the effects of the whiskey wore off and the hangover set in, he felt like someone had strung a pigging string around his head and drawn it up tight. His eyeballs throbbed and his mouth was as dry as a buffalo wallow in August, and about as odoriferous.

His saddle pals felt much the same. In a show of support and solidarity, they had unspooled their bedrolls in the town square. Some spent a fitful night, others slept like calves with full bellies. When morning came, all awakened hungover. Half-closed eyes could not filter out the pain of the rising sun, and soaking their heads in the water trough offered little relief for fevered brows. Empty pockets meant empty stomachs, but few of the cowboys could have looked a fried egg in the eye if given the opportunity.

Worst of all was the waiting. They bided their time, idling around the town square to keep Red company. The conversation was scant and mostly whispered, with brains too fragile for serious talk and ears too sensitive for disquiet. It was not until nearly dinner time that Luther moseyed up with the key to Red's shackles.

"On your feet, cowboy. You've got an appointment with Judge Payne." As they walked down the main street toward the Cactus Thorn Saloon, Luther commiserated with the erstwhile roughstock rider. "Good golly, fella, you're in a heap of trouble. That steer tore up the judge's saloon real bad and he ain't none too happy. Don't recollect when last I seen him so mad. He's fit to chew up horseshoes and spit out horseshoe nails."

Red said nothing, only groaned.

"Just so's you know, if he passes sentence for you to be horsewhipped, I'll be the one runnin' the whip, and he don't allow me to let up none."

Red moaned.

"But it ain't nothin' personal. Just doin' my job is all. I hope you won't hold it ag'in me."

A sizable crowd had congregated in the saloon by the time the marshal and prisoner arrived with a string of soft-stepping cowboys following along like a gaggle of goslings. Most of the crowd stood, as few chairs had survived the steer's mad attack in working order.

Luther had put a three-legged table on the dancehall stage, a tenuous fourth leg nailed on to keep things steady. Luther hoped the judge would not bang his gavel on the table hard enough to make the whole thing crumple. Twah, from his perch on his stool, studied the arrangement in wonder.

With Red seated before the bar—the judge's bar, not the saloon bar—Luther read from his card to call court into session. The judge banged his gavel and called for order, advising the bartender and barmaids to keep the booze flowing, but to do so quietly.

Whack!

"You there! Stand up!"

Red followed the judge's order, rising slowly from the chair as the bones in his joints and every vertebra in his back snapped and crackled and popped in memory of a wild steer ride and a night on the hard ground.

"What is your name, Son?"

Red cleared his throat and struggled to speak. He raised his cuffed hands and signaled Luther to step over. "Might I have a glass of water?"

he whispered. "My talker seems to need lubrication." Then, with a weak smile, "A beer might work better."

Luther explained the delay to judge.

"Oh, what the hell! Get the man a beer!"

Whack!

The beverage went down in an uninterrupted series of long gulps, followed by a satisfied sigh and a head-to-toe shudder. "Red."

"Red?" the judge said.

"Red."

"That is all? Just Red?"

"Far as I know, Mister Judge, Sir. I ain't been called nothin' else for so long I can't rightly recall what I went by before that."

"Well, Red, I suppose you know why you are here, before this court."

Red squirmed. "I reckon it's got somethin' to do with that ornery roan steer I got into a altercation with yesterday."

"That is it precisely."

The judge opened his big black book. Luther held his breath as it slid across the table, concerned the movement might upset the cobbled-together table. As he was wont to do, the judge thumbed through the book's pages, running a finger up and down the columns, flipping from one section to another, and finally slamming it shut with enough force to cause Luther to gasp.

Whack!

"Red, you are charged with being a public nuisance, disturbing the peace, destruction of property public and private, endangering the public, animal abuse, inciting a riot, violation of the noise ordinance, holding a public exhibition without a license, causing havoc on a public thoroughfare, impeding traffic, and being drunk and disorderly."

Whack!

"How do you plead?"

Red stood for a long moment, head bowed. Then he raised his head and smiled at the judge. "I reckon I'm not guilty, Judge. Well, except for the drunk and disorderly part. I suppose I was a mite tipsy at the time."

Whack!

"Not guilty?! Do not insult the intelligence of this court!" Justice waved his gavel over the crowd. Red-faced, he said, "Why, most every person in this room witnessed your destruction of a goodly portion of this town!"

Red only smiled.

"Well? What do you have to say for yourself?"

Red smiled wider and cleared his throat. "Well, Judge, it weren't me."

"Wasn't you? What the hell do you mean? Am I to call every man in this room to testify they saw you—and it was most certainly you, you being the only black cowboy in a red bandana seen on the streets of this town of late!"

"No, Judge, Sir, that won't be necessary. I was there and I saw it myself. But like I said, it weren't me."

The judge, baffled beyond words, could only stare at the cowboy. But the question was plain on his face, and the tension so thick in the room you could bounce a ball off it.

"Here's the thing, Judge. Like I said, I never did none of that stuff. It was that steer that done it all. You know the one—big red roan mossy horn with a wide rack of droopy antlers. I can point him out to you if you want."

Justice Payne stuttered and spit and stammered before words formed. "You are attempting to lay the blame on an animal?"

"Well, it was him that did it all. I never broke nothin'."

"But you were on the animal's back! The whole time!"

"Yessir. And I'm damn glad I was—and so should you be. If I hadn't of been there, that steer would've done a whole lot worse. Hellfire! If I hadn't of controlled that mad cow what little bit I could, he'd have wrecked a whole lot more stuff. You'll recollect that it was me what rode him out of this very barroom 'fore he could do any more damage than what he already did."

Again, the judge struggled to speak through the anger that had beads of sweat popping out on his forehead and upper lip. "That is nothing but a lot of nonsense!"

Red raised his hands and spread them as wide apart as the handcuffs would allow. "Take a look at me, Judge. There ain't a scratch on me. There ain't no way a man could bust up all the stuff you said without gettin' busted up some hisself. Like I said, it was the steer what done it."

Justice Payne huffed and puffed. He hissed and miffed. He opened up his big black book and closed it again, then opened it back up and slammed through the pages and kept at it for several minutes.

Red, and the rest of the crowd, waited. Some looked on with faint smiles, amused at the judge's discombobulation and in admiration of the cowboy's defense. Others waited with bated breath to see how the judge would talk his way around this one. For his part, Red hoped his line of bullshit would keep Luther's blacksnake whip at bay.

A change in the judge's demeanor led to a change of atmosphere in the room. He closed the book gently and pushed it aside. He looked at Red and smiled. He spread the smile around the room.

"Red, the court accepts your explanation of the events in question. We concur with your assertion that, in actual fact, it was the steer that caused the aforementioned damage as outlined in the charges."

Red's saddle pals whooped and hollered, clapping and stomping and tossing their hats into the air. Others in the assemblage joined in the celebration.

Whack!

Whack!

Whack!

"Order!" yelled the judge. "Order in the court!"

Whack!

Whack!

Whack!

"You will come to order, or I will clear the room!"

Whack!

The tumult died down.

"Now, then, Red. As you have asserted, and as the court has agreed, it was the steer that caused the damage. Do you understand my finding?"

Red nodded. "Yessir."

"Now, then. Since the steer caused the damage, said steer belonging to whatever ranch it is you work for, and you being a representative of said ranch, and having escorted said steer into the confines of the city, the court finds you nonetheless responsible for the damage."

Whack!

Red cleared his throat. "Judge?"

"What is it? I am about to find you guilty and pronounce sentence."

"But that ain't right, Judge."

"What 'ain't right'?"

"That steer don't belong to the ranch."

"What?!"

"Like I said, that steer, it don't belong to the ranch."

Justice and Mercy

As before, Justice Payne stuttered and stammered, searching for words. "Who, then? Who?" was all he could muster.

Red smiled wide. He turned to the right, then the left, spreading his smile over all assembled. "Why, Judge—that steer, he belongs to *you*."

"W . . . wh . . . what?"

"He's yours, Judge." Red turned and pointed to one of the cowboys on the sidelines. "That feller over there—the one in the blue bib-front shirt with the gravy stain on it and wearin' that big black hat, he's the foreman out at the ranch. And he's got a bill of sale right there in his pocket showin' that the steer we been talkin' about, and all them other beeves we brung to town, was sold to the butcher shop three days ago. And unless I been misinformed, that butcher shop, it belongs to you."

Again, the crowd erupted into applause and celebration, led by the cow punchers. Even Twah lifted his snout skyward and let out a happy howl.

Without a word, without so much as a whack of his gavel, Justice Payne backed away from his table, picked up his big black law book, and left the bench with the woolen Navajo blanket he wore as his judge's robes waving like a flag of surrender behind him.

Later that same afternoon, Mercy O'Malley sat in her upper rooms at the House of Passion, watching out the window as the river flowed by. A snippet of a Bible verse came to mind, one she remembered for some unknown reason. Somewhere in Ecclesiastes, she thought. "All the rivers run into the sea; yet the sea is not full."

Sort of like Justice Payne's bank account, she thought. *The money flows in, but it is never full. At least not full enough to satisfy Justice Payne.*

Then she smiled, thinking of the judge's comeuppance in court that morning. She had stayed at the Cactus Thorn afterward, celebrating with the crowd and going so far as to buy a round for the house. She even passed out chits to Red and his saddle pals, redeemable for a stroll through her flower garden and a pleasurable session with the bloom of their choice.

Still, the judge's embarrassment would likely lead to a crackdown on the citizens of the town. One did not beard the lion without consequence. Increased taxes for business owners, perhaps. Higher rents for his tenants, maybe. Upping the prices in his shops and stores, perchance.

But she did not allow the realization of troubles to come to dampen her mood. For in her hand she held a letter. The letter was a battle plan, of sorts, in the second front of her war against Justice Payne. The envelope bore a Philadelphia postmark, and the return address of a law firm she employed to oversee her investments as well as handle routine legal matters that might arise.

There was nothing routine, however, in the task she had laid out for them.

The missive informed her that the senior partners understood her desires and would immediately undertake their fulfillment. Success was unlikely, they informed her, based on cursory research, but they would still do as instructed.

That was fine with Mercy, for she knew failure was a near certainty. And yet in that failure there was also success, for the work of the law firm would further stir the pot that was just beginning to send tendrils of steam into the air.

A few days hence, with the arrival of a Philadelphia lawyer, the pot would no doubt heat up to a rolling boil.

Chapter Twenty-Four

The Philadelphia lawyer, all decked out in his three-piece suit, boiled and starched shirt, and shoes polished to a mirror finish, sat across the desk from the bank manager.

"So, you are interested in investing in real estate hereabouts," the banker said.

"No, sir, you misunderstand me. Not hereabouts—here." The lawyer tapped his walking stick on the floor twice to reinforce his point.

The bank manager rocked back in his big chair and laid his hands, fingers interlaced, atop his protruding belly, and studied his guest. "I am a banker. This is a bank. We are not in the real estate business, either buying or selling."

"Of that I am fully aware, good Sir. The same can be said of myself and the law firm that employs me."

"Why, then, are we here?"

Scooting his chair closer to the desk, the lawyer propped his walking stick against its lip, leaned forward, then placed his hands, fingers interlaced to mirror those of the banker, atop the desk. "We know, from long experience, that the man who carries the keys to the bank in a town most generally also has his fingers on its pulse. He knows whose property may be ripe for picking, whose financial situation would benefit from an infusion of cash through selling off assets, such as real estate." He waved his hand. "And so on. I am sure I need not elaborate."

The lawyer leaned farther forward. "Here is the gist of it. My firm represents a client with an interest in the future of this town. It is believed growth, and the resulting commerce that will come, offer an excellent opportunity for prosperity. Our client would like to share in that wealth." The lawyer sat back in his chair.

"Hmmm," the banker said. "Are you aware—and are your firm and your client aware—of the ownership situation here?"

"Indeed, we are. We know through our research that title to the entire island is held by one man. Justice Payne." The lawyer smiled. "I must admit, finding that information was no small achievement. With no governmental or administrative relationship with the adjacent counties—Adams and Jefferson, I believe they are—locating records at either courthouse proved impossible." The lawyer shrugged. "Our man was forced to rummage through the records at the statehouse—which are in an abominable condition, by the way—to locate the recordings of titles and deeds and the like."

The banker smiled. "Yes. Of course. Justice Payne likes it that way. The less he sees of bean counters from Adams or Jefferson Counties, or the state capital for that matter, the better." The banker's chair squeaked as he rocked forward and propped his elbows on the desktop. "Another thing you ought to know about Justice Payne is that he has a purpose for owning the island in its entirety. There is a method in the madness, so to speak. His reasons are of no consequence to you. All you need to know is that it is not in his interest to part with any of his property on the island. In a word, it is not for sale. None of it."

With a smile, the Philadelphia lawyer stood and picked up his walking stick. He reached out and retrieved his hat from the hat rack, placed it just so on his head, and settled it with the tap of a finger to the crown. "Every man has his price, sir. I suspect this Justice Payne of yours is no exception."

The banker stood, walked around the desk, and opened the door for his guest. "I believe you will find that Justice Payne *is* an exception."

With a smile and a slight bow, the Philadelphia Lawyer stepped through the doorway, walked through the bank lobby, and out the front doors. He paused on the boardwalk and looked up and down the main street. He inhaled deeply of the clear, clean Western air, noting the difference between it and the thick, humid, fetid, smoky Philadelphia fog he was accustomed to breathing. He could see why his firm's client preferred living in the otherwise uncivilized Wild West.

Unfortunately, forbidden as he was from making any contact with said client, or acknowledging any familiarity or relationship with anyone in the town, he could not share that observation with Miss Mercy O'Malley.

The lawyer spent the remainder of the afternoon walking the business district. He entered door after door, inquiring after the owner or manager. He asked questions about the state of business in the town, their view of future prospects, their satisfaction with conditions, and the like. The inquiries were carefully considered, meant to divulge a more than passing interest, make known the seriousness of the probe, and imply that things could be better. All while acting just brash enough to almost offend—especially in businesses owned by Justice Payne.

The plan worked. The afternoon had not passed before the judge was aware of the man meddling in his affairs. Justice wondered at the sudden interest in his island. No such thing had ever occurred before. Oh, there had been inquiries about property ownership, but those had been individual in nature—the one doing the inquiring wanting to set up shop of one kind or another. When apprised of the situation, they were happy enough to move along and seek opportunity elsewhere.

But this—this was different.

After worrying throughout a fitful night, the judge decided to confront the situation head on. He moseyed up and down the walkways lining the shops and stores hoping to encounter the inquirer. And he did. He almost collided with the lawyer as the man stepped out of the tobacconist's shop—the tobacconist being one of those independent owners dependent on the judge for the roofs over their heads.

"I beg your pardon, sir," the Philadelphia lawyer said, stepping back from the near miss. He reached up with his walking stick and tapped the brim of his hat as he bowed slightly. He recognized Justice Payne from descriptions of the man. Then, with a smile, he held up the other hand, which held a bunch of just-purchased cigars. "Care for a smoke? The man inside insists they come from Havana, but I suspect the Connecticut River Valley to be a more likely point of origin."

Taken aback by the man's proximity and familiarity, Justice could only shake his head. He took another step back and studied the man, knowing without a doubt he had found who he was looking for. But before he could stake a claim to the conversation, the lawyer spoke again.

"A lovely day. Simply lovely. This dry Western climate is invigorating. He leaned in close and almost whispered. "Although I confess, the aridity of the air is wreaking havoc with my sinus! Nor is it treating my eczema rubrum kindly."

Again, the lawyer's forward manner and familiarity rattled the judge, further inhibiting his ability to speak.

The lawyer, on the other hand, was fully aware of the effect his behavior had on the judge, which was fully intended.

"Tell me, sir—are you an inhabitant of the town, or a visitor, such as myself?" He did not wait for an answer, and pressed on. "I find it a most quaint town—village, if you will. Of course, being from the East, I am accustomed to a more refined way of living. Not that there is anything wrong with the somewhat uncivilized nature of the town."

The judge tried to interrupt, but only managed to insert half a word before the lawyer continued.

"Having arrived only yesterday, I am not, of course, fully familiar with the town—but I have seen its like before in my travels and it is—how should I say it?—of a kind."

By now, Justice Payne had forgotten his carefully rehearsed approach to the man. "Why, then, are you so hell bent on buying property here?"

This time, the Philadelphia lawyer stepped back, florid with feigned indignation. "I beg your pardon, sir! My business here is my own affair, and none of yours."

"That's what you think!"

"Why, pray tell, should I lend credence to what you say? Who are you? To whom am I speaking?"

Justice took a deep breath, seeming to swell up like a game cock as he did. "For your information, I am Justice Payne. I own this town. I own this island. I am the law on this island. You had best rein in your insolence, or I will haul you into court!"

The lawyer smiled his biggest smile. "Payne, you say? Justice Payne? Why, you are just the man I am looking for! It has been my intention since arriving here to seek an appointment with you, but I thought, first, to get the lay of the land, so to speak." He slid his walking stick under the arm with the cigars and held it there, then offered his free hand to the judge. "It is a pleasure to meet you, Mister Payne—or should I say Judge Payne? Or, perhaps, Your Honor?"

"Judge will be fine." Justice took the proffered handshake, and found the man's grip firm and his pumping vigorous. Somehow, this dandy was outmaneuvering him at every turn. Every time he thought he was getting his feet planted firmly in the encounter, this fop pulled the rug out from under him. "You want to meet, you say. Well, follow me down to the Cactus Thorn Saloon."

"Saloon? Oh, no. No, no, no. No, sir. No, Judge."

"Why the hell not? What is the matter with you?"

The lawyer pulled a gold pocket watch—linked to a gold chain that passed through the bottom buttonhole on his vest and into the opposite pocket—and flipped it open. "It is not yet eleven o'clock in the morning. Fourteen of, according to my watch—which is always right, by the way. Much, much too early for me to imbibe. I do not know the custom here, or your personal—"

"Never mind that. I am not inviting you for a drink. I own the Cactus Thorn, and keep my office there. My living quarters as well."

Raising up and tipping his head back a touch the lawyer looked down his nose at the judge. "A saloon? Your domicile is in a drinking establishment? Oh, my. Oh, my, my."

Justice snorted. "It suits me. Don't worry about it." He turned on his heel and walked away. If the popinjay chose to follow, fine. If not . . . well, he would worry about that later.

The lawyer did follow. He strutted along behind the judge as if on his way to the Walnut Steet Theater in his home city to take in a performance.

At the Cactus Thorn, despite the early hour, Twah was already keeping watch—in his usual fully prone position—at his accustomed place atop the bar. Al the bodyguard and Luther the town marshal had apparently given guard duty over to the dog, despite their presence there. Al stood behind the bar, just beyond the dog, forearms folded atop the bar and leaning across until her nose almost touched the marshal's, him standing on the opposite side of the bar and mirroring her position. They whispered and smiled, giggled and sighed.

Twah sat up and propped himself on his front leg when the saloon doors swung open, and the judge stepped through. He did not wait for his guest, and the lawyer had to wait as the doors swung shut, past shut, rebounded, and swung to. Then, he pushed them open and followed the judge, who had stopped a few steps inside.

While the dog noted the entry, neither Al nor Luther paid any attention.

"Al!" the judge said. "Luther! What are you two up to?"

They did not hear. Or, if they did, it did not alter their activity in any way. The judge walked closer. "Al!"

As if awakened from sleep, the girl stood. Her eyes darted around to get her bearings, then landed on the judge. She cleared her throat. "Mister Payne, sir. Sorry." She nodded toward Luther. "Just talkin' to the marshal here."

"I see that." He shook his head. "I told you not to spoil that damn dog and you did not listen. Now it looks like you are bound to do the same to Luther."

Luther, slow to be distracted from his dreaminess, turned to the judge, blinking his eyes and looking unsure of the situation. "Huh?"

"Never mind." Justice again shook his head and set off toward his office in the rear. He assumed the lawyer would follow.

Chapter Twenty-Five

The Philadelphia lawyer smiled and bowed slightly in the direction of Al and Luther, tapping his walking stick to the brim of his hat, then set off through the saloon on the trail of Justice Payne. He caught up with his prey at the doorway into the judge's office, where Payne stood propping the door open.

"Have a seat," the judge said. He hung his hat on the rack then removed his jacket and hung it on a hook.

The lawyer stood and looked on, hands stacked atop the handle of his walking stick. He noted the paperwork spread in disarray across the desk. He saw the big black book and gavel, and the Navajo blanket hanging on a peg, curious about their reason for being.

"Sit," Justice said.

Turning toward the judge and smiling, the lawyer cleared his throat. "I shall stand, if you please. A touch of lumbago, you know."

"Fine. Now, suppose you tell me why you are here. And I want the truth of it, not this cockamamie story about buying property."

The lawyer sniffed. "I assure you, good sir, there is nothing 'cockamamie' about my stated purpose in visiting your fair community. As I have said clearly to all who have inquired, my firm represents a client interested in investing in real estate."

"The West is overrun with land. There is no shortage of property going for a song. Why here?"

The lawyer decided to sit, and grimaced as he eased into a chair. "You are right, of course, about the availability of property elsewhere. But our client was very specific about where the investments should be made. Unfortunately, the law forbids my revealing any information concerning our client's purposes, or the client's identity. I am free to say, again, that the request was very specific, and the interest is in owning property here, on this island, as I have said." He cleared his throat. "I am not at liberty to say anything further. As I said, the law forbids it."

"I suppose you have a point about the law," the judge said. "Here, however, the law operates somewhat differently than what you Easterners are accustomed to."

"Oh? How is that?"

Justice leaned forward. "*I* am the law here."

"Of course. I am told that you sit as the judge in this community. But, surely, you are bound by the canons of law, the statutes, the decrees, the ordinances in effect here locally."

"Not in the least. I am guided by my own opinion. Common sense. Directed by an overriding concern for the good of the community. That, and nothing more."

The lawyer mulled that over for a long moment. "I am aware that you are not affiliated in a governmental sense with either of the counties which surround you—Adams and Jefferson Counties, I believe. A most unusual situation, for certain, although somewhat understandable. But surely there are state laws that govern you. And, of course, federal regulations."

Justice laughed. "The state attempts to stick its nose into our affairs from time to time. But, without fail, they go back to their hallowed halls of government in the capital city with their noses out of joint. We brook no nonsense from them." He smiled. "And as for the national government—well, suffice it to say that Washington is a long, long way from here. So far as I know, there is no one in that city who is even aware of our existence."

"Hmmm. So, in effect, you make it up as you go along."

The judge raised both hands in surrender. "You have me there. Guilty as charged."

The lawyer thought it over. He asked if the judge considered it fair to exercise unfettered rule over the people. He questioned the wisdom of unchecked power. He wondered aloud about the possibility of corruption—of the judge acting in his own interest, rather than that of the citizens.

Justice Payne acknowledged the danger. Then, in no uncertain terms, said that nothing untoward had ever happened and that no such thing ever would—as long as he was running things.

"And that," the judge said, "is the nub of the matter. That is why you—your client, rather—will never own a square inch of my island. Nor will anyone else."

"The people accept this?"

The judge shrugged. "They have no choice. That is the way it is. If they find it unacceptable, they are welcome—invited, encouraged, even—to move on and find some other place more to their liking."

Again, the lawyer mulled over the judge's assertions. "So, then, I take it there is no hint of opposition among the people. That the people are pleased with your administration of the laws."

This time, it was the judge who paused to ponder. "For the most part, I would say that is true. Although . . ."

The length of the pause grew, then lengthened some more. The longer he waited to continue, the more the judge fidgeted. A flush crept up from under his collar. Beads of sweat glistened on his upper lip. Vertical lines appeared and deepened where his forehead met his nose.

"So!" the Philadelphia lawyer said. "All is not as rosy as you implied!"

The judge slapped the desktop. "No, it is not, now that you mention it. There is this woman. A businesswoman. She runs a brothel, a high-class house of ill repute, here on the island. I know of a surety she is out to get me. I suspect she is taking advantage of me financially, although I cannot prove it. I believe she is going behind my back as well, launching some underhanded scheme to assume control by wresting it from me!"

After letting it lie for a moment, allowing the tension to build, the lawyer asked if the judge had any evidence of any of this.

"No, dammit! And that is part of the problem! I know she is up to something, but I cannot figure out what it is."

"But with no evidence, it is only suspicion." The lawyer took in a long, slow breath then let it out the same way. "I am reminded of something Shakespeare wrote. In one of his King Henry the Sixth plays. The third one, if I recall correctly. 'Suspicion always haunts the guilty mind,' he wrote."

"What!?" Justice Payne launched himself out of his chair. He shook his finger in the lawyer's face. "Guilty mind, you say? Guilty mind? I assure you that such is not the case." He sniffed and sat back down. "Guilty mind my—. I think it best if you leave me now, sir. In fact, I demand it." He pointed to the door. "Get the hell out of here."

Al and Luther were still making moon eyes at one another over the bar. Twah, the three-legged dog, opened one eye in the slumbering head hanging over the edge of the bar to watch the dandy stroll through the Cactus Thorn Saloon and out through the swinging doors. He may have noticed the hint of a smile on the Philadelphia lawyer's face.

The lawyer strolled down the sidewalk, tapping his walking stick, swinging it in a circle through the air, then tapping it again, repeating the motion over and over as he walked. He turned into the Overland Stage and Express office to inquire about the next outbound coach. Although he had failed in his mission, he knew he had succeeded in achieving, or at least furthering, his client's goals.

Back at the Cactus Thorn Saloon, Justice Payne still sat at his desk, where he steamed and stewed, fretted and fussed, fumed and seethed.

Upset that he had voiced his fears to the stranger, he took some comfort in the fact that the Philadelphia lawyer, being a stranger, was unlikely to share his discovery of the judge's suspicions with anyone in the town.

Little did the judge know that, at that very moment, the lawyer sat in his hotel room penning a letter to his client, not to be posted, of course, until the next stop on the stage line. Armed with that information, Mercy O'Malley would step up her campaign to rally the business community to rebel against Judge Payne and his uncommon law.

Step up, she did. Rally the troops, she did. It was only a matter of days until Mercy O'Malley stirred up enough support to confront Justice Payne. At the appointed time, shortly after the breakfast hour, every independent business owner in the town (except the dentist, forced to miss the festivities to attend to an abscessed tooth) as well as several who operated businesses in the judge's employ, converged at the Cactus Thorn. A sizable crowd of other townspeople who had gotten wind of the pending showdown were among those assembled, as were a few curiosity seekers who noticed the unusual amount of traffic headed toward the saloon and followed along.

"Al, where is that table Justice uses when he holds court?" Mercy said as she breezed through the swinging doors.

Al, surprised at the stream of people following Mercy through the doors did not respond. Even Twah stood up on all threes in surprise. He did not growl or bark. Instead, a series of whimpers of a sort sounded as his head wagged back and forth watching the passing parade. Al hurried through the barroom to a table in the rear where Luther sat, his feet propped on another chair, arms folded across his chest, head bowed and hat brim pulled low, snoring.

"Luther!" Al said in a loud whisper, jostling his shoulder. "Luther!"

Luther stirred slightly and groaned, swatting at an imaginary fly. "Go 'way, Al . . . you know I like to sleep off breakfast."

Al shook him harder. "Wake up. Luther! Somethin's goin' on!"

Luther snorted and plopped his feet to the floor. He sat up and slid his hat up his forehead and ground at his eyes with his fists, then forced them open. His jaw dropped. "Good golly gracious sakes alive! What's going on, Al? Where'd all these people come from?"

"I don't know, Luther. Miss Mercy brought them all here, near as I can guess. You had best go find her and see what's up."

When the marshal found Mercy she again brought up the question about the judge's table. Luther, unhinged by the demand, the gathering crowd, and a half-awake mind, fetched the table in question, fully repaired from its earlier insufficiency, and put it in place on the dancehall stage, then fetched the chair.

"I dunno, Miss Mercy. The judge, he might not be too happy about you sitting here."

"Be that as it may, boyo, we're holding a meeting here this morning and I am taking the lead in the proceedings. Justice Payne can go suck eggs."

Luther blanched. "For heck's sake! Don't go lettin' the judge hear you sayin' that. He'd likely pin your ears back."

"Not a chance."

People were still coming into the Cactus Thorn, the crowd pressing forward to where Mercy O'Malley stood on the platform. Luther swam upstream to reach the end of the bar where Al and the dog were. He had no idea what was afoot, but wanted no part of it. He hoped the judge would not hear the hubbub.

No such luck.

Justice Payne had heard the dither and disquiet, and even now was putting on his suit coat. Outside his door he stopped and listened. He pondered and puzzled over the sound of the sizable crowd, wondering why such an assembly could occur without his knowledge. He walked down the short hallway and stopped where it opened into the saloon proper. The sight of the crowd proved more upsetting than the sound of it, as the townspeople were crowded chockablock around the dancehall stage, the crowd thinning only slightly toward the fringes of the room. No one was seated, everyone standing around and amongst the islands formed by the empty tables.

Standing on the stage, behind *his* table was Mercy O'Malley, both hands raised petitioning the congregation for quiet.

The judge walked into the room and quiet flowed through the crowd like a wave, washing away small talk, whispered conversations, hushed questions. All eyes were on Justice Payne, standing with his legs spread and hands clasped behind his back. Mercy followed the gaze of the people and locked eyes with the judge.

After a moment, he shifted his glare to take in the crowd. He would talk to them, not to the firebrand on the platform. They were, after all, his people. His employees. His tenants. In a sense, his subjects.

Or so he liked to think.

But there was a movement afoot. And he was about to step right into the quagmire it would create. Still, this was *his* town. *His* island. *His* law. And these were *his* people.

He stepped forward, as near to the stage where Mercy stood as the crowd allowed. His eyes swept the gathering. He cleared his throat. "Would someone care to tell me what the hell is going on here?"

Chapter Twenty-Six

Mercy O'Malley had spent weeks, months, quietly stirring up discord on the island and convincing her fellow citizens that life—and business—could be better. Now, with one question, thirteen words—*Would someone care to tell me what the hell is going on here?*—from the mouth of Justice Payne, she feared it could all come undone.

She said, "I would be pleased to do so, Justice."

The judge shook his head. "No. Not you, Mercy." He swept his hand over the crowd. "I want one of them." He pointed at the hatmaker. "How about you, Francesca?" The milliner only hung her head, concealing her face behind the floppy brim of her flowery hat. "You, Giacomo?" he said, his finger pointing out the town drunk. "What have you to say?" The alcoholist only shifted his weight back and forth from one foot to the other, stuffing his hands deeper into his pockets. "You?" the judge said, calling out another townsman. Then another. And another. And yet another.

Justice threw up his hands. "What is this? Will no one speak up?"

"I damn well will, and you know it," Mercy said.

"Oh, I do not doubt it, Mercy O'Malley. I have never known you to suffer a shortage of words. Quite the opposite, in fact."

"Well, then, how about you quit lording it over these folks and listen."

Justice snorted. "I suppose it is you who called this meeting, or whatever it is."

"You suppose right, Judge. And I'd say it is well past time that we done so."

"What is it you hope to accomplish?"

Mercy smiled. "I'm glad you asked. For it has to do with you. With you, and with all of us." The madam, with outstretched arms, took in the whole of the crowd. "There are a few things we would like to clear up. And that's just for starters."

Murmuring and muttering spread through the crowd as its members regained some measure of the courage lost earlier to the judge's intimidating presence.

Justice sensed the change in the air. He said, "Suppose I ask you to leave? This is, after all, my saloon in which you are gathered. And, as the sitting judge in the town, I could declare this an unlawful assembly and require its breakup."

Mercy smiled. She detected a hint, however slight, of uncertainty in the judge. "You can try," she said. "But I don't know as we would pay any attention to such a request—or order." She turned to the crowd. "How about it? Anybody here likely to leave this meeting on the judge's say-so?"

The word "no" and its many variants rose from the crowd and hung heavy in the air over the judge's head. Justice sagged, dragged a chair away from a table and sat.

"Here's the thing, Justice," Mercy said. "You run this island like it was your own little fiefdom. Kingdom, even. Now, we know you settled this island. We know you built this town. We know you own it all, and that we are here, in some sense, at your pleasure. But it can't go on that way no more. This town has outgrown all that, Judge. This town has outgrown *you*."

Scattered applause and words of agreement punctuated Mercy's oration. As she continued her declamation, enthusiasm, vocalized agreement, and ovations grew. Mercy listed generalized complaints, reading from a list not on paper, but inscribed in her soul. She complained of the low wages paid to the judge's workers, and of inadequate compensation for managers of his successful businesses. She denounced the burdensome taxes levied against independent business owners, and the onerous rents charged for occupancy of his buildings and lots. She protested the application of Justice's justice as arbitrary and capricious, unfair and inequitable. She sounded off about the appearance and disappearance of so-called laws at the judge's whim. She opposed the levying of fines as injurious and discriminatory. She objected to the antiquated punishment of the lash, and the unjustifiable and haphazard practice in the sentencing of stripes.

Then there was the haughtiness and dismissiveness of the judge's manner in answering complaints from the citizens. The disdain he demonstrated for the opinions of others. The expectation that his every utterance would be obeyed without question, his every whim treated as an edict from on high. His abuse and mistreatment of, and his demeaning attitude toward, well, everyone.

Mercy had the assembly fired up to a fevered pitch, the excitement brought to a boil. Others from the town stepped forward to offer their own complaints. Courage multiplied, encouraging still more complainants to state their case. Only a few withered under the judge's stern gaze; most withstood the implied threat and spoke their minds. Some offered specific grievances, others uttered gripes of a more general nature.

For the most part, Justice Payne sat silent through the onslaught. His occasional attempts to answer charges, to dispute claims, were met with scorn and with behests to stay silent until called upon. Mercy O'Malley, without benefit of gavel, robes of office, intimidation, badgering, bullying, blustering, browbeating, or showboating was able to maintain calm and control, and conduct an orderly assembly. All who wished to speak were heard, all complaints were voiced, and all opinions noted.

And then it was time to hear from Justice Payne.

He rose from his seat and studied the crowd. He stepped up onto the dancehall stage. He scowled for a long moment at Mercy O'Malley. He turned his attention again to the assembly with a frown and a glower, casting his eyes across the crowd and creating the feeling—the fear—in one and all that he was looking at them, and them alone. Again, the air seemed to leave the room. Nervous shifting and shuffling spread among the people.

Mercy knew it was now or never. "C'mon, Justice. Speak your piece or climb down off this stage."

"It is *my* stage, Mercy O'Malley, and I shall stand on it or not, as I like."

"Well, what is it you've got to say to these people?"

The judge took in a deep breath and stretched himself to his full height. "So, you are dissatisfied with conditions, are you? Are you? Or have you been browbeaten into thinking so by this . . . this . . . rabble-rouser, this instigator, this agitator standing beside me?" He sniffed. "While I, guided by nothing but the well-being of every one of you, have devoted my every waking hour to the betterment of the community—your betterment!

"I have kept the peace. I have maintained law and order. I have served the public interest. I have promoted business. I have averted attempts at governmental influence from Adams County. From Jefferson County. From those in state government who would meddle in our affairs. Who among you believes he—or she—could do better? Could have done more?" Justice turned and pointed an accusing finger at Mercy. "This woman? This keeper of a house of ill repute? This procuress? This woman who, herself, is a prostitute?"

Luther, of all people, stepped out of the crowd. "Now, hold on there, Judge. There ain't no need for talk like that. Golly sakes, everybody knows Miss Mercy is a fine lady, never mind her way of makin' a living. Besides, I ain't never seen you turn up your nose at all the money she pays you for this, that, and the other. I know I've collected a right smart of money from her house at your say-so."

"Hold your tongue, you blithering idiot! Luther, every man jack in this room knows you consort with Miss Mercy's whores! You are hardly fit to speak objectively."

"Oh, for heck's sake, Judge! You know darn well most of the men in this room visits Miss Mercy's place—even if their name ain't Jack!"

A collective gasp filled the air, and wives in the audience looked askance at their husbands.

Luther said, "Heavens to Betsy! You've been known to sneak in the side door over there your own self."

"Luther, I told you to shut up! You haven't the sense God gave an oxbow stirrup, so you had best keep quiet. Do not forget which side your bread is buttered on."

"Well, tarnation! If you don't think no more of me that that, you can keep your ol' badge." The now former town marshal pulled the pin on the badge and lifted it from his shirt, then sailed it onto the floor of the stage, where it bounced and clinked and clanked and jangled and jingled and came to rest at the feet of Justice Payne. Luther turned and took the arm of Al. "C'mon Al—let's get on out of here."

The crowd parted for Luther and Al, sending them on their way with hearty applause. Twah trotted along in their tracks and kept his three legs moving despite the judge's calls and whistles and remonstrations for him to return.

As the batwing doors of the Cactus Thorn Saloon swung shut, Justice told the audience not to worry—he would appoint a new town marshal and things would return to normal without a ripple.

Somewhere in the middle of the audience, a hand went up. Attached to the other end of the arm was Giacomo Moretti. He waved the hand back and forth to get the judge's attention.

Justice sighed. "What is it, Giacomo? Your glass empty? Your bottle all gone?"

"Never you mind all that," Moretti said, bolstered by newfound, if fragile, courage. "Long as you get paid for what I imbibe, you got no call to complain. What I want to know is, how come *you* get to appoint the marshal?"

"Whatever do you mean? Is the fog in your dipsomaniac brain so thick you've forgotten I am the judge? The mayor? Who is better suited to appoint a law officer?"

Giacomo said no more, the judge's insult having cowed him. But the rudeness Justice had shown to Mercy, Luther, and now a helpless drunk stirred the crowd, causing much grumbling and mumbling.

Mercy said, "I've got an idea, Justice. It's a little thing that here in America they call an election."

"Election!"

"Election. Surely you've heard of it. It's where the people gets to vote to choose those who are to lead them." Mercy smiled. "You might find mention of it in that big law book you're always looking at."

Words of agreement filled the air as the audience took up the idea of an election, culminating in a repeated chant of VOTE! VOTE! VOTE!

Justice Payne faced the onslaught in silence, his voice lost. Mercy allowed the chant to continue for a time, then held up her arms for silence.

"Sounds like the people are in favor of an election, Justice." Mercy paused to let the applause and cheers dissipate. "Seems to me that as long as we're at it, we might as well fill some more offices besides town marshal."

Justice said nothing, but the question was on his face.

"What say we vote us in a town board, Justice? What do you think?"

"I cannot imagine what for! What on earth could they do? Nothing helpful, I say."

Mercy recited a litany of ideas an elected town board could take on. She suggested the establishment of laws and ordinances, rules and regulations to govern the town. She proposed guidelines for fines and sentences for those who ran afoul of the law. She advocated formalized and fair tax rates. Others in the assembly stepped forward with suggestions of their own, the result being a full and busy schedule of activity for the prospective town board.

All the while, the judge fumed, his face florid and forehead furrowed.

And then someone lit the fuse.

"How's about we elect ourselves a mayor while we're at it?"

"NO!" Justice's explosion of denial liked to have shaken the chandeliers and dusted the ceiling beams in the Cactus Thorn. "NOT ON YOUR LIVES!"

The audience listened to the judge rant and rave that there was no need for elections, for a town board, for written laws, or anything else under discussion—and certainly not a mayor.

"It seems apparent that some among you have forgotten that you already have a mayor! I am the mayor of this town!"

A voice in the crowd said, "That's just the trouble—you're the mayor, the judge, and every other damn thing there is to be in this town!"

The comment drew jeers and applause.

The judge signaled for silence. "Have you forgotten whose town this is? Need I remind you that *I* built this town! Me! This island was nothing more than a weed patch when I first set foot on it! Scrawny trees and scraggly brush and mud. I have guided its development. I built the bridges. I laid out the streets and roads. I built the buildings. I own many of the businesses. I provide opportunity for others of you to run businesses of your own. Now, then, let us reason together! Is not all I have reminded you of reason enough to allow me to govern my own town? To do so as I see fit?"

The hush continued as the crowd considered the judge's words. Again, Mercy sensed the shifting tide and stepped forward. One by one, she called out to business owners in the town and asked them to reveal the tax rate Justice Payne demanded of them to conduct business in "his" town. She asked leaseholders and renters of the buildings housing businesses and homes to declare the rents they paid. Some even divulged the wages and salaries paid by the judge for their labor in or their management of his enterprises.

The variance, the disparity, the inequality shocked the community anew with each revelation. Without further suggestion or encouragement, the crowd once again took up the chant, VOTE! VOTE! VOTE!

This time, it was Justice Payne who held up his hands asking for silence. It took some time, but the chant diminished then died. The audience looked on expectantly.

The judge cleared his throat. "Ladies and gentlemen, friends and neighbors, I have heard and listened to your complaints. I understand your frustrations. I feel your pain." He paused and studied the crowd. "I promise to consider what you have said. I pledge to give serious thought to your concerns. And I vow to take appropriate action."

After a long pause, the judge continued. "But—"

The audience interrupted with catcalls, jeers, and hisses at the conjunction.

The judge waited for the cacophony to quiet. Then, "But, there will be no election! Not for mayor, not for marshal, not for any office!"

Again, derision rocked the rafters.

Mercy O'Malley had sat in silence long enough. She stepped forward. The crowd quieted.

"Haven't you said enough?" the judge said. "Haven't you caused enough trouble?"

Mercy smiled a stiff, determined smile. "I think it is you who has said more than enough. Too much, if truth be told. You have pushed us too far, Justice Payne. Your bullheadedness leaves us no choice."

The confused look on the judge's face lightened Mercy's smile and it turned to one of joy.

"Justice Payne," she said, then raised a clenched fist. "From this very moment on, this town is on strike!"

An affirmative roar went up from the crowd, and raised fists sprouted from the crowd like grass after rain, accompanied by another chant: STRIKE! STRIKE! STRIKE! . . .

Chapter Twenty-Seven

Mercy O'Malley stood looking out the window from her rooms on the upper floor of the House of Passion, watching the river flow under the bridge. She mused over the old adage that you cannot step into the same river twice, wondering if that applied to looking, as well as stepping.

She turned to her guests. "What will you two do now, now that you're both out of work?"

Luther, former town marshal, sat on a plush sofa, hat in his lap, looking around a room at the House of Passion he had never visited before. "Oh, gosh, Miss Mercy—there ain't nothin' for it but for me and Al to pack up and leave."

"I, myself, have often considered leaving this island. But, for some reason, I seem to have taken root here." She sighed. "With the strike on, Justice might come to his senses and things may get better. Mayhap you two can return one day soon."

"I reckon we'll be doin' just that, Miss Mercy," Al said. "But it'll only be to buy supplies such as we need, which won't never be much."

"Sounds like you have something in mind."

"We do for a fact. You knew I grew up on a ranch up the valley yonder."

"Yes. You've said so before. But I thought that with all your brothers the place was overstocked with mouths to feed and you saw no future there."

Al nodded. "Just as you say. But I got an aunt out in the same country who's got a spread. She's Pa's sister, see, and her and her man homesteaded out there same time as Pa. Built up a right nice little ranch. Her man died a while back, and she's poorly—gettin' up there in years, y'know. They never had no kids, so there ain't no one to take over the place, or even take care of it."

Al smiled from ear to ear. "No one, that is, 'cept me. Aunt Alice—I got my name from her, see—she's always taken a likin' to me. Treated me like her own daughter, much as she could, only most all she ever tried to teach me 'bout womanly ways got lost amongst all the boys I was with at home every day. But she never give up on me, and asked some time back if I would be willin' to take over runnin' the ranch, and take title to it once she passed on.

" 'Course I said yes. And she never even flinched when I took Luther here in on the deal. Said if he was good enough for me, he was good enough for her."

Luther blushed, studying the inside of his hat as if the answer to some great mystery might be found within. He looked up and said, "I never had much luck at cowboyin' back home, what with Pa gettin' after me all the time. But I sure do like it out on this here ranch, Miss Mercy. Gee willikers! There ain't nothin' like climbin' onto a horse and goin' for a ride out amongst the cows and calves. Twah, he likes it too—runs all over the place like he's got four legs!"

Al patted him on the thigh, then linked an arm through his and smiled. "My aunt says all you got to do to run a ranch is be smarter than what a cow is—and they ain't all that smart. I reckon we got time to teach Luther the way of it." She reached over and poked Luther in the ribs with a finger. "She said Luther'd have to learn one thing, though."

The girl paused until Mercy prodded her to go on.

"She says he'll have to learn how to cuss good and proper and leave off all this namby-pamby pretend profanity he's partial to. She says cows don't understand no other way of talkin' than good old-fashioned cowboy cussin'."

Luther blushed again. Al and Mercy laughed.

The young couple stood to take their leave. Luther asked Al if he could have a private word with Miss Mercy, and the girl made her way down the stairs and into the parlor. The former lawman, the blush lingering on his face, shifted his weight and fiddled with his hat brim.

"Well, Luther, what is it?"

It still took some time for Luther to find words to prime the pump. "Oh golly, Miss Mercy . . . it's about Miss Rose."

"Miss Rose?"

"Yeah. Miss Rose. Not the Miss Rose you got now, or some of them others that has been here." He swallowed hard. "You know the Miss Rose I mean, don't you?"

"I believe I do, Luther. You were rather sweet on the girl, weren't you?"

"I was . . . . But now, what with Al and all . . . well, if Miss Rose should come back . . . gosh . . . well, would you tell her that I've found another and I can't keep them promises I made to her? Tell her I never meant to tell no lies, and I'll likely burn in heck for it. But, well, Al—there's somethin' different with her, y'know . . . somethin' special . . ."

Mercy smiled and patted Luther on the shoulder. "Don't give it a second thought, boyo. I'm sure she'll understand."

The town had been quiet since the strike was called. It had been weeks. Businesses—at least those not owned by Justice Payne—continued to operate, but the owners withheld any taxes due. Rent and lease payments were likewise held back. As for the judge's enterprises, they were boycotted as much as possible, with customers limiting purchases to goods not available elsewhere. Sympathetic managers at some of those places conducted business out the back door, out of sight of Justice's watching eyes, or those of his spies.

A few enterprising souls capitalized on the scarcity by filling wagons with wares from Adams and Jefferson Counties. They set up tent stores alongside the roads across from the island bridges, offering their merchandise at prices lower, even, than those at the judge's stores and businesses. He, of course, retaliated by dropping prices to the point of selling at a loss, but most citizens held to the boycott as much as possible and his businesses floundered. Managers and workers took no hurt, however, as townspeople supplied them with necessities, returning favors through back doors and after dark.

As promised, Justice Payne had appointed a new town marshal. A relative newcomer to the town, he arrived the afternoon following the town meeting, taking up a seat at a poker table in the Cactus Thorn Saloon. There he sat. And sat. Throughout the afternoon he played solitaire, expecting business would pick up and he would find a game come evening.

It did not happen.

At some point, Justice Payne wandered out of his rooms, surprised at the emptiness of the saloon. But he doubted the strike and boycotts would hold for long, and was determined to withstand the demands of the citizens. He struck up a conversation with the gambler and offered him the job of town marshal.

The cardsharp accepted the appointment, figuring it would put a little money in his purse. Besides, after listening to the judge's explanation, the situation in the town amused him and he thought it might be interesting to watch it play out. After pinning on the badge and making a few tours of the town and talking with folks, he would have taken odds that they would prevail over the judge.

For their part, the people of the town treated the new marshal kindly, but ignored all and any of his orders. Citations were shredded into bits and tossed away. The citation for littering that inevitably followed was treated likewise. Only when the marshal walked away was the refuse retrieved and properly disposed of in a trash receptacle.

Whenever the judge, in a continuous dither, ordered his lawman to take a malcontent into custody, a crowd of citizens would gather between the marshal and the offender, feigning confusion, misunderstanding the lawman's orders, offering assistance, using their feigned good intentions to interfere with the arrest, and getting in the way until the fugitive could be spirited away.

Justice could only take so much. Likewise, his new town marshal. For his part, the judge berated and rebuked the man, chastised and castigated him, reprimanded and reproached him, even going so far as to question his manhood. For his part, the lawman only smiled, unpinned the badge from his vest, and handed it back to the judge. Thereafter, he contented himself with sitting alone at the disused card table at Mercy O'Malley's House of Passion, playing solitaire and the occasional game of cribbage with the flower girls for stakes best not mentioned.

Justice Payne's irritation grew with the lengthening strike. Repeated meetings with his bank manager verified a serious slowdown in deposits into the judge's accounts, which further irritated him. The banker's insistence that there was still money to burn did nothing to douse his anger. In an attempt to shore up his finances, the judge jacked up prices for the goods and services he offered in the town. He decided competing with the temporary merchants across the bridges was a lost cause, and that it was better to sell less and make a profit than to sell more and lose money.

Most people were unaffected by the retrenchment in prices, but when Justice cut wages and salaries for his workers and managers, the community became more determined than ever and cut off all trade with him. Mercy O'Malley, sensing a crack in the judge's defenses, opened her coffers and made up the lost money and more to keep citizens from serious harm. Where Justice Payne reproached, reprimanded, and reviled his workers—and anyone else he encountered in the town—for their actions and activities, Mercy offered appreciation, admiration, and adulation for their being stalwart and stouthearted.

While the judge forecast doom and the demise of the town, Mercy predicted better days ahead. As Justice declared and declaimed a series of laws forbidding continuation of the strikes, Mercy presented petitions signed by a majority of townspeople nullifying his edicts. When he had tollgates built at the island's bridges to prevent trade with the temporary tent stores, she rebuilt the old ferry and offered free passage for all comings and goings. Whatever moves Justice made to bring the citizenry to bay, Mercy's countermoves rendered him impotent to effect change.

Late one morning—late according to the clock, but early by the hours Mercy O'Malley kept—a messenger arrived at the House of Passion. He carried a note addressed to Mercy, sealed with wax and the words "Personal and Confidential" scrawled on its face. She recognized the handwriting as that of Justice Payne. Seated at the table with her morning coffee, she broke the seal and unfolded the sheet.

> *You are hereby summoned to meet with His Honor Judge Justice Payne in his offices at the Cactus Thorn Saloon this day at three o'clock in the P.M. to answer complaints referred against you and for purposes of consultation concerning community affairs.*

Mercy smiled and set the missive aside. After finishing her coffee, she retired to her desk and took up the pen and a sheet of stationery.

My Dear Justice,

I am in receipt of your order to appear this afternoon. I regret to inform you that I am unable to comply owing to the press of business. However, should you find it convenient to call on me at the House of Passion at or before 5:00 o'clock today, I shall be pleased to confer with you.

Your Obedient Servant, Mercy O'Malley

Lacking the formality of sealing wax, Mercy sealed the folded note with a dab of paste, then bridged the join with a bright red lipstick imprint of a kiss, personally applied.

A stream of similar orders and invitations, requests and refusals, flowed between the Cactus Thorn and the House of Passion for several days. Finally, a compromise was agreed to. Justice and Mercy would meet on neutral ground—or the nearest thing there was to it on the island—in a conference room at the bank. Mercy arrived first and the bank manager showed her to the room. Justice came in a few minutes later to find her seated in the stuffed and upholstered chair at the head of the table—the very seat he was accustomed to occupying. A sizable stack of papers and documents sat before her on the tabletop. Miffed at her occupation of the superior seat, he sat in one of the wooden railback chairs at the side of the table, two seats away from Mercy.

"Ah, c'mon, Justice. Sit up here by me," Mercy said, patting the table in front of the nearest seat.

The judge slapped the table with the palm of his hand.

Whack!

"I will not!"

Whack!

Justice engaged in a round of name-calling, accusations, allegations, threats, and recrimination. He smacked the table with the ball of his fist.

Whack!

Mercy smiled. "No need to get angry—or to pound on the table like it's your judge's bench. I expect to be treated civil, and if you ain't going to, I'd just as well leave now."

Flushed and flustered, Justice waved a hand as if to sweep away the hostility in the air.

"Now, then, Justice—what is it you want of me?"

Chapter Twenty-Eight

After the table pounding and vehement, vicious, vituperative invective, Justice Payne got down to business. He started with his usual recitation of reasons he did not deserve to be treated the way the people of the island were treating him—his founding of the town and all the good deeds that followed and the rest of the accustomed litany.

Then, "What I want of you is to stop all this, Miss O'Malley."

"What makes you think I can stop it?"

"Do not play games with me, Mercy. I know you are behind it—you started it, you stirred the pot, you call the shots. And you can stop it."

"And why would I want to do that?"

The judge scooted his chair around until it faced Mercy. He leaned forward and spoke in a hushed voice. "I will cut you in. We can work together. You and I will run this town. Twenty percent. Twenty percent for you, free and clear, for doing nothing more than stopping all this nonsense and allowing me to get back to controlling things as I have always done. And supporting me as needed. People listen to you."

Mercy laughed. "You've got be joking! Me, coming out in favor of the way you do things? Hell's bells! You've just now accused me of bein' behind this uprising—and now you want me to do a turnabout? What'll I say? 'Never mind, folks. I didn't mean none of it. Just a joke. All in good fun, you know.' D'you think anybody would fall for such nonsense?"

"Think about it. Twenty percent. I can assure you that your cut will be substantial."

Mercy snorted and told the judge he could keep his twenty percent.

"Thirty percent."

Mercy said nothing.

Justice and Mercy

"All right, then. Forty. Forty percent and not a penny more."

The woman only stared.

Justice sat back in his chair and sighed. "Have it your way. But, no matter. You have to put a stop to this strike. It cannot go on, and you know it. You are killing this town. Only you can save it. Stop it. Now."

"I'm afraid I can't agree with you. There's only one person who can stop it."

"Oh? And who might that be?"

Mercy smiled. "You, Justice. You're the one. You can stop it, right now."

This time, Justice Payne laughed. "Me? Stop it? I did not start it, and I cannot stop it."

"Sure you can. All you have to do is agree to the demands of the people."

The judge snorted. "Me? Acquiesce? Not a chance. This is *my* town! *Mine!*—to run as I see fit." He smacked the tabletop.

Whack!

Mercy leaned forward and folded her arms on the tabletop. She locked eyes with the judge. "It *was* your town. *Was*. But now it has outgrown you. People are no longer satisfied with having you call all the shots. They're fed up with dancing to your tune."

Fuming, face so florid Mercy feared he might burst a blood vessel, jaws clenched and breaths coming fast, Justice sputtered and spit searching for words. "You know nothing woman! Why—why—why—you are nothing but a common whore!"

Whack!

Mercy suppressed the rising laugh, but could not help but smile. "I may well be a whore, but there ain't nothing common about me."

He offered no reply.

"That's your trouble, Justice, at least part of it—you always think ill of people. It wouldn't hurt you to say something nice now and then."

The judge sat and stewed for several minutes. He sighed long and loud. He asked, in a voice barely audible, what it was the people wanted.

"You know good and well what's wanted. It's all right here," Mercy said, tapping the pile of papers before her with a fingernail. "You've been handed a copy of everything here, what the people are asking for. If 'ask' be the right word—demand is more like it. You've been given every petition, every demand, every appeal."

The judge sniffed and said every sheet of paper he had been given went directly into the firebox in the stove in his offices at the Cactus Thorn Saloon, unread.

"Well, then, I guess we start at the beginning." Mercy went through the papers, page by page. The demand for elections for all positions of authority in the town—including mayor, marshal, and tax assessor. The election of members of and formation of a town board to formulate laws, codes, rules, regulations, statutes, tax rates, budgets, and other functions necessary for orderly operation of the town. Elimination of the whipping post and whippings, to be replaced by a proper jail and sentencing guidelines. Establishment of formal courtroom proceedings, including prosecutors to present evidence, representation for defendants, and trial by jury for higher crimes.

Justice Payne listened to it all without comment. For a time, his flush deepened, then faded, until his visage was as pale and pasty as pancake batter. He sagged in his chair, shoulders stooped, head bowed. He sat silent for a time. He released a long, slow breath. "Is there any room for negotiation? For compromise?"

"I'm afraid not. The people have spoken. It's what they want, and they'll accept no less."

"I guess I'm out, then."

"Likely. But you're welcome—as is any citizen of the town—to try for election to any office on the ballot."

Justice could not even muster a wry smile. "Could I count on your vote?"

"I'll tell you what, Justice. If I have any say in the way things gets done—that's a mighty big 'if' mind you—I'd do my best to persuade the town board and mayor and whoever to appoint you judge."

The man perked up. "Me? Judge? You would do that for me?"

"Like I said, I ain't makin' no promises. But if you promise to play ball and run things like a regular courtroom and follow the laws and such as the town board comes up with, I'll do what I can." She leaned toward the judge and spoke softly. "Between you and me and the back fence, I think I can get it done."

"Why? Why would you do it, Mercy?"

"Aw, hell, Justice! You and me go way back. We've weathered many a storm together in this town. Underneath it all you ain't such a bad sort—just full of yourself, is all. Besides, I know how you like drapin' yourself in that Navajo rug and poundin' that little wood hammer of yours. Then there's that phony lawbook. I reckon you could do a fine job as the law in this town if you was to put your mind to it."

"I guess I owe you my thanks."

"You don't owe me anything. There ain't no guarantee I can get it done."

The judge managed a weak smile. "I don't believe that for a minute, Mercy O'Malley. Somehow, you can get people to do whatever you want them to." He sighed. "It must be feminine wiles or some such. I cannot imagine how else you do it. Whatever it is, it seems to work better than bluster and bullying."

"It ain't no big secret, Justice, the difference between me and you." Mercy smiled. "It's like me old mamó back in Ireland—my granny—used to say: 'A spoonful of honey will catch more flies than a gallon of vinegar.' "

About the Author

Writer **Rod Miller** is a four-time winner of, and six-time finalist for, the Western Writers of America Spur Award. His writing has also won awards from Western Fictioneers, Westerners International, and the Academy of Western Artists. A lifelong Westerner, Miller writes fiction, history, poetry, and magazine articles about the American West's people and places.

Read more online at:
writerRodMiller.com
RawhideRobinson.com
writerRodMiller.blogspot.com

Coming Soon!

SPUR AWARD-WINNING AUTHOR
ROD MILLER

WITH A KISS I DIE

With a Kiss I Die is a love story entwined in the tragedy of the Mountain Meadows Massacre. Polly Alden, a young California-bound Arkansas emigrant, falls in love with Tom Langford, a Mormon boy she meets in the settlements of Utah Territory. Caught between the fear and hatred of the persecuted Saints for the emigrants, and the hostility of the emigrants toward Mormons who will not replenish their dwindling supplies, the young lovers defy mistrust and opposition as they aspire to a life together.

Follow the trail of the Arkansas emigrants and the blossoming affection of the star-crossed lovers in a compelling, engaging tale inspired by history—and the eternal conflict between good and evil, hatred and love.

**For more information
visit:** www.SpeakingVolumes.us

Now Available!

SPUR AWARD-WINNING AUTHOR
ROD MILLER

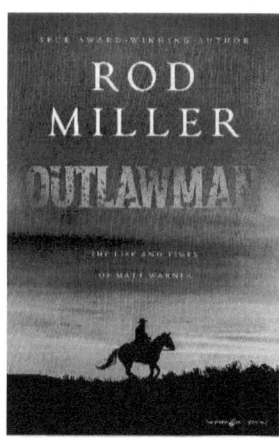
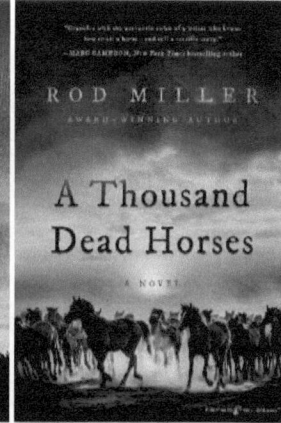

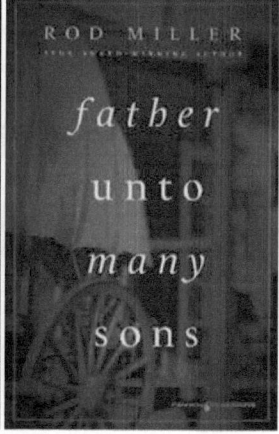

**For more information
visit:** www.SpeakingVolumes.us

Now Available!

DICK BROWN'S

UNDER THE CANYON SKY SERIES
BOOKS 1 - 3

 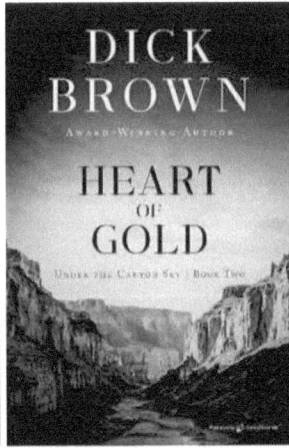 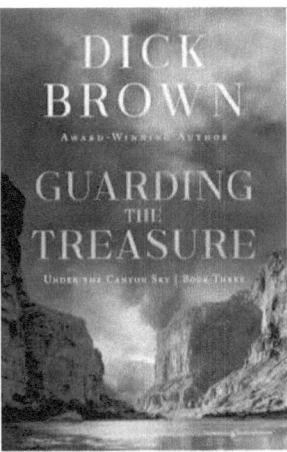

**For more information
visit:** www.SpeakingVolumes.us

Now Available!

AWARD-WINNING AUTHOR
JIM JONES

ACTION/ADVENTURE WESTERNS

**For more information
visit:** www.SpeakingVolumes.us

Now Available!

Winner of the 2024 Spur Award

THE HEART BENEATH THE BADGE
BY
GEORGE T. ARNOLD

**For more information
visit:** www.SpeakingVolumes.us

www.ingramcontent.com/pod-product-compliance
Lightning Source LLC
LaVergne TN
LVHW091634070526
838199LV00044B/1068